Triple Crown Publications
presents

D1400293

Keisha

By Darrell DeBrew

This is a work of fiction. The authors have invented the characters. Any resemblance to actual persons, living or dead, is purely coincidental.

If you have purchased this book with a 'dull' or missing cover--You have possibly purchased an unauthorized or stolen book. Please immediately contact the publisher advising where, when and how you purchased this book.

Compilation and Introduction copyright © 2004 by Triple Crown Publications
PO Box 247378
Columbus, Ohio 43219
www.TripleCrownPublications.com

Library of Congress Control Number: 2005909345
ISBN: 0-9767894-3-4
ISBN 13: 978-0-9767894-3-7
Author: Darrell DeBrew
Associate Editor: Cynthia Parker
Editor-in-Chief: Mia McPherson
Consulting: Vickie M. Stringer

First Trade Paperback Edition Printing
10 9 8 7 6 5 4
Printed in the United States of America

Dedication

This book is dedicated to Linda Williams, Juan Muza (Papo) and Dolly Lopez

Acknowledgements

My most important acknowledgement goes out to Linda Williams. When a lady steps in your life and says let get this done, by all means necessary, it's time to step it up and handle yo' business like a true playa and do the right thing in all facets. Without your assistance, Linda, I would not have been able to turn this book in like I wanted to. Thank you.

My second acknowledgement goes out to Juan Muza. You hooked me up with Linda. I also have to fit Dolly Lopez in here.

To the Triple Crown family – I have to thank Vickie Stringer for the stepping stone and tolerating my everything-has-to-be-right ass. I can see us laughing about this years from now. Keep getting it on all four corners. There is no other way for a hustler. When you see Nikki Turner, thank her for *Stacy* and *Keisha*.

My man Fitzdaine Gordon – thanks for your support and I can see us making some good money in the future. You will get the first five (5) copies of *Stacy* as soon as it comes off the press.

To my editors – without y'alls comments and criticisms I don't think I'd be able to complete my projects. Thank you for taking out the time to read my terribly typed manuscripts: Tawan, Tank, Rodney Moss, Michael Crews, Eddie G. Jackson & Wilburn.

To my girl Phyllis Rush – I just know we are going to get together on something. Peace and Love.

I hope y'all enjoy this book.

I can be hollered at:

Mr. Darrell James DeBrew (Da'Rel-Da'Rel)
Reg. No 14102-056
FCI Loretto
P.O. Box 1000
Loretto, PA 15940

www.darrelldebrew.com

◆ ◆ ◆ ◆ ◆

"Please don't kill me, I don't know where the money is." For ten minutes, non-stop, Karyn endured kicks from Timberland boots and blows from brass-knuckled fists. At any moment she knew that her husband, Sherlock, was going to walk through the door. She had no idea that he was dead, and had been for several hours.

"All we want is the money," Danny Boy hollered while connecting a hook against Karyn's left temple. The blow was so powerful; it sent Karyn out of the chair, spinning one-hundred-and-eighty degrees, before hitting the floor. Her head hitting the oak dresser hurt as much as the right hook. Before Karyn could soak up the pain from the head blows, Danny Boy broke one of her ribs with a thunderin' kick. "Bitch, where the fuck is the money? If you want the pain to stop, just tell me what I want to know." Danny Boy was a big dude with a big booming voice that commanded attention.

Sherlock, I need you baby, she thought. *Where are you?*

Sherlock and Karyn were together for over twenty years. Sherlock was one of the most respected hustlers in the streets. He was never sent to jail because all he did was run numbers and gamble. He took great care of his wife Karyn, and their daughter, Keisha. Karyn was that red-bone that all men in the community desired. She received many offers to model but turned them down. All she cared about was being good to Sherlock and Keisha, who was the spitting image of her. Many thought they were sisters.

Danny Boy was getting impatient. With a handful of her hair he pulled her up off the floor. There was too much pain running through her body to resist his will.

"Let me go. I'll tell you where the money is," she said, barely audible. Pain was coming at her from all parts of her body. Her entire face was swollen and bruised. She could barely talk with a split lip and a few chipped teeth.

Danny Boy threw her on the bed like she was a wet paper towel. For months, he and Clarence waited to make a major lick. They wanted to get into the drug game in a major way. That meant they needed cash so they could buy their way in. Working their way up was going to take too long and they didn't want to follow orders from another man in the streets. Nobody was going to front them but so much because they were always short with the cash. It was always Danny Boy's fault. He thought about robbing, extorting and getting over on everybody. Clarence stuck by his man's side, no matter what he did.

It was about ten seconds since Danny Boy had thrown Karyn on the bed. "You need to get to telling me where the money is." It was rumored that Sherlock had a few million dollars. Danny Boy knew that by the look of the house, inside and out, that the old head had some serious cash. It had to be stashed up in there somewhere. Sherlock was known for paying off the numbers in cash, within a matter of hours, no matter what day it was or how much.

Karyn knew exactly where the money was. Sherlock always told her to give up the money unless she knew the robbers were going to kill her afterwards. Though it was unlikely to happen because he had so much respect in the streets, Sherlock trained and prepared his ladies for the worst of situations. He also kept them informed about all the cats that ran the streets. Danny Boy and Clarence were suspected of several murders and burglaries.

She was hoping to get in position to grab the .380 that was strapped to the bottom of the bed on the left side.

"So you wanna play games with Danny Boy. Didn't anybody tell you not to play with me?" He got a kick out of inflicting pain. Everyone who showed a sign of weakness around him was either robbed or extorted. At the age of 19, he was feared all over DC. Clarence was just a few months younger than Danny Boy. They were two of the few gang-banging teenagers that survived. People expected them to end up dead any day. Many tried to get them but D and C always seemed to get them first.

Karyn determined that the only way that she was going to survive was to kill Danny Boy and Clarence. Still, there had to be something wrong. Sherlock was always home by eight o'clock on Sunday mornings. The nightstand clock read nine fifteen. Getting to the left side of the bed was all she had to do to make her move.

Danny Boy grabbed her by her hair and lifted her head up off the bed, about two feet, and punched her in the back of her head as hard as he could. She intentionally rolled her body to the left, off the bed, and onto the floor. The blow almost knocked her unconscious. She could feel her heartbeat in her head along with what felt like the throbbing of three migraine headaches. Her will to live kept her moving. With both of her eyes looking like rotted plums, there was no need to try looking for the gun. Everything was blurry and red.

"Yeah bitch, I might as well rape you and kill you so you can be with Sherlock. He got killed at the skin game last night. I saw it all," Danny Boy snarled. Sherlock caught the houseman cheating with a deck that had shaved cards. Every time a certain deck was used the deuces would be the last card and the winner of the most money. It was a common trick at skin games and Sherlock wanted his money back. When Cedric wouldn't give him his money back an argument ensued. The houseman killed him so he wouldn't have to give everyone back their money. Plus, if word got out that he was cheating, someone was going to kill him for sure. It was either him or Sherlock.

Her hand found the gun just as he finished saying "rape." Quickly she put a bullet in the chamber. With the gun aimed, she waited for him to show his figure. It would be a matter of seconds for him to come at her again.

His mind went to getting the pussy and conquering her. "Fuck the money," he growled as if he were a werewolf. "We'll just sell your jewelry and the cars." He started walking over to the left side of the bed. "But first I'm going to get some of that –" He ducked just in time. She fired two shots. There was no time for him to pull the gun out of his shoulder holster. The bullets just missed his head.

It took all of her strength to stand up. Just as he cut the corner to go in the bathroom, she fired off two more shots, again just missing him. She was using her hearing to guide her.

Boom. Boom. Boom. Shots from her gun rang out again, but his shots hit her. One bullet ripped through her stomach and the other hit her in the shoulder, making her fall back up against the wall. The last one caught her in the chest and made her fall to the floor.

Clarence ducked when he saw her gun aimed at the bedroom door. By the look on her face, he could tell that she couldn't see him. When she fell back and dropped the gun he figured her for dead.

"Danny, where the fuck you at? Let's get the fuck out of here, I got the money." Clarence was looking for the money in the next room when he heard the shots. From the sound of the gun he knew that it couldn't have been Danny Boy firing the gun.

"Damn, that bitch almost killed me," Danny Boy yelled as he came out of the bathroom with his .45 Glock in hand. He was mad that his slippin' kept him from stealing some pussy. She was dead now and sticking around wasn't a good idea because of all the shots that were fired.

"How the fuck she get a gun? We got to get the fuck out of here. Yo' ass must have really been slippin'." Clarence was the cool headed one of the pair and the one making the right decisions that kept them alive.

"Hey man, what about Keisha?" They agreed that they would have to kill Keisha and her mother after the robbery. Danny Boy had to say something about her before they started the job because Keisha and Clarence were friends from high school and used to kick it a lot on the phone. Clarence, not hesitating to say that it was mandatory, meant a lot to Danny Boy. Loyalty is everything in the crime game.

"Keisha might walk through the door any second, so might the police. She can't testify to what she hasn't seen and the only witness is dead. You don't want to wait for the police do you?" Clarence didn't want to have to kill Keisha. He called her that morning and told her to meet him so he could give her a gift. She already two-wayed him, twice, trying to find out where he was. If Danny Boy ever found out, Clarence would have to kill him.

"That's the reason that I fuck with you. How much cash

we got?" Danny Boy was happy and started putting his gun back in its holster.

"There's got to be at least two hundred thousand in this bag. Let's hit the back door." They were out.

In the District of Columbia they were known as D & C. Opposites attracting couldn't have been truer in their case. Danny Boy was a hot head who was willing to battle with any and everyone, at anytime, anywhere, with or without guns. Clarence was the quiet, thinking type, who only said what was needed to be said. He was always thinking so he could be ahead of his enemies. Clarence didn't mind Danny Boy being the leader. Psychologically, Clarence was the leader because of all the times he saved them from being murdered. Things were always split equally and they never argued. This was because Clarence was good at using psychology. Everybody knew Clarence could make it big in the game without Danny Boy. Danny thought he had Clarence hypnotized, so it didn't matter what people said. He also felt that he could make it without Clarence.

They played their roles well. Danny Boy always picked the jobs and Clarence always planned things and kept up with their enemies' moves. Their plan was to make a big lick without disrespecting anybody in the drug game, regardless of what their hustle was. Robbing a drug dealer would mean a temporary supply and a war to fight. Fighting a war and making money didn't exactly mix well.

The perfect opportunity presented itself when Sherlock was murdered. Because it happened at a gambling house, Danny knew the houseman and the fellow gamblers weren't going to report it to the police or tell anybody what happened.

◆ ◆ ◆ ◆ ◆

"It's our time Clarence, Sherlock is dead." It was six o'clock when Danny Boy made the phone call. He hung around a little while so that the other gamblers and hustlers wouldn't be suspicious of him after they found out that Sherlock's house was robbed.

Clarence knew exactly what he meant. The first thing he thought about was Keisha. She was trying to get him to come back to school and work for her father to keep money in his pockets. Sherlock even propositioned him one time while he was visiting Keisha.

"Okay, when are we going in?" He was trying to buy time so he could make a plan.

"Hey man, we got to do everybody. No witnesses." If it weren't for Keisha he wouldn't have said this. Danny Boy didn't know how serious Clarence and Keisha's relationship had become. Still, he knew that Clarence had feelings for her. That could present a problem.

"Remember you're talking to a vet. I'll call you in an hour after I take this girl home." Clarence wasn't with a girl. He had to buy some time for the very reason Danny asked the question. There was no way he was going to kill Keisha, no matter how much money was involved.

"Why the fuck is that going to take so long?" Danny was in a serious rush.

"She don't live in DC. She lives in Maryland."

"Shit, a'ight." There was no need to argue. He knew that his partner was going to be there.

Clarence immediately made moves to get Keisha out of the house. At least three or four times a week they would meet in the morning, usually before she went to school, and once over the weekend. They were having a beautiful romance that few knew about.

◆ ◆ ◆ ◆ ◆

When Keisha saw her back door open she knew something was wrong. Neither of her parents would leave the back door open. She was already upset with Clarence for standing her up and not two-waying her back. She grew tired of calling and waiting.

"Mama, where you at Mama? Daddy, where you at," she hollered as she entered the kitchen. Everything looked normal. Walking farther, she noticed the living room was torn up. This was a sign of a robbery.

"Mama, Daddy," she called out again. There was no answer. Before she went upstairs she went in the front closet to get her gun. Sherlock trained his wife and daughter well. With gun in hand, she proceeded up the steps.

Her bedroom was ransacked and the money hidden in her closet was missing. Her father's den was also torn up. She almost dropped her gun when she saw her mother slumped against the wall. "What the fuck happened," she hollered. The possibilities of the robbers still being in the house slipped her mind. The sight of her mother ran a jolt of pain through her entire body.

Keisha didn't care that there was blood all over the bed and the carpet. All that mattered was helping her. She laid her gun on the carpet and hoisted her mother's lifeless body into her arms.

"Mama what happened? Don't die on me, I need you Mama. I'mma call an ambulance." Seeing her mother in that condition made her feel like it happened to her. Her pretty face was gone. She couldn't help but to think that she would never be the same. The sight of anyone else in that condition would have caused her to keep her distance.

It took about a minute to get connected with an operator and another minute to inform her of the situation and describe the house.

"Is that you Keisha?" Karyn mumbled the best she could.

"It's me, Mama." A slight smile came to her face. "You're going to make it Mama." She rocked her back and forth. "The ambulance is on the way. You are going to make it."

"I'm in a lot of pain. Baby I'm hurtin' all inside. I can barely see you." The sound of her voice revealed just how she was feeling.

"Mama tell me what happened. Who did this to you," speaking with her voice full of urgency. Keisha was also wondering where her father was and why he wasn't home.

"I'm so tired and sleepy baby." Drool was coming out the left side of her mouth. "It hurts so much, I just want to sleep."

"No Mama." She shook her. "You can't go back to sleep. Who did this to you?"

"It was D & C. They wanted money."

She didn't want to believe that Clarence had something to do with her mother's condition. "Mama are you sure?"

"D & C baby, they wanted money. Don't worry though, Sherlock will get them."

Keisha felt betrayed and tricked. That made the pain that much worse. "Wake up Mama. Wake up Mama," she yelled over and over, but it was no use. When the paramedics came through the door Keisha was still telling her to wake up.

Keisha sat on her bed in shock and dismay as the paramedics and police worked to save her mother.

Danny Boy and Clarence had to pay for what they had done, especially Clarence. As soon as her father came home, they would go on a mission. Sherlock taught her that telling the police about street beefs wasn't the thing to do. She didn't want to see them go to jail or have an easy death. There would have to be much pain. It was mandatory that they paid for what they did and feel what she was feeling. She didn't know what she was going to do, or how she would do it, but

Triple Crown Publications presents . . .   Keisha

for now, she knew that she needed to talk to her father.

Ya'll gon' pay the price like nobody ever has for fucking with my mother. Ya'll's pain is gon' be greater than mine. These words kept going over and over in Keisha's head.

◆ ◆ ◆ ◆ ◆

♦ ♦ ♦ ♦ ♦

DC's most efficient homicide detective, Sally, arrived on the scene at ten o'clock. Out of six hundred cases over a twenty-year span, she solved eighty-five percent of them. She also made sure she didn't convict any innocent people. Born and raised in the district, at the age of forty-six, Sally knew the streets well and all of the players just like a DJ knows his records. She knew how to play them all for information.

Before she approached a new crime scene, she had a ritual. First, she would take a medium sized Black & Mild cigar and rub it back and forth between both of her hands to loosen up the tobacco. Next, she would break the cigar down to the tan wrapper and put the tobacco in the plastic wrapper the cigar came in. This is a process that takes about fifteen minutes if a person isn't in a hurry. The wrapper was believed to cause headaches. Once the tan wrapper was removed from the cigar casing, the tobacco would be poured back into the hollowed out cigar. To pack the tobacco, the tip had to be tapped against a hard surface.

When Sally walked through the front door she was tapping her cigar against her watch. Once inside, she lit her Black. When the aroma filled the air, fellow officers knew better than to disturb her by telling her that the body was upstairs. They just kept quiet. When she entered they just made way for her to do her thing. Sally did things her way and copped a nasty attitude if somebody interfered with her process. As always, she walked around the first floor if the crime scene was at a house.

She started walking, smoking, looking around and saying, "Umm," every two to three steps. All year round, whether she was or wasn't at work, Sally wore pinstriped suits. It was rumored that sometimes she didn't wear a bra or underwear underneath. Officers would make bets on what color suit she would wear the next day. Today she was wearing dark lavender, with dark black pinstripes. Her pink pumps went great with the outfit. Because of her style and attitude they called her "The Pinstriped Bitch." She knew it and didn't give a damn. She always spoke her mind; in fact, she loved her title.

Nobody said a word when she started walking slowly up the stairs. From the scent of the cigar, which made its way upstairs before she did, her arrival was anticipated. Every few steps, Sally would let out an "Umm" that was just loud enough to be heard in the silent room. All of the officers were standing still and waiting for her to finish making her preliminary investigation. Her footsteps and her "Umms" were the only sounds that could be heard.

She knew Sherlock for years and was intrigued by how elegantly his house was furnished. She paused at the entrance of Keisha's bedroom, noticed the look on her face and called her into the hallway.

"Hello Ma'am. Who are you?" Keisha didn't feel like

talking to another officer, she just wanted to leave.

"Hello young lady. My name is Sally, and I've been assigned this case." Seeing worry in her face, she spoke as she took a long drag from her cigar. "Don't worry, I plan on solving this crime." Sally took note of Keisha's beauty. Reflecting back to the pictures she saw downstairs, she thought to herself that the camera didn't do her justice. She continued, knowing people were listening to her. "Everybody calls me Sally, or the Pinstriped Bitch, and homicides are my expertise. I need to ask you a few questions." She knew this wasn't a good time to talk to Keisha, but with everything fresh in her mind, she may have been able to provide some assistance; although, more questions would only be more aggravating for the young girl. The officers wouldn't let her do anything because they said she was part of the crime scene. Her gun on the floor made them suspicious. It would be up to Sally to let her go. Keisha thought to herself that Sally really didn't look like an officer.

She already knew the story that Keisha told Bambi. There would be plenty of time to see if the story was true. "Keisha you have just been through something tragic. Do you have a relative that you can stay with?"

"My Aunt Jessica is on the way from Maryland and should be here in a few minutes." The look on Keisha's face told how much stress she was feeling. She was tired of sitting in her room, unable to leave, like she was a suspect.

"Keisha, we can't let you leave with anything except a few items of clothing." If Sally let her pack a bag, some of her fellow officers would be complaining to the Captain, saying she was letting evidence go, but it was the least she could do.

"Okay, thank you," Keisha said as she went back in her room to gather a few things.

Sally waited until Keisha was downstairs to continue

with her investigation. Sally usually talked to her assistant, Bambi, who talked to officers and other personnel. "You all know the routine, Sally is in the house and handling business, so get lost," Bambi snapped.

Her colleagues hated the way Sally went about doing things. Most of the time she didn't recognize their presence. The most she would do was speak, and that was only if it was absolutely necessary or job related. Still, Sally made sure she never said anything to offend them, in front of or behind their backs. There was nothing they could do to sabotage her. She kept them at a distance and did her thing.

The next stop was Sherlock's bedroom. She looked up at the ceiling just as she fully stepped in the door. Then she looked at the walls. As an African-American female, she chose to put extra intensity into her job because it was a field that was dominated by males, mostly white. Her desire made it easy to get convictions. Her successes allowed her to do things her way without any problems.

"Okay Bambi, let's talk about this."

Bambi was a white girl with severe acne who knew very little about the streets. Looking beneath Bambi's physical features and lack of street knowledge, Sally saw loyalty and a fresh, fertile female mind. Because of this, Sally made Bambi her assistant. "It looks like an attempted robbery, or rape, that turned into a homicide."

"I think Keisha is holding back information from us. The sound in her voice when she left was the sound of a woman who was on a mission." Sally was still looking around the room.

"A mission to do what," Bambi countered.

"Look around. Think about it," Sally said coolly as she took another drag.

It registered what Sally was implying. "Nah, she doesn't seem like the kind of girl who would help her house get robbed. It looks like she was living a really good life. She said she wasn't here when her mother was murdered … or from the looks of it, tortured." Bambi was the type who looked for a motive for a murder, then at the suspect's background to determine possible behavior. Many people in the streets kept her fooled.

Sally couldn't get Keisha's voice out of her head. Her behavior seemed strange. "Umm," Sally murmured as she walked over to Karyn's lifeless body. "From the position of the body the shooter was probably in the doorway."

"What makes you think that," Bambi questioned.

"There are several bullet holes in the walls over there and over there. There are two by this door and two by the bathroom door." Sally didn't look at the report that told where the bullet casings were found. She was trying to live the scene out in her mind with the least amount of information.

"That means that the deceased fired shots too, but couldn't see."

"How do you know she couldn't see," Bambi asked, as her main job was to find holes in Sally's theories.

"Look at her face, her eyes are black and swollen shut."

"Didn't you see the movie, 'Ray'? When a person looses one sense the other senses step up. Just think, she had the shit beat out of her but was able to get her hands on a gun or two. We have a nine millimeter and a .380." That was the simple part, almost too simple.

"Well, Keisha said that she had the nine, so her mother must have had the .380. Plus the shells that were on the carpet over here were from a .380." Bambi could see Sally's logic.

"So what about the shells by the door?"

"They are from a 10-millimeter."

It was rare that a person got shot with that type of gun.

"Umm, that's pretty serious. I can't remember the last time I heard of a cat carrying something that big. How many times did she get shot?"

"She got hit three times, two of them went straight through her. I think she died from internal bleeding. The last one lodged in her chest."

"Umm, this is unusual. The deceased gets beat up really bad, to the point of disfigurement, but somehow she gets off at least four shots. Then she gets shot three times." Sally wondered if Karyn was shooting at more than one person.

"Well, I can help a little bit. The .380 came from up under the bed. At one point, she was probably in that chair and on the bed. There's blood in those places. The daughter says she came upstairs with the nine when she thought there was a break in." Bambi did her part by gathering all the possible information.

"Umm, all of that fits together. Did the pussy get tapped? She was a very beautiful woman," Sally said, eyeing the picture on the wall. Using crude language meant nothing to her. She was as hard as they came, but she carried herself like a lady.

"She still had her panties on. We'll wait to see what the pathologist has to say. It seems like an attempted robbery, although Keisha says there was nothing missing."

"It all makes sense, except for one thing." Sally took a long draw on her cigar. "There's something that girl isn't telling us. I know she didn't kill her mother but she knows much more than what she's saying." The intense look on Keisha's face told Sally that she was doing some serious thinking instead of just grieving. It was the same look that she saw many times in the past. Finding the killer, or killers, would be a matter of finding a 10-millimeter and/or watching Keisha.

The next thing on the agenda was to find Sherlock. Sally

could see Sherlock and Keisha trying to find and get revenge on the killers.

A week later, Karyn's funeral was held at Harmony Cemetery. Her entire family from Maryland was there. Since she lived in DC for over seventeen years, they didn't mind having the funeral there. All of DC's players were there, including Danny Boy and Clarence. They arrived late and didn't show their faces until Karyn was put in the ground. Being seen at the funeral could have caused a shoot out with some people who were looking for them. They made no attempts to stop any beefs.

Sally showed up also because she wanted to speak with Keisha.

Clarence waited until the funeral was almost over before he approached her. "Keisha, may I speak with you in private?" People that he had never seen surrounded her. They might think that it was rather wrong for him to question Keisha at her mother's funeral.

Keisha wanted to say no but knew that wouldn't be the way to get information – information that would be helpful in getting her revenge. She decided to put on a slight smile. "Okay." They stepped to the side. "You look real nice in that suit. Is it brand new or did you just break it out to impress me?"

Clarence ignored the comment. He was there to test the waters. "Why haven't you called a brotha back? I've been trying to get at you for a week. Are you mad at me or something?"

She started nodding her head, "You damn right I'm mad at you."

She thought to herself that he looked really good in the

suit. She wanted to ask him how much of her father's money he spent on it. "You picked one hell of a day to stand me up."

"Maybe I saved your life. If you were in the house you would have probably been killed too. Did you think about that?" Clarence was feeling really guilty over the past week. He wished there was a way for him to explain and make her understand.

Damn this nigga is good with words. She smiled a little bit to go along with what he said. "Maybe you have a point, but you lied to me and that makes me feel that I can't trust you anymore." She had to come up with something that went with the situation to keep him thrown off balance. There was the possibility that he wanted to know if she implicated him by telling the police about their little date that he didn't show up for. She wouldn't say a thing until he asked.

"I understand, and you're right. I was wrong. The last thing that I wanted to do was hurt you. If you can find it in your heart, please forgive me and call me tonight." Clarence was partially acting but he wanted to keep her in his life because of her looks and loyalty. Part of him wanted to know if she suspected that he killed her mother.

Sally was watching their expressions with deep interest. Intentionally, she made sure she was in Keisha's full view. No matter how long it took she would wait to talk to her.

"Listen Clarence, tell me who killed my mother and kidnapped my father. I know you keep your ear to the street. You've always known the 411." Finding out what happened to her father was the most important thing for Keisha. She didn't want to think the worst. There was the possibility that Clarence would slip and say that he did it and tell her about Sherlock. Her love for him was causing much inner turmoil.

Sally positioned herself so Clarence had to walk past her.

"I haven't heard a thing. Nobody has seen Sherlock since last weekend. What I'm concerned about is you and I. I really miss you." Keisha wasn't like the other girls in the streets. Not only was she beautiful, she was mad intelligent and knew how to treat a man in the game. Feeling guilty, he still wanted her to be a part of his life.

"Clarence, things are different now. I'm scared that whoever killed my mother may come back to get me. After today I'm not going back to the district." Her heart didn't fully accept that he had something to do with it although she wasn't able to erase the love she felt for him. Feeling betrayed, along with losing her parents, was making it hard to keep from saying what was on her mind.

"When you need me, I'll be here waiting for you. All you have to do is call me." He wanted to say much more but decided against it. He figured she would call him after a month or so.

"Bye," she said dryly while she was turning to walk away. "Bye," he said as he turned to walk to the car.

"That's a very nice suit, Clarence," Sally said as they crossed paths. "I'm surprised to see you in the open. You ain't bangin' no more?" She knew it would be a matter of time before she caught him and Danny Boy. Their names were ringing all across town. Sooner or later a trail would lead to their doors.

Looking at her up and down, Clarence walked past her without saying a word.

As Sally was walking and trying catch up with Keisha, she hollered back at Clarence, "You should let me get some of that young thang before you get killed. I can make you a man." She was down for having a good time but men her age weren't able to please her. She didn't care who knew about her sexual exploits but when she got buck, there was no stopping her.

"Keisha, wait up, I need to speak with you." Sally had to pick up her pace because Keisha was walking rather fast.

Keisha wanted to avoid her. Seeing Clarence first, and now having to deal with Sally was too much too soon. What she knew about Sally's reputation made her a little tense about getting her revenge. She was famous throughout Maryland, Baltimore and Virginia. All week, Keisha wondered if she was going to be able to get her revenge before Sally cracked the case.

Pausing and looking into Keisha's face she said, "You sure are a very pretty young lady, just like your mother." Sally always seemed to be in a good mood. It was part of her game.

"Thank you Ms. Henderson. You look stunning in that suit." Sally was wearing a black suit with white pinstripes.

"First, let me apologize for the behavior of my fellow officers. Everybody is a suspect to them." Sally sensed that Keisha didn't trust many people. Her sources told her that Keisha was only close to her parents and Clarence. She no longer had her parents and things weren't looking all that well with Clarence. This was a sign that Keisha was going into a shell.

"Well, that part is over. Do you have any suspects yet?" Keisha knew exactly what Sally was trying to do. She expected such.

"Not yet," she responded as she took a small puff on a cigar. "I think you are holding back on me. You seem to know something that you aren't telling."

Damn, she's smart, Keisha thought. "What makes you think I'm holding something back? I know you don't think I killed my parents." Sherlock taught his daughter ways of controlling a conversation while getting information without revealing anything.

"Parents, huh? What makes you think your father is dead?" This question was asked just to hear her response. Sally also felt like Sherlock was dead because a major player disappearing, and his house getting burglarized, couldn't just be a coincidence.

"I can't imagine there being too many other reasons for my father not coming home." Keisha knew the response when she made her last statement. It was not hard to imagine what a cop would ask next.

"I still think that you are holding something back." Sally considered Keisha's response evasive and slick. She didn't mind her diverting from the subject for a second. This was a means of getting to know a person's inner feelings better.

Keisha's instinct told her that she was going to be seeing a lot of Sally. "I don't know what to tell you, but I hope you solve this case. Your reputation says that you will."

"Umm," Sally murmured. "I'll be on the case. Trust that! By the way, you're staying in Maryland, right?"

"Yes, My Aunt Jessica felt that I needed to get a fresh start." Keisha's attention went to Clarence as he was getting in the gray Impala that was waiting for him. She could tell that Danny Boy was at the wheel.

"So that means you won't be seeing much of your boyfriend anymore?" Sally let out rings of smoke in the air.

"I don't have a boyfriend and it's time for me to go." All of the day's activities took a lot out of Keisha. She also learned a few things about Sally and Clarence.

"Here's my card, call me if you have any questions or have any new information." The relationship between Clarence and Keisha seemed like the best place to further her investigation. There was something there. All sources said they had a special relationship. Plus, Clarence wouldn't have been talking to her for no reason.

"Have a good day Ms. Henderson," Keisha said as she walked away.

"You too." That was the second time Keisha called her Ms. Henderson. Keisha didn't get it off the card because she didn't look at it. She had to have questioned some people. Why would a seventeen year old be asking questions about a homicide detective?

"Hey man, you look like you just lost your best friend," Danny Boy said to Clarence as he was getting in the car. The question was meant as a test. Sally speaking to him wasn't a good sign, even though it was only for a second. Sally was known to hound a dude if he was a suspect.

What the fuck are you talking about? You my best friend." They were debating if they should, or should not, kill Keisha to make sure their trail was safe. Danny Boy kept saying that he had a feeling. Every time he had some alcohol in him, which was just about every day, he brought up the subject.

Danny Boy and Clarence did everything together since they were in diapers. Their Mothers lived across the hall from each other in Potomac Garden Projects. Both lived in single parent homes, without any brothers, sisters or fathers. Thus, they became brothers to each other.

Danny Boy started getting in trouble on the first day of Kindergarten. Another boy reported him to the principal for taking his lunch money. Danny Boy was gifted with size and extraordinary strength to go with it and used both to his advantage every time he could.

The only time Clarence got in trouble was when he was with Danny Boy and they had to fight together. Clarence did his homework and left people alone unless he was disrespected. Most people thought Clarence was Danny Boy's younger brother. People said this because it wasn't natural for them to hang out together and get along so well. Clarence kept an easy "B" average and was the star point guard for the basketball team. Danny Boy played running back for the football team and could barely keep passing grades. He was put up a few grades because of his athletic abilities and because teachers didn't want to deal with him. Danny Boy missed many days of school when football season was over and nobody complained.

Danny Boy loved to run the streets and talk to the hustlers. Clarence was intrigued by the stories but he wasn't going to skip school to hang out with them like Danny Boy. It was seldom that Clarence didn't listen to his mother.

As he got older, Danny Boy started hanging in the streets more and more. When he started drinking MD20/20, Wild Irish Rose and smoking weed, he knew that the streets were where he belonged. Once he pledged himself to the game, there was no turning back. No matter how much his mother whipped and talked to him, he wouldn't change.

Danny Boy convinced Clarence to take his first drink and smoke his first joint. He would not have done any of that with anyone else. Drinking wasn't that bad to him, unless there was a hangover. Smoking weed was out of the question. Having the munchies and laughing all the time was not for him. A few times was enough.

Clarence was showing a lot of promise in school. His mother and teachers were expecting him to go to school to be a lawyer or a doctor. They also urged him to stop hanging out with Danny Boy. It seemed like every week Danny Boy was in a fight with someone. The only fights he lost were the ones with guys who were much bigger.

Just as everyone expected, Danny Boy ended up in Juvenile at twelve years old. He was the only one in a shoplifting ring that got caught. This was the first time that Danny Boy and Clarence were ever separated. They kept in touch with each other by letters and a few phone calls. Life just wasn't the same for Clarence without Danny Boy near-

by. Clarence was still doing good and representing his basketball team, averaging forty points per game. His Mother
was the proudest Mother in the projects.

Danny Boy's street credibility went up because he didn't
rat on the other members of the shoplifting crew. All of DC
knew about him because he was always getting into fights.
Reformatory School was just like another home to him.
There was plenty to smoke and drink, along with plenty of
violence. Most of the boys there were older and were into
using weapons - mostly knives. It was what they called a
Gladiator school.

Danny Boy gained a lot of respect because of his reputation from the streets. He also knocked a few niggas out when
they got in his way. With respect comes the power to run
things. That's exactly what Danny Boy did. He put together
a crew and demanded a cut from all activities going on in the
prison: storemen, housemen that ran card games to the cats
that were bringing in weed and wine. If there was a problem
he sent one of his soldiers to shank the cat. Danny Boy had
half the prison locked down. Jarvis had the other half sewed
up.

Jarvis was also a big fellow. He was seventeen and had
been there since he was thirteen, and had to stay in Juvenile
until he was twenty-one because he killed another kid for
stealing his sneakers. Jarvis had several people doing things
for him but was not happy with just having half of the spot.
With Danny Boy moving with so much steam and aggres-
siveness, Jarvis felt that a confrontation was imminent.

Danny Boy did have thoughts of taking him out and
toyed with the idea, but with only a year left to serve there
was no need to take the risk. He figured he could use Jarvis
when he got out. Danny Boy figured there was more money
to be made on the outside than on the inside and he put his
greed in check.

Jarvis' paranoia caused him to challenge Danny Boy to a knife fight. It was a common thing that happened when a beef couldn't be settled in the boxing ring. Danny Boy wasn't just strong and fast; he knew how to handle a knife. When he was alone, he practiced until he perfected his technique. Danny Boy had no choice but to kill Jarvis or get killed. He stabbed and ripped Jarvis's guts loose like he was taught. This was his first kill.

The rush he got caused him to take advantage of anybody who showed any sign of weakness. He changed – for the worse. He would take everything, then sell a dude to another set in the prison so they could do as they pleased with him. A monster was created.

When Danny Boy got out, at age fifteen, it didn't take much to convince Clarence to run the streets with him. This is when the name D & C was created. Going to school and playing basketball became boring to Clarence. He craved the action that Danny Boy was getting and telling him about for so many years. He couldn't resist having a ringside seat and being part of how Danny Boy planned to take over the district and the streets.

"I don't want you to think that I don't trust you. Once we get to moving that shit I don't want to have to look back." Danny Boy could see that he was about to start getting on his man's nerves.

"Look man let's get out of here. We have a few cats to make peace with." Clarence was always smart enough to keep Danny Boy out of his head and business.

"At times I think you want to be too cautious." Danny Boy had to wonder if there would ever come a time that Clarence would try to outsmart him. Clarence stood stronger than he expected. Waiting to spend lots of money, and go get a package, made a lot of sense. Clarence explained that they needed to put some time between the murder and their come up. Danny put the car in motion but he couldn't wait to get a Benz.

"Like you said, we don't want to have to look back."

"Yeah, let's see if we can make peace with these youngsters."

The dudes they had beefs with were all young, trigger happy, wannabe thugs, trying to make names for themselves. The district was full of them. It was a real simple thing. If they couldn't be put to work, or weren't agreeable to squashing the beef, elimination was the only other option.

Only two cats had to be bumped off. Danny Boy took care of one with his Colt .45 and Clarence took care of the other with his Glock Model 29 10 mm. Usually they would sell their guns to some out-of-state cats after they put in work but this time they had their pieces melted down.

Leaving the district couldn't have happened fast enough for Keisha. For a week she wondered what she was going to say to Clarence when she saw him. Seeing him at the funeral was totally unexpected. It took all of her strength to keep from jumping on him and accusing him of killing her mother. At this point, the missing money didn't matter. It was a miracle that she was able to keep a tap on her lust for revenge. As of yet, she hadn't figured out a way to make him pay that would satisfy her.

Jessica could see that Keisha had a lot on her mind. "Are you alright Keisha? Wasn't that the guy that used to be your boyfriend?" Jessica had to ask because Keisha wouldn't take her eyes off of him. She was sure it was the same guy that she saw in a picture and met a few times.

"I'm a'ight. He's from of DC. I don't want any more parts of DC." Though Jessica was just like her sister, she couldn't tell her what was on her mind. There was no need to tell anyone. Sherlock taught her that many things were never to be said.

"Okay, we'll be outside of the D in a few minutes." Jessica was Sherlock's younger sister.

Maybe in the future Keisha would talk about her feelings for Clarence with Jessica. It just depended on how long it was going to take to get him out of her system.

Keisha and Clarence were close since Junior High. It all started when she asked him to tutor her in English. She really didn't need his help. It was her way of getting him in her house for her parents to approval. Her mother knew it was game but she went for it because Keisha told her so much about Clarence that she wanted to meet him instead of just watching him play basketball while she cheered. They would be studying right in the living room. What harm could that be? At that time they were in the seventh and eighth grades.

Sherlock was extremely strict and protective of his daughter and only child. He really didn't care for the studying thing. He went for it until the summer came. Their friendship was maintained by using the telephone.

Keisha was extremely attracted to Clarence's light brown eyes and bronze skin. He was her Adonis. When he cut his hair in a low cut Caesar she loved his look, especially the waves. She would always tell her mother that just looking at his hair made her seasick. Her mother understood and encouraged the relationship. Their mission was to convince Sherlock to accept him as well.

When school started back the study sessions resumed. On his own accord, Sherlock decided that he wanted to meet Clarence alone and talk to him. Sherlock let him know that he knew that his daughter didn't need a tutor because she was a straight "A" student. Still, he approved of the relationship because Clarence seemed to have his head in the right place. Sherlock knew that his daughter was going to start seeing boys, with or without his approval, in some manner or the other. Holding a young girl back wasn't a reasonable possibility. Keisha always obeyed him and conducted herself with respect and class.

Keisha loved everything about Clarence - the way he walked and the way he talked. The sound of his voice captivated her. The things that he talked about and the dreams and ambitions that he had made her want to be a part of his life. Most of all, she loved him because he loved her for being herself. At no time did he try to make her submissive. She didn't mind him being in charge, as long as he did it with finesse and respect. They talked about having sex on several occasions. It was mostly him trying to get her to give up the cherry but he respected her decision to wait until she at least graduated from high school. There was absolutely nothing that they couldn't talk about no matter how the other one felt.

Keisha admired Clarence's will to wait for them to have sex. She and her mother had lengthy conversations about it. Karyn convinced her that it was in most men to have multiple sex partners, no matter what a woman did. This was hard for Keisha to accept, but she did, though she was jealous as hell when she heard about Clarence having sex with other females. For a few weeks, she wouldn't speak to him in school or accept his phone calls. Keisha was about having her way and that included having her man all to herself. Still, no matter how much she wanted Clarence to be all hers, she wasn't going to sleep with him. She would never disobey her parents like that.

When he stopped calling, and started acting like she didn't exist, she picked up the phone and called him. It was her first lesson in compromising. Her love for Clarence was stronger than her pride. Her mother told her that she would one day get tired of Clarence and take an interest in other boys. She tried to explain to her that was how puppy love went.

It didn't turn out to be that way. They fell deeper and deeper in love with each other. At no time did they call each other boyfriend and girlfriend. Keisha was still keeping her options open even though they spent as much time on the phone as possible. Seldom did a day go by that they didn't talk to each other. Many girls chased Clarence and sexed him to make Keisha jealous. Many of them hated her because they knew her father was a major player and bought her everything. Keisha took it all in stride. Clarence treated her like a queen and put her before any other girl, and they all knew it. He didn't hesitate to keep them in check. This let her know that she really had a hell of a man. In the end she planned on having Clarence all to herself. Her mother had to give her a lot of guidance and advice to keep her head right. Keisha had to put a few females in check, though, when they said something about her not being able to keep her man satisfied. Once she showed that she had skills she never heard anything else. Sherlock taught his daughter, and his wife, how to fight on the punching bag in the basement.

Since Keisha didn't own her man physically, she decided to own him mentally and spiritually. She kept him interested in her by challenging his mind and stimulating his intellect. They both loved to read and share information over the Internet. She gave him her old computer and paid for his e-mail service. On a daily basis, over e-mail, she wrote him poems and letters and he would do the same. She always made sure that she had something to talk to him about, even if it was sports. Whatever interested him, interested her. Her mother was teaching her how to mentally seduce him. Keisha could see that it was working. She had his total attention just about whenever she wanted it.

No matter how many girls he fucked, he always made time for her and did things to make her feel special. No matter how much they were seen together at school, they continued to tell people they were just friends. However, it was hard to hide the obvious that they were in love. When they were together they had a glow that was hard to disguise.

Keisha's plan was to be so good to him, without sex, that when they started having sex he wouldn't be able to think about anybody else. All was good until he decided to quit school to run the streets with Danny Boy. When Sherlock found out, he forbade Clarence from coming over. Keisha didn't care about him being in the game. She even convinced her father to give him a position in his organization. Sherlock agreed, only if Clarence decided to go back to school. Clarence kept saying yes, but he never went back.

Keisha accepted and respected his decision although she still hoped that something would change his mind. They had to start seeing each other without Sherlock knowing about it. He didn't want his daughter catching a stray bullet. Seeing Clarence behind her father's back was okay, until he spoiled it.

Keisha knew that Danny Boy talked him into robbing her father. It wasn't like Clarence was on dope or something. One day she planned to ask Clarence why, while she was getting her revenge.

"I don't think you sleep Sally. You are twice my age and you always look fresh like you're ready to take on the world," Bambi said when she walked into the office.

"At my age I've learned to disregard the bullshit and enjoy life. I know what I enjoy and I get it."

"Some good, young dick and a crime makes for a good orgasm," they said in unison, and laughed. Most people couldn't deal with Sally's straightforwardness. Some loved her because she kept it real and loved to talk shit, others did their best to avoid her.

"Damn, I wish I could enjoy life like you do."

"Girl we got us a good-ass case here." She got up and started walking around. It was time to get to work. "Why would a seventeen-year-old investigate a homicide detective," Sally questioned as she looked at pictures of all of the possible suspects.

"That's a good question. You must be referring to Keisha," Bambi said as she picked up a picture off of Sally's desk. "Damn she's one hell of a pretty girl. If I looked like her I would be a model and get paid."

In Bambi's mind, she knew Keisha was smart, but something else kept pulling at her and couldn't put her finger quite on it. She felt that Keisha was thinking about hiring her own private detective to solve the murder but there could be more. The way Sally asked the question made it sound a little more peculiar. Most of the things that Sally said sounded different until she put the whole picture into perspective.

"I was talking to her yesterday and she called me Ms. Henderson, twice. How many people, let alone kids, have you heard call me that?" Sally knew the answer, it was her way of provoking thought.

"Did you think that she was just trying to be respectful," Bambi replied as she took a seat at her desk. They had their own private office, where nobody else was allowed. Bambi really wanted to say that it couldn't be pertinent to anything but kept the thought to herself.

"Okay, let me go a little further. She said that Clarence wasn't her boyfriend. All of her schoolmates say that they were close and they were in love with each other, but she denies that all the time. She keeps on saying they were friends, but I know that's not true."

Bambi was very familiar with Clarence. "So you think that she's trying to protect him or something?"

"It's possible, but it's too simple. What girl would protect her mother's murderer," she said as she walked over to the window. She still had to consider that angle for a minute because it would make her correct and that was a real possibility. Bambi was starting to think that Sally was tripping. "If she ain't protecting him, then what do you think she's doing?"

"Umm, let me tell you a little more. I watched them talk. She didn't seem too pleased with him. As a matter of fact, she seemed a little upset. You would think she would have been glad for him to be there for her." Sally took out her lighter and lit up a Black. "Imagine this, they planned to rob Sherlock, things didn't go right and the mother got killed. So Keisha is being quiet to keep from getting jail time." Sally had to admit to herself that what she just said was rather a far stretch of the imagination. In the past, some of her wild guesses ended up being correct.

Bambi had to think for a few seconds. It was a hell of a theory that deserved some thought before a response. "Let me get this straight, Clarence and Keisha planned a robbery on Sherlock but the mother ends up getting murdered."

"That's exactly what I'm talking about. I can tell that she has serious feelings for him. He could have talked her into it."

"Clarence is cool but ain't all that," Bambi said with her nose turned upward. "They're both smarter than that. If they wanted to get Sherlock's money, they could have come up with another plan that would have gotten her out of the house." Something else came to her mind, "She could have just had Clarence and his partner go in the house when nobody was home, like during a game." Karyn and Sherlock loved to see their daughter cheerlead.

"Shit," Sally hollered with disgust. "You have a point there." Many of the officers loved it when one of her theories got shot down. This was her reason for only working with an assistant. She hated negative energy. "On the day of the murder the girl had a look on her face that I couldn't figure out. She also said there was nothing missing from the house."

"Let me tell you what I'm thinking. All we have to do is find a hustler that carries a 10-millimeter. That should be simple because very few people have them." Bambi was great at using deductive reasoning.

"Guess what, I thought about that two days ago. It's been rumored that Clarence has a Glock Model 29. If I'm not mistaken, it's a ten. That's a big ass gun that usually leaves a hole in the target." Two cats in the northeast had been hit like that. Because it happened outside, and no slug could be found, there was no trail that led back to Clarence.

"I still say Clarence is smarter than that." He used hollow points so that there wouldn't be a slug for comparison. "He isn't going to keep the same gun that he used to shoot several people with."

"He's probably using hollow points and not thinking about circumstantial evidence." Sally had already thought about this, but it still meant that the killer was smart.

"Oh yeah, check this, why rob the father of your girlfriend when there were other people you could have robbed? Clarence doesn't seem like a gully cat." From listening to Bambi, one wouldn't have thought that she was from the better part of the district.

"Damn Bambi, you right." She started pacing and smoking. "Clarence isn't like that at all, but Danny Boy is. He's the kind to take what he wants."

"Danny Boy would have to have some serious control over Clarence to get him to rob Sherlock. I can't imagine

Clarence being scared of Danny Boy. Word on the streets say that Clarence really doesn't need Danny Boy to make it. In fact, they say he needs to stop hanging around Danny Boy." Part of Bambi's job was to keep profiles on every hustler and gang banger in the district and surrounding areas. She knew them like an author knows the characters in a book.

"I said this was a good mystery." Sally was still pacing.

"Let's look at what we haven't looked at – Sherlock and Danny Boy."

"That's a damn good idea." A smile came to Sally's face as she patted her perfectly relaxed hair and tugged on her ponytail. That was how she wore her hair most of the time.

"It was the weekend and Sherlock was known for gambling. If he wasn't at a gambling house my name ain't Bambi."

"I got to find out what happened to him," Sally exclaimed. She really didn't have the right to inquire about Sherlock because he was still just considered a missing person. With his wife dead she was supposed to seek him out to question him but she knew there was a piece missing to the puzzle. The question was, who had the correct piece?

Sally had the feeling that the answers to the questions were right at her fingertips. There was no doubt that Clarence was involved with the murder. If Clarence had something to do with it then Danny Boy had to be in the picture. There was no doubt in her mind that Keisha knew something that she wasn't telling. The information she didn't tell had to be the key. Sally wasn't sure of how she was going to crack the case and get into Keisha's head, but for now, finding Sherlock was her number one priority. As time slipped away, he was more than a missing person.

◆ ◆ ◆ ◆ ◆

◆ ◆ ◆ ◆ ◆

A little over two weeks had passed since Danny Boy
and Clarence made their move. During their down
time, they planned how they were going to hit the streets
without being questioned.

"Man I'm ready to put a down payment on that Benz,"
Danny Boy said with a grin on his face. When he smiled he
resembled a cute gorilla. Girls got a kick out of his size and
ruthless-looking grin.

Clarence grinned also. They were on Pennsylvania
Avenue, looking at a building they were going to make their
spot. "This is going to be perfect. We have three floors and
the rent is cheap." They were standing at the window and
looking inside while some of their new recruits were in the
vehicle, smoking weed and drinking.

"Damn man, all you talk about is saving money. We're
about to be major playas. Spending money ain't a thang." If
it hadn't been for Clarence they would have been at the
malls and clubs splurging.

Clarence laughed, it was hard to hold his man back. Since they made peace with the streets, Danny was getting drunk and smoking dro on a daily basis. This left Clarence to plan and put all things in place.

"Danny my man, you're right, money ain't about to be a thang." Clarence could see that changing wasn't going to be as simple as he thought. The hardest things that he needed to do were already done. That included keeping Danny Boy from spending a wad of cash, and convincing him to just sell dro, instead of cocaine and heroin, to start out.

"Shit man, we could be flipping ounces of coke right now." Danny immediately wanted to go out and purchase four kilos but Clarence had to convince him that them moving that hard and that fast meant people would wonder where they got the money, especially being that their pockets hadn't been that fat from the start.

"You know we don't want people suspecting that we stole Sherlock's money and murdered his wife. The streets are still talking about what happened." Clarence was getting tired of telling Danny Boy the same thing. Being patient was also hard on Clarence because he was in a rush to move his mother out of the 'hood.

"Yeah, yeah," Danny responded with impatience in his voice. "Well we have these youngsters ready to go to work. We've sold them a dream and need to get started." The recruits were made into soldiers and lieutenants and they would only work under cats that were also gang bangers or former ones.

"They okay. We told them that it would be another two weeks before the shipment would be in. We have plenty of time to pacify 'em." Clarence disliked the tone of Danny's voice. In a few weeks Danny Boy would be thinking that he was on top of the world.

"So let's put the down payment on this spot. It ain't like

we don't have the money." It was aggravating to Danny to just sit on one hundred twenty thousand dollars. Burning a hole in his pocket was an understatement. No matter his desire, he stuck with Clarence because he always stuck with him, no matter how grimy he had been with people. He knew that soon he would be able to splurge like he wanted to.

"That sounds like a really good move. Next week we'll pick up a pound of that dro." They were starting out like they only had a few dollars even though Clarence had spoken to all of the suppliers to get the best price and the best connect. He told them that D&C planned on having a twenty-hour dro spot to start with. No one took his plans of parlaying seriously but Clarence didn't mind. He did all the talking while Danny Boy sat in the car. None of the suppliers wanted to talk to Danny Boy. His griminess and style preceded him.

"Damn it's about time that we made a move so we can get that cash." Danny was grinning.

"We are about to turn ten thousand dollars into a multi-million dollar operation." Clarence knew that making the money was the easy part once respect was established. His statement was made to appease his partner's ego.

The groundwork had been laid. If anybody asked any questions about how they got the money, they would say that they saved. They were starting with the minimum amount of dro that they could get started with, and they had dedicated soldiers that were ready to get paid. It would look like D & C were struggling, though they were strapped with cash. They even planned to leave the building raggedy. Clarence knew it would be a matter of time before the suppliers would front them whatever they wanted.

Clarence also knew that there were going to be problems with his partner because Danny Boy never handled his money well. He also liked to start needless and meaningless beefs with other drug dealers and playas. There was also the possibility of there being a power struggle between the both of them. The maxim of 'More Money Problems' was another factor. Though these bridges could only be crossed when the time came, Clarence was the kind to always think ahead.

Danny Boy was seeing D&C becoming the biggest set in the district. Once they got started, there was nothing that could stand in their way. He wanted people to say his name with the respect that a Don deserved. Whatever whip on rims that another cat possessed would look like nothing in comparison with what he was planning on buying. It would be just a matter of time before he was respected as one of the baddest hustlers on the East Coast. Soon all the street magazines, *Don Diva* and *F.E.D.S.*, would want to interview him. He wasn't going to be satisfied until they were able to purchase a hundred kilos of heroin. Being solo, like Frank Matthews, was also appealing. Money definitely wouldn't be a thang.

5

◆ ◆ ◆ ◆ ◆

"All I need you to do is stay hard," she said while positioning herself on her latest plaything. Sally loved to ride a big dick. "Ooh that feels so good." She was going up and down slowly and wiggling when her G-Spot was hit. "Yeah young buck, just like that. This is some good ass dick." He grabbed her waist and thrust upward, "I could ride this thing all night long."

Kevin thought that he was the shit because he was getting it on with a female that was old enough to be his Mama, and a cop at that.

It was time for her switch positions to keep him from cumming. She knew when he was getting close to a nut and she loved to fuck for at least thirty minutes. Plus, she needed to get two more orgasms. "I'm switchin' positions, baby." She was letting him know that she was going to let him get his after a while.

She came up off of him just enough for his tool to be out of her. Her left hand was gently holding his tool in place.

Older women knew the significance of not losing contact with a lover. She turned around with her back was facing him, like they were about to do it doggy style but with him laying on his back. She hadn't known him long enough to let him have control of her like that.

Slowly she reinserted his tool and moaned as she slid down. Her pussy contracted enough for her to feel a tensing sensation because of his size. Still moving slowly, she was able to take it all back in. "Damn you got a big dick, and it feels so good." Her tongue was licking her top lip as he pushed up and hit her spot. "Ooooh that feels so fucking good." She jumped up a little bit while she balanced herself with one hand on his stomach and one on the bed. Her feet were placed on the bed, up against his thighs.

She was still moving up and down slowly. The slow motion made her feel like she was about to cum all over him at any moment. "Yeah that's it. That's the way Sally likes it." They had found a rhythm with a tempo that was pure pleasure to her.

"Ooooh that's the shit, young buck." She was on an upward stroke almost causing him to slip out of her. The head of his dick crossed the sensitive part of her pussy. "We got to get that one more time." With the head of his dick just inside of her they found another rhythm. "Oh yeah," she said between moans. "That's the motherfuckin' shit." They were throwing it back and forth at each other with short strokes. "Yes Kevin, Sally loves your dick. Keep stroking just like that." Their tempo had quickened, with the same length strokes. Stroking the entrance to her pussy was driving her into ecstasy.

Kevin decided to push all the way up in her, again. "Oooh Kevin, I can't last much longer. That feels so fucking good." Kevin grabbed her by the waist and flipped her over while still stroking her. His dick was all the way up in her and the short strokes were keeping her turned on.

Before she realized it they were doing it doggy style. Kevin started banging her hard and slapping her ass. "Oh Kevin fuck me harder," was all she could scream while trying to catch her breath. "Oh I'm cumming! It feels good as a motherfucker, please don't stop!" Kevin was banging her as hard as he could.

It made her feel good to know that she could take all nine inches of him. "Right there. Yes that's it." Kevin had it all in her and was moving her hips from side to side, grinding at the entrance of her pussy and hitting her G-Spot.

She was surprised that a seventeen-year-old knew so much about fucking. "Now fuck me slowly Kevin." Kevin complied. When it felt like he was about to back out she pushed her ass toward him. "That's it Kevin, now fuck me harder," she growled between clinched teeth. If she could get one more orgasm she would be able to make it for another month.

With all his might, he slapped her ass and stroked her as fast and as hard as he could. "Oh that feels good. Please don't stop. Please don't stop. I need one more nut." Turning back to look at him, she squinted her eyes and bit her bottom lip as she grabbed his thigh, giving her all.

She tightened her pussy as much as she could and wiggled because it was feeling so good. Every time he hit her spot it made her lose her breath and took her to another level. This was the best fuck she had in a long time. "Shit, I'm about to cum." She could barely get the words out. "Damn, that's it." They climaxed together.

Just as soon as they were able to stand up, she slapped the shit out of him, right across his left cheek with her right hand. "That was for fucking me doggy style. Just because you have a big dick doesn't mean you can fuck me the way you want."

He just held his face with a look of confusion. No one taught him the ways of a bitch.

She was having her way and she loved it. Experience trained her to use young dudes so that she wouldn't get used or hurt. The young ones were easy to control and use for sexual purposes because they thought they were getting over.

"Put your clothes on so I can talk to you." She wanted to laugh at the expression on his face. If he were a real man she would have taken the chance that his ego would be bruised.

It was time to get some information. When she came back in the bedroom she gave him a few shots of Barcardi Rum. "Tell me what's happening with D & C." She sat in front of him, showing her bare thighs, which she kept toned by using a Stairmaster on a daily basis.

Kevin bought into the D & C dream and that called for a certain amount of loyalty. Loyalty is compromised when some good pussy has a cat wide open. Her experience with her pussy, and her mouth, had him ready to tell it all. "They are about to start a dro spot over on Pennsylvania."

"Dro," she questioned. "Why ain't they selling coke or heroin? The real money is in heroin."

"Clarence said that they only have a few thousand dollars to get started with." Kevin didn't care what they started with, as long as he was making money. He still preferred dro because he could get his smoke on and still keep the money straight.

Sally was tempted to say that she didn't believe that shit but she kept quiet. A few thousand dollars wasn't a lot of money to be starting a spot with. It seemed that they only had enough money to get started. That didn't seem right.

"They say they are going to have an endless supply." He made this comment because of the look on her face.

Might as well get to the point, "Where do you think they got the money from?" She knew that nobody was going to front a lot of drugs to young dealers. There was too much of a possibility that they might end up dead the next day. "You think they robbed Sherlock," she questioned. The Barcardi seemed to have kicked in because his tongue had gotten loose.

"Nah, Sherlock was like Clarence's father-in-law. He would have given him a few thousand if he stopped fucking with Danny Boy. To be down with Sherlock, and have Keisha, would have been enough for me to say fuck Danny Boy." He was thinking about all the guys that wanted to get next to Keisha and Sherlock.

"So what's the word on Sherlock?"

"I hate to say it, but Sherlock is probably dead. His operation is still running smooth as a motherfucker, but when your house gets robbed and you can't be found, you have to be dead." He was glad that she didn't ask him anything that would make him feel uncomfortable. He finished off his drink.

"Word is that Sherlock loved to gamble on the weekend." It was an indirect question as she was satisfied so far with his information. With her foot she started rubbing on his shin.

"Everybody knows that Sherlock loved to play skin at Cedric's gambling spot every weekend. Shit, that was his hobby." The look on his face said that he admired Sherlock.

With a sexy voice, she said, "I have one more question for you Mr. Big Dick."

He started smirking, "What's that?"

"Does Clarence have a gun that's bigger than average?"

What a stupid question, he thought. What could that have to do with anything? "Yeah he carries a big gun. It's bigger than a nine and loud as a motherfucker." Clarence had taken

a few shots at him one time when they had a be
'hood rat. Kevin threatened Clarence because he
Clarence was really harmless. It was one of the be
was squashed.

"Mama is satisfied. Now she wants some more of th
dick."

Sally wasn't certain if Clarence had a ten, but she
pretty sure by hearing Kevin's description. No matter, it
enough for her to think that he murdered Karyn and robbe
Sherlock. There was also the chance that somebody else
committed the murder to frame Clarence and Danny Boy,
but what would be the benefit? Plus street cats weren't that
sophisticated.

All the angles she came up with had problems. For five
or ten grand, she couldn't imagine Clarence going through
the trouble of robbing who would become his father-in-law,
and killing his mother-in-law. Though their relationship
wasn't that, that's what people considered them because of
Keisha. All the facts didn't add up to a conclusion that was
plausible or couldn't be contradicted. The most perplexing
was Keisha's behavior.

There were only two constants to go off of - Sherlock
loved to play Georgia Skin on the weekend and Clarence
carried a big gun.

◆ ◆ ◆ ◆ ◆

Keisha turned into a 106 & Park freak. It was three
weeks since the funeral and she figured that her love for
Clarence would have subsided, but it hadn't. The only thing
that did change was her deepened intensity to see him suffer.

Her mother's voice saying that it was D & C kept popping in her head.

al nights she woke up in a cold sweat after having
e dream –

rence shooting her mother. She knew that his Glock
s favorite weapon because they talked about it on
occasions.

Vaking up from the dreams, it was like she knew every-
g about him but nothing at all. Hope was telling her that
r mother made a mistake. Clarence was like a son to her
d she was like a mother to him. People with feelings like
that just don't hurt each other. She could have fully understood if it had been anybody else or just Danny Boy, but not
Clarence.

Talking to Jessica helped the situation a little bit. At best,
she could only be seen as an ear

to burn up. Jessica would want to call the police if she
was told the truth.

"Jessica, have you ever been so deeply in love with somebody that you can't make yourself hate them?"

"Oh, so that's why you were looking at Clarence like
that." Jessica mused.

"Why would you want to hate a good-looking boy like
that?" Jessica was thinking that Keisha was just trippin'.

"Girl, it isn't like I really want to hate him. I just want to
have less love for him but I can't get him off my mind."

"If your ass was looking for a good man, like I am, you
wouldn't be saying that." Jessica was a decent looking red-
bone. She was one of those independent career type females,
mostly lots of work and little play.

"He did something that I can't forgive him for.
Something in me wants him to convince me that he didn't
do it. Isn't that rather backwards?" She bit into a slice of
pizza.

"You've been talking about this for three weeks. Did he
cheat on you or something?" Jessica just couldn't imagine

Clarence doing something that bad, especially hearing Keisha talk about him for so many years. "Maybe you should call him." Jessica grabbed her second piece of pizza.

"Nah, it ain't that he cheated on me. We ain't ever had sex."

Jessica started laughing. She was laughing so hard she had to put her pizza down. "Damn girl, you got love for a dude like that and ya'll ain't even made love? Ya'll on some Romeo and Juliet shit." Jessica really didn't mean it to be harmful. It was a response to something that wasn't expected, especially nowadays.

Keisha found it to be funny as well, but she was not laughing because it was humorous, it was that messed up for her. "Girl stop laughing at me and no, I'm not calling that motherfucker."

"I'm sorry about laughing. In the twenty-first century you don't hear about love like that. They say that it's better to be in love and get your heart broken than to never have been in love at all." She picked her slice of pizza back up.

"Seriously Jessica, is it possible to stop loving somebody when you have feelings that deep?" Danny Boy wasn't that important, but the love she felt for Clarence was keeping her from figuring out how to make him feel the pain she was feeling.

"If you love Clarence, like you say you do, you'll probably never get him out of your system." Jessica had enough experience to know.

Keisha had a look of astonishment on her face. What Jessica just said seemed to fit the situation. Alicia Keys' song "Fallin'" came to mind.

"You can't be serious Jessica, I could have these feelings for him forever." It was a question put in the form of a statement. She put her pizza down, leaned back on the sofa, tucked her feet up under her shapely butt and went into deep thought.

"It happens like that. A woman must be careful about the first man she gives her heart to." Jessica hadn't noticed that Keisha drifted in thought.

Keisha knew for sure that her mission was going to be extremely hard. Her love for Clarence was something she now knew she couldn't get out of her heart. Making him feel pain was just going to be that much harder. She didn't know if she would be able to complete her mission. Maybe it would be simpler to put a bullet in his head and get it over with. That is, if she would be able to do that. Killing him would be too easy of a punishment. What he deserved was lots of pain and suffering, the kind that would make a cat regret that he crossed the line.

Wanting to hurt Clarence, and hurting him, were two different things. That was her biggest problem. Not being able to tell anyone was the other problem. Who was there that she could trust and would believe her? It came down to controlling her emotions to put work in. She had to do it for her mother, for her father, and mostly, for being betrayed. But could she?

6

♦ ♦ ♦ ♦ ♦

It took Sally a week before she was able to catch up with Cedric. He just walked into his poolroom on Pennsylvania, which was three blocks away from D & C's spot.

She was parked across the street in her dark blue BMW with gold pinstripes. All one hundred and thirty-five pounds of her five-foot-seven frame was moving fast to get across the street.

When she walked in the poolroom all the action stopped and all eyes were on her. "Ya'll just act like I ain't here. Just don't kill anybody while I'm in the building." It was a known fact that all she investigated were murders.

At Cedric's they did like they wanted to. After the spot was closed they played dice on the pool tables. A crack head or two had been known to get gang-raped there. All the major playas did their thing upstairs, in the back rooms, mostly gambling.

Sally walked straight to the back. After her announcement they acted like she wasn't there. The smell of weed was all over the place. Sally walked past the lady that ran the counter like she ran the place. When she got in the back she banged on the door that said Manager. "Open the door Cedric. You know who it is."

She turned the knob to see if it was open but it was no use. She banged on the door again. "You don't want me to come back with a search warrant."

"Why the fuck are you stressin' me," Cedric demanded as he opened the bathroom door, which was right across from his office. Cedric was a tall, decent looking, dark-skinned brotha and had a hell of a deep voice.

She turned around and gave him a nasty look, like he shouldn't have been in the bathroom. "In your office," she pointed. "We need to talk."

"What the fuck you want girl? You know that I run a clean establishment." He just walked past her after unlocking his office door.

She followed him and closed the door behind her. "I need to know what happened to Sherlock." Her voice was saying that she was expecting to hear a lie.

"My name is Cedric, not CNN." There was some hatred in his voice as he took a seat behind his desk.

"Okay you want to be smart. I wonder how some people downtown are going to feel about you selling alcohol to minors." She was pacing back and forth. Her black two-piece skirt suit with gray pinstripes was making her feel sexy.

He wanted to say, "fuck you bitch," but that would only cause problems. "Why are you on me about him? I'm not your type. Why ain't you sweatin' a young cat." He was trying to be funny.

"Cedric you need to be careful," she said yawning, bored with his response. You are a prime suspect in his murder, considering this was the last place he was seen. We know you run a skin game on the weekends." With the utmost intensity she was looking at him.

"Sally, who the fuck do you think you're talking to. Who the hell said Sherlock is dead?" He almost said that she didn't have Sherlock's body. His partners buried the body across the Virginia line.

"Listen here Cedric, you need to tell me what you know. Was Sherlock here the night before he was missing?" There was no way for her to win an argument about whether or not Sherlock was dead because his body had not been found.

Cedric was an older cat that did a few bids for burglaries and attempted murder. He and Sherlock had come up together. Cedric wasn't good at anything and was always in financial trouble. His girlfriends kept him having ups and downs. He had to always get it the best way he could. If it weren't for running a gambling house he would have been broke. He was a super trick all his life, with his biggest weakness being young pussy.

"Every time somebody is missing or killed in this part of town, you want to harass me and I don't never know shit." He was exaggerating to make it sound good.

"Listen Cedric, you might as well stop frontin' and trying to make me out to be a bad bitch. What happened to Sherlock?"

"Shit, if you know that he was here you should know what happened to him. I want to know my damn self." He was wondering what the other cats that attended the game were going to say. He also knew it had to have been a cat at the skin game who murdered Sherlock's wife. He had a real good idea of who it could be.

It was time to change direction. "Was Sherlock at the skin game?" She sat down and lowered her voice. Years ago when she arrested Cedric for burglary it was easy to trip him up. That was twenty years ago and he had gotten smarter.

Cedric wanted to say no, but too many people knew Sherlock came to his spot every weekend, religiously. Saying 'yes' was out of the question because there would be more questions. Since the conversation started, he was inclined to say something. "Maybe he was, maybe he wasn't."

"Okay Cedric, I see that you aren't going to cooperate. It's cool. You know I'm going to be on top of this, so I'll be talking to you later." It was time to go. Because she knew that he was watching she switched her hips and her delightful looking ass a little harder than usual. She didn't want to attract him, she just did it because she could. The door slammed.

He knew she would be back. All the cats at the card game and his people were thorough. None of them would tell the police anything. In his younger days he would have felt safe with that knowledge, but as an experienced criminal, he knew that thorough cats said things to people they felt comfortable around. This meant that information still got back to the police. Any small piece of information getting back to Sally was a really dangerous thing. As a two-time loser, a murder charge meant a life sentence in the district.

Sally was happy with her investigation. If he didn't do it, he knew who did. Her findings weren't in what he said, they were in what he didn't say. Usually a suspect is going say something to justify that he wasn't involved in the crime. The police watched Sherlock go to the game for the past six months. Also, Sherlock's Mercedes was impounded from down the block. With Cedric's place being the last spot Sherlock was seen, he would have had to say some really good things to undermine being a suspect.

If Cedric said Sherlock played all night and left, Sally would have been thrown off. Sherlock was known for leaving his cars on the streets, then getting them out of impound. Cedric would have a good defense that would have lessened her suspicion. No matter what, she knew the streets would talk soon. They always did, even if just by mistake. If they didn't talk she knew how to get them to talk.

D & C stacked over one hundred thousand in just two weeks. Their reputations changed and they attained the respect of playas. The dro was moving and business was growing.

"It's time for us to step this thing up and start making some real money." Danny Boy had been waiting patiently. "What we're doing so far is cool, but we can do so much better."

"Yeah, it's been about six weeks and our names are ringing the way they should." People were coming in lines and their supplier was now frontin' them three pounds at a time, sometimes twice a day. Supply was a phone call away. Clarence was glad that he could finally say to Danny Boy that it was alright to do his thing.

"The money we making now is nothing compared to what we could be making." Danny Boy was fully ready to do the damn thing. Clarence's plans made perfect sense to him now that no one was questioning them about where they got the money to get started.

"I've been thinking about that too." They were upstairs in their office, where no one was allowed, unless invited, or there was an emergency. "I think it's best you use another spot. There are going to be two different kinds of clientele."

"Yeah that sounds really slick. How much you think we should spend?" Danny Boy asked, putting his feet up on his desk as Clarence looked out the window. "A lot of the workers and lieutenants want to get into something that moves faster and makes more money."

"Danny Boy, let me tell you the best thing that I'll ever be able to tell you." Clarence turned around and moved closer to Danny Boy's desk. "We can get what we want. We don't have to pay for it." They dapped each other on that.

"Damn Clarence, you've been doing some really good politicking." He was thinking that he needed to be a part of these sessions. He could see the balance of power swinging.

"All the suppliers have their eyes on us. The respect that we have in the streets is better than having a Platinum American Express."

Danny Boy started laughing. It all started from the things that he had done in the streets and in Juvenile. "Okay that sounds good. There is something that it's time for us to do."

"What's that?"

"What good is it to make money without spending any of it." It was time to go shopping among other things.

"You right and you better know it. Ain't no time like the present." The foundation that they needed was laid. "We might as well take the entire crew with us."

"Yea—" There was a loud knock at the door. They looked at each other and instincts told them to grab a weapon but that wasn't possible. They hadn't been carrying any since they got their spot rolling. There was no need because they had plenty of soldiers and no beefs in the streets.

"It's Sally," she hollered.

Their eyes opened wide. "What the fuck is she doing up here," Danny Boy said in a low tone. Clarence just shrugged his shoulders.

Clarence wasn't surprised. She was known to show up at people's spots to harass them. Coming around was part of her game. "Might as well see what she wants. She can cause trouble if she wants to." He opened the door.

"Damn, it took ya'll long enough." She was leaning on the doorframe like she was getting tired of waiting. She was wearing a dark blue, two-piece skirt outfit, with white pin-stripes. She loved the way it showed off her curves. She walked in with a big grin on her face. "What ya'll had to do, put away a few grams of dro before ya'll opened the door?"

"Sally, what do you want and why are you accusing me of selling dro?" Danny Boy put his feet on the floor. What he really wanted was to stand up and get in her face but that wasn't the way to get rid of her.

"Well since you asked," she responded with a sassy voice, "I came to see Clarence." She was standing in front of Clarence with a pose that was meant to be a sexual chal-lenge. With her right hand she was slapping her purse into her left hand. "Do you mind Danny Boy?" The look she gave him said they needed some privacy.

This reminded Danny Boy of all of the other women that flocked to Clarence. It seemed that they all wanted to talk to him. With much reluctance, he left and shut the door.

"To what do I owe this visit?" Clarence was trying his best to sound friendly while letting her know that he really didn't want to talk to her.

"I've been wondering where ya'll got the money to start this dro spot. Nobody in this town would front ya'll that much dro a few weeks ago, so where did you get the money?" Her lips were talking, but she was wondering to herself what it would be like to do Clarence, for just one night.

This was the first conversation that he ever had with Sally. Whenever he saw her in the past, if he saw her first, he went the other way. "What are you talkin' about?" He knew better than to break eye contact. Her demeanor said she was taking a lot of mental notes, but what she was really doing was sizing him up for her own personal pleasure.

"Listen youngsta, I was sending cats to jail in this town before you were born. I know who sells what and who sells for who." Her arms were now crossed over her chest with her gaze still intense.

"If you know all of this why are you asking me questions?" Having the police up in his spot wasn't a good thing, no matter how it was looked at. Telling her to leave would have been a waste of breath and time.

"Well, Clarence, I know that you're the mastermind behind this. Two street niggas, turned playas, is almost unheard of."

Clarence just kept looking at her.

"You have the entire town fooled except for me. I know you killed Sherlock's wife and robbed them. You were practically a part of their family," she said trying to make him feel guilty. "Who would suspect you?" She was thinking that he had to be a good poker player because his expression hadn't changed one bit. She hated it when she couldn't read a man.

Sitting at his desk, Clarence just took deep, easy, slow breaths and glared back at her. She walked toward the window with an attitude. "You made one small mistake." She wanted him to reply as she continued to look out the window. Clarence wasn't going to say another word. She was the one who wanted information, not him. She also reminded him of Columbo.

Minutes passed and he was still silent. She walked over to his desk and he motioned for her to take a seat but she refused. His silence was getting to her. "But you made one mistake Clarence," she repeated. Clarence leaned back in his chair as he locked eyes with her. She wanted what she had to say next to really sink in. "The gun you shot the mother with is going to bring you down. You should have picked up the shells."

"Are you finished? If not, say what you have to say, and

get out." Clarence wasn't trying to hear what she was saying. There were no slugs, no witnesses, and no gun. This all meant no case.

"Actually, no I'm not. It doesn't matter that you used hollow points. I'm still going to get you." Walking over to him, bending over she whispered in his ear, "I still want some of that dick to go with it." She turned and sashayed her way out.

Though Clarence's ego was big, he wasn't going to take Sally's visit for granted. To him, she just used the element of surprise and used it well. Showing the gun to a few cats in the streets was the only thing that worried him. He did it for intimidation purposes and to show off a little bit. People in the streets weren't for sure what he was carrying, but they all said it was bigger than the average gun. No one in the street, except Danny Boy, knew for a fact that the gun was a ten. No matter how he looked at it, he couldn't see her having enough evidence to put a case together.

"Yo Clarence, what was that all about?" Danny Boy asked as he reentered.

"She thinks that she can put something on me. I just listened to her." The more details that he gave the more questions Danny Boy was going to ask. He knew that it involved something that they had done because they did everything together.

Danny Boy figured it was about the murder because that's the only thing she investigated. "Do you think she has anything?"

"Nah, she came to dig for reactions. That's how she starts her investigations. She's the kind that tries to see where a cat's heart and head are at. That's why I always act cold toward her." He remembered a story about a dude she pressed so hard that he started slippin' and got caught for another body that wasn't his.

"You know she's going to be back." Danny Boy was also wondering if Keisha was going to come back to town and how Clarence was going to react.

"Does that mean you don't believe in a brotha anymore?" Clarence didn't like the sound of his voice. They weren't looking at each other.

"Nah, it isn't that. It seems like you're about to get brand new and shit. Shit is about to really change." What Sally just did made him feel a need to speak up. He felt that Clarence was getting too much attention for them to be a team.

Clarence really didn't need to answer. Lately, much of Danny Boy's body language revealed his inner tension. It was only a matter of time. "What's really up? Go ahead and say what's on your mind."

Danny Boy knew what he wanted to say, but couldn't really put it in words. "All I'm saying is don't go changing on me. We've been a team and we need to remain a team."

Clarence came from behind his desk and sat on it, "Check this out Danny Boy, what I've been doing is what's best for us, not just for me. We're still playing the same roles as before."

That was the real problem. People showing more respect for Clarence over him, was really itching his ass. "All I'm sayin' is that I don't want to see you change." Danny Boy took a seat behind his desk.

"Nah man, there's more to it than that. Say what's really on your mind." Clarence was trying to keep negative emotions from building up between them.

"I ain't feeling what the fuck is going on. Since we started this spot you've been calling all the shots. It seems like you might want to take over." Danny Boy knew better and that he was being paranoid, but he put the shit out there.

"Oh so you mad because Sally came at me and not at you? You want her to come at you, accusing you of murder?

Man, don't even trip. We just pulled off a hell of a heist." He knew that Danny wasn't ready to be a player. Having peace wasn't something he was used to.

"It's like this man, I need some control. All of our people are running around saying 'Clarence said'. They act like half of this ain't mine." It was always that way when people thought about D & C. With them running a spot it was much clearer.

It was the truth. "So what do you want me to do?" Clarence was feeling disrespected. To be questioned about his intentions and actions wasn't sitting well with him. The moves that he just put down put them on another level of playahood that few reached, especially in such a short time. It looked like they started with a pound of dro and were about to make millions.

"I ain't for sho'."

"You mad at me for making moves for us and don't know what you want me to do." Clarence knew that it was all jealousy. He walked over to the window to look at the traffic. He hadn't just started practicing psychology on Danny.

Danny Boy was feeling like he really shouldn't have brought the subject up. He knew that he couldn't out-think and out-talk Clarence. "I'll tell you what, how about I run the coke spot while you run this spot." He felt that he needed to have more say-sos in the decision making without having to consult with his partner.

Telling him 'no' is what his instincts told him to say. "Okay, that's a bet. We'll find a spot and get a brick on the front. I won't even show my face at that spot."

Danny Boy smiled. "That's a motherfuckin' bet." He stepped out with such enthusiasm that he slammed the door behind him.

The situation was terrible any way Clarence looked at it. Selling cocaine brought the greed out of cats and turned many of them into users. That was his main reason for starting out with weed because it was hard to smoke up the profit. Plus, starting out with weed was the best way to let their workers prove themselves. This is something he didn't mention to Danny Boy. More than likely it wouldn't have made a difference since he was thinking about his reputation.

Clarence knew that the crack spot was going to be some trouble, sooner or later. There was no way Danny Boy would be able to handle his business like a player. Things were going to be like they were in the past. He could easily break them and mess up their names in a matter of weeks. There was no way Clarence was going to go for that.

Clarence was also sure that Danny Boy would soon go behind his back to get at the suppliers. Although he had every right to meet with them, doing it without Clarence knowing would be grimey and disrespectful. At that point there would be real problems between them.

Hopefully, Danny Boy having a spot to control would make him feel better. If it didn't, there was no telling what he would do.

It was true that Clarence was clearly perceived as the leader of their crew. Everyone knew that he was the one with the business mind. It was his planning moves that allowed them to make major moves without people thinking they robbed Sherlock. Things could not be sweeter.

For now, it was time to go shopping and move Ma' Dukes up out of the projects.

Sally rode in the BMW with Bambi driving. "How are we going to prove that Clarence had the gun that killed Karyn?" Bambi asked.

"I'm not exactly sure, but I know Keisha can help us."

Bambi didn't even want to try to think of what the angle was. "Why are you making me ask? Just tell me."

"Usually when a parent gets killed I get a call about every week, for at least three months, to see if anything has turned up. That girl knows that Clarence had something to do with it."

"That makes a lot of sense. She hasn't called one time and she hasn't called about her father missing." It made sense, but why? "But what is the motive?"

"Damn girl, I have to tell you everything? Danny Boy and Clarence needed money to get a drug spot started. Robbing a major playa was out of the question unless they could avoid suspicion."

"Keep going." Bambi's ears perked up. The story was beginning to sound like a book.

"Who would suspect Clarence of killing the two people he would eventually call family?" The more she talked about it, the more it made sense.

"Hold on, let me think for a minute." She processed the thoughts and angles through her brain. It wasn't hard with a one-sixty IQ. "What about the money. How do we know they found some money in the house?"

Sally started laughing. "Only two rooms in the house were ransacked, Keisha's bedroom and the living room. There was no sign that the main bedroom was searched and that should have been the first one searched."

She looked over at Sally. "So you're saying that Clarence knew that the money was in one of those two rooms."

"Exactly." Sally snapped her fingers. And that means Keisha knew that Clarence was in the house." Sally could see the crime being solved in a matter of weeks. There couldn't be that many more missing pieces to the puzzle that needed to be found to prove it all.

"Now hold up." Bambi wasn't ready to just accept that

theory. "What you are saying is that Keisha is an accessory –after –the fact."

Sally wanted to tell her to think outside the college degree but decided to help her understand her theory. "What did I tell you about having an open mind? She don't know shit about no accessory –after –the fact. Plus, her father probably told her to never take her beefs to the police." That statement made her theory sound that much more plausible.

Bambi couldn't help it, she came from a world where things made sense in different ways. "Now that you put it that way, I see your point. I have to be more open minded," she confessed. "I still can't see her knowing that he did it. I can't help it."

"Just think about the look she had on her face at the house. That was pure anger." No matter how much she talked to Bambi, the small details always got by her.

Bambi thought back to the crime scene, and seeing Keisha's expressions. "People are supposed to hurt when a relative dies."

"There's a difference between being hurt, sad and angry. She was really angry; angry with somebody and that some-body has to be the killer." Keisha's look was plastered in her mind.

"So that somebody has to be the killer," Bambi repeated.

"Yeah, I'm feeling you."

"I'm going to smoke a Black to that." Sally was satisfied that Bambi finally agreed with her reasoning. She pulled one out of her purse and tapped it on the dashboard.

Watching Keisha and Clarence at the funeral helped her put it all together. There were still missing pieces though. Neither of them was acting like they should have. Seventeen-year-old girls don't get mad at their boyfriends when they should be turning to them for comfort, especially in their time of need. It was obvious that Clarence was there to ask questions, instead of being there for her. Putting the rest of it together would be the hard part.

They rode for about ten minutes without talking. "Where does Sherlock fit into all of this? He's got to be missing or dead," Bambi said to restart the conversation.

"We both know he's dead." Sally waited for Bambi to think about it for a few seconds. "Maybe this case is a little to sophisticated for you."

"Okay, let me think. If Clarence went in the house that means Danny Boy also went in. So you're thinking that they wouldn't have disrespected Sherlock like that if he were alive." She decided to rely on her common sense and street knowledge versus her textbooks.

"Damn girl, that was tight." She smiled and looked over at Bambi while taking a long drag on her Black.

Bambi started to like the smell of the cigars and was tempted to ask for a drag. Her family would kill her if she tried one. "It still doesn't make sense to me."

"Aw shit, at least some progress was made," Sally mumbled. "Danny Boy isn't the kind to work for another dude, so they needed to rob someone that was already set to get start up money. They knew if they robbed the wrong cat, they would never get another chance. That would defeat the purpose. They might end up dead or locked up. Clarence isn't just street smart, he's book smart, and playa smart." At times it seemed that Bambi was really on point but at other times, it seemed like she was lost in space. Today she was totally on another planet.

"Damn Sally, I don't know how you do it. You should go to school to teach this." The Black smelled more and more tempting. "Hey let me try one of those."

"What? You think it's going to help you think? You just need some dick. Girl, yo' ass ain't worth shit today." She gave her a Black that wasn't broken down. Maybe if she caught a headache she would not make it a habit.

Bambi laughed because she wasn't being deprived of sex. "I can't help it if I can't think like you. They don't teach this shit in college."

"You got that right." Sally laughed, blowing smoke into the air. She considered going to college but dismissed the thought most of the time. The book training might change what she was already able to do naturally. Why take that chance? "We have to find the missing pieces to this puzzle. We have to go see Keisha."

Keisha was parked on Pennsylvania for an hour. There was something she had to see before she left. The sign on the spot said D & C in black and silver letters, and there were all kinds of people going in and out. Most of them were decently dressed. There were a lot of cats walking around wearing black jackets with silver letters. On the back it had 'D & C'. Many of her friends told her that they had started a dro spot but she had to see it for herself. They also said that Clarence, specifically, was sportin' a new black Lexus. She was pissed because she knew it was her father's money that financed the business and paid for the car. Though she saw most of what she came to see, she had to lay eyes on him for just a few seconds. The trip just wouldn't be complete until she saw him.

Waiting for him to come out was a test of her patience. She was sure he was in the building because a black Lexus was parked out front. She didn't want to ride around the neighborhood or the projects. She also didn't want to be seen by any of their friends. Nobody knew what she was pushing and she wanted to keep it that way.

After a three-hour wait, she saw him come out of the building. Keisha practically stood up in her seat to get a closer look. He walked out of the building and was standing to the left of the entrance to stay in the shade. Keisha could feel herself perspiring watching him as he stood there, looking back and forth. "Damn!" she hollered as she grabbed the steering wheel and shook it. He was looking too good. "I should kill yo' ass for just looking that good." It was an expression she couldn't resist saying.

All of her feelings for him hit her like she did not think possible. Even her pussy was reacting to the sight of him. Her knees were feeling weak and her nipples were already standing at attention. She reached up under her seat for her nine and placed it in the passenger seat. When she looked back up she saw a girl walking out the front door heading toward him. It was Diamond.

Diamond had a honey complexion and loved guys that were straight paid. She knew she was sexy and always flaunted it.

Clarence turned to her when she tugged on his jacket. Diamond tongued him down with a kiss that looked so passionate that passing traffic started slowing down. Diamond did what she had to do to keep her man's attention.

Keisha's temperature went up ten more degrees. There was no competing with Diamond if she had no contact with Clarence. There was nothing rational about Keisha's jealousy; she couldn't stop feeling what she was feeling, no matter how much she tried. Keisha's jealousy pushed her to make a quick decision. "Clarence you and that bitch are going to die today!!"

When they stopped kissing, they got into his car that was parked at the curb. Keisha flipped her ignition and waited for them to take off.

Clarence headed west on Pennsylvania, toward the DC/Maryland line. There was quite a bit of traffic on Pennsylvania but Keisha managed to stay about four vehicles behind. She had her nine in her lap, with one in the chamber. They were almost to the Anacostia Freeway. Keisha thought that would be the perfect spot to execute her plan. The idea was to shoot him up then take a left on Anacostia. Before anybody could report anything, she would be back in Baltimore. They were almost there. Traffic thinned out and she was right behind them.

Before she could turn on her signal she saw his left signal light start flashing. That plan was spoiled, just like that. Continuing to follow him, she turned on her left turn signal. She was almost on his bumper and was close enough to see his eyes when he looked in his side view mirror. Instincts already told her to put on her baseball cap so he wouldn't recognize her, though she felt that she was sitting up too high for him to see her.

The road up ahead was clear and there was no traffic. Her plan now was to pull up on the side of them and start firing. With the passenger window open and a little leaning, it would be easy. Three shots should do it, she thought. The first would break the window. The second and third would hit the mark, right at the top of his head. From there she could just speed off.

"On the count of three," she said out loud. She tensed herself as the count began. "One, this is for my mother. Two, this is for you betraying me and my father. Three." She floored the accelerator. Just as she was about to get in the left lane, she saw another truck pulling out of a driveway, into the other lane. She had to hit her brakes or run into the back of the Lexus. Damaging the car wasn't good enough and she wasn't about to mess up her truck.

"Shit," Keisha hollered. "You ain't gonna keep being that lucky Clarence!"

The Lexus sped up and got out of sight.

Clarence knew that whoever was in the black Escalade tried to kill him. He noticed it when he came out of his spot. When the Escalade made the same left turn, his red flag went up. He was certain when the Escalade rode up on his bumper, twice. The only thing that he could see in his rear view mirror was a baseball cap pulled down over the driver's eyes. This also meant something to him.

Diamond never noticed a thing. He thought about telling her when they got back to their condo but decided against it. It wasn't like he would be talking to a down-ass chic like Keisha that understood certain things about the game.

When they got inside, Clarence went straight to the bedroom to be alone so he could think. Somebody tried to do him. Two main things were on his agenda; one, figure out who and why; two, what to do about it and be prepared. He knew that the biggest problem was going to be figuring out who. He didn't have any beefs in the street and didn't know of anyone who owned a plain black Escalade. It wasn't paranoia because he was looking at the Escalade for three hours. The only thing that he could do, he determined, was to tell his man and get ready.

Lately, he hadn't been riding around with a gun but that was changing immediately. He had two nine millimeters at his mother's crib. For at least two weeks he would carry one with him and keep the other one in the car. That was about all that he could do. If he told his whole crew they would act crazy and tell the entire city and that wouldn't be good.

Clarence knew that they may start acting too aggressive with anybody to protect him, so he kept quiet.

Just wait and watch is what Clarence decided to do. Whoever it was would have to come around again. At least he could rule out it being an attempted robbery. Seldom did he carry money on him.

After about an hour, Clarence let Diamond in the bedroom. She knocked on the door every fifteen minutes. To Clarence, Diamond was good for two things - being a good showpiece and sex. Sex with her was all good. She went out of her way to please her man and would do anything to satisfy his sexual desires. She even suggested they have Ménage a trios. Besides that, she looked better than most women in the district. She pushed his playa status up a few more notches. All she wanted from him was to keep her in the latest fashions and buy her some jewelry to make her feel special. She was a worthy investment for the meantime.

She was making him look good in front of all of the old-time playas. People always said they looked good as a couple, especially since they had the same complexion. They looked like they were made for each other.

They were having sex two and three times a day. She wouldn't give him any rest. She also loved sucking his dick while they were riding around the city. He loved the attention she gave him but love her, he didn't. Keisha was still on his mind.

A day never went by that he didn't think about Keisha. With all of Diamond's attention he figured that Keisha would become a distant memory. Not. Diamond couldn't relate and speak on things that interested him. He would have been able to talk to Keisha about certain situations. While Diamond was doing a striptease in an aqua-blue thong, Clarence's mind wandered to how to get Keisha back into his life.

Finding her was a matter of finding out where Jessica lived in Baltimore City.

Jessica expected to see Keisha by five o'clock but it was eight o'clock when she finally arrived.

"Damn girl, you look like some shit," Jessica commented when she walked in.

Keisha threw her keys down on the living room table and sat on the couch. "I saw Clarence today," she said like she was out of breath.

"Why did you go see Clarence? You have a boyfriend who is about to be an engineer. Girl, don't mess this up." Jessica wanted to see Keisha get Clarence out of her system. With summer school almost over, getting ready to go to college in the fall and having a new boyfriend, Jessica thought that Keisha might be too busy to think about Clarence, let alone go see him.

Keisha wanted to tell her the whole story. "I didn't see him like talk to him. I just watched him to see how he was doing." Her voice was raised a few pitches to make herself understood, like what she was saying needed justification. "You know what I mean?"

"All I can say is that love will make a girl do some crazy things." Jessica grabbed the remote and started watching television.

"I was so happy to just look at him and he was looking so good. Then he had this girl named Diamond with him. He ain't supposed to be with that hoe," she screamed, getting louder.

"So you still love him." Jessica had a grin on her face. As she expected, Clarence would be the topic of conversation again.

"No," she sighed.

"You might as well admit it because you sure are sounding jealous." Jessica laughed a little bit.

Keisha was getting frustrated because it wasn't supposed to be like this. Thinking about Clarence while she was having sex with James didn't seem like a big deal to her. She figured that he moved on and it was time for her to as well. Just going through the motions with James, she knew her heart was with Clarence.

"Okay, maybe I'm a little jealous. Now what am I supposed to do?" She didn't want Jessica to dominate the conversation.

"I'm glad you asked. If you love Clarence so much, then go get your man. Believe me, love doesn't change just like that," she snapped her finger, as experience ruled the words that came out of her mouth.

"You don't understand." Telling Jessica that she just tried to kill Clarence and why, was something she was so tempted to do, but it would only complicate matters. More than likely she wouldn't understand why she still felt this way, but she had to say something. "We've been apart for a while. Why would he want me back? Diamond is so damn sexy that it should be illegal. I may not be able to compete."

"Are you saying that you want him back?"

She paused for a few seconds, "No." Jessica decided to stay quiet. "Yes I do." Jessica was still quiet. "No I don't."

Jessica stood up to walk back in the kitchen. "You might as well go get your man. I'm willing to bet that he still loves you too." That was an interesting thought. Getting Clarence back and breaking his heart would be a good way to pay him back but what if he had other things on his mind and what if he were in love with Diamond. He could also be suspicious of her because he hadn't seen her in a while. Maybe hurting him was the way to get him out of her system. If it weren't for that truck it would be all over. Maybe trying again was the thing to do, just to get it all over with. All of these choices and thoughts were frustrating Keisha. Her emotions were getting in the way of her mission and she didn't know what to think, feel, or what to do. She still knew what she wanted. Getting it done was the problem along with figuring out how to do it.

She knew there would be plenty of chances to get him. Killing him like she tried to do might have been too good for him. There wasn't going to be the kind of suffering that she desired for him. She wanted him to feel the kind of pain that she was feeling, without killing his mother, something she could never do. Keisha was sure about one thing, she was determined to not let her feelings for him get in the way in the future. She knew she had to admit to her love for him but make him suffer ten times more.

"Keisha you have some visitors," Jessica hollered from the front of the house.

It wasn't a good time to deal with James. Giving her virginity to him wasn't anything like she hoped it would be. In fact, it was a total regret. Though he was decent looking, plenty of money and a bright future, he just didn't fill the bill. As Destiny's Child would put it, "If yo' status ain't 'hood." Keisha fully understood this now. At best, James was a good person to be with just to pass time, nothing more. Telling him about the things that she was used to talking about, like the streets and the game, was out of the question. Today would be a good day to dump him and find a cat that had an edge to himself. After seeing Clarence, she knew that James wasn't the answer. From now on everything had to be about handling her mission.

"Hello Keisha," they said in unison, like it was natural for them to visit her.

Keisha was cautious to not act surprised. First she had to

see Clarence and Diamond together, and then she missed killing him by three seconds. Now, she had to deal with Sally and Bambi.

"Oh it's so good to see you Sally." Sally was wearing a dark green, two-piece pants suit with light green pinstripes. She came to dig at Keisha's reactions. Sitting down, she continued. "Did you find my father? Do you have anything on who killed my mother?" she asked excitedly. Keisha was putting on an act. It just dawned on her that she never called Sally since her mother's death. "Sit down please," she motioned toward the couch.

"I wish I could say all of that," Sally responded as she took a seat. Bambi took a seat also, to the right of Sally. She was all eyes and ears. "But I've made some real good progress." Jessica was also all eyes and ears as she walked back into the room with crackers and iced tea.

"So tell me what's up," Keisha asked.

"We have every reason to believe that your father is dead." Waiting for a reaction, but seeing none, she continued. "We think we know who killed your mother."

Keisha thought Sally's visit was going to be about all bullshit, but she was thrown off guard with the news regarding her father. Even though she felt something happened to him, she wasn't prepared to hear the words that came from Sally's lips. Gathering her thoughts, she asked, "Well, would you mind telling me?" She took off her sneakers and put her feet up under her.

"We think, well we're almost positive that Clarence killed your mother."

Keisha looked at Sally with a blank expression on her face. Then she looked at Bambi to see the inquisitive expression on her face. Jessica was looking suspiciously at Sally until the silence was broken.

"You must have good reason to believe that it's

Clarence." Keisha didn't change any of her facial expression. "Mama and Clarence were very close."

Sally liked the answer, it was in the range of expected responses. "Well I'm trying to prepare you for what may happen." Sally was baiting Keisha to say more about Clarence.

"I don't understand." As she expected Sally came to play games and digging for information was the apparent purpose.

"I know that you know Clarence, and I don't want you to be surprised when he gets arrested," she spoke with a concerned tone in her voice, for effect.

Keisha wasn't exactly sure what to say but she did know what she wasn't going to do and that was reveal information. She figured she'd go with the direct approach, "I'm surprised, so tell me why you think this."

"Clarence left something in the house that practically leads back to him. They were 10-millimeter bullet shell casings." A little bit of information at a time would help her read Keisha and her responses.

"Please finish, there has to be more to it than that." Keisha already knew what she was going to say. Responding like she was satisfied with the answer would have been out of character.

"Our sources say that he's the only one even seen with a gun that resembles a 10-millimeter. It's a rather big gun." Sally wanted to hold back that information for a few more minutes but Keisha's direct answer totally threw her off her plan of action.

Keisha put on a fake smile and wanted to ask when Clarence would be arrested. "It's hard for me to believe that Clarence killed her. They were really close."

"I think it's natural for you to see things that way. Many people say that Clarence was like a member of your family, but facts are facts." If Keisha took the stance of defending Clarence, it might mean that she knew more than all thought. The stance wasn't strong enough to infer that.

Keisha would have given anything at that moment to not hear Clarence's name anymore that week. Her memory registered that he did have a ten. He purchased two of them because he tried to give her one. He told her that tens were more powerful than nines and looked intimidating.

"Explain to me how you know he had this type of gun?" Keisha asked to keep up her front. The direct approach was perfect for her act. This information was permanently placed in her mind. It meant something. There was definitely no doubt now, that Clarence was the murderer.

"I can't exactly tell you everything my informants have told me, but I can assure you that they are reliable." She started chewing on a cracker. Sally felt that they were having a stalemate.

"I might as well be honest with you, it's hard for me to believe that Clarence killed my mother. We were planning on getting married." There had to be more that Sally might like to expose and Keisha was attempting to make Sally defend her position.

Bambi looked at Sally. She didn't realize that her look tipped the scales in Keisha's favor.

Sally, if necessary, would have had to admit that Keisha's comeback was good, too good. "I fully understand your position. If I were you, I'd probably feel the same way."

Jessica wanted to ask Sally why she came so far to deliver such little information that was still not fact.

"Please, Sally tell me this, if you're able to." Keisha decided to take advantage of being in control. "Can you tell me what happened to my Daddy?"

Sally still had the same expression she had when the conversation started, though she lost control. "We're about to close in on that. I'm pretty sure that I'll have it closed in a few weeks." Much confidence was in her voice.

"Would you mind telling us what you know?" Jessica asked. They were now talking about her older brother.

"I'm afraid I can't because the evidence that I have isn't concrete."

Jessica wanted to ask her why she said something about Clarence killing Karyn because there wasn't much difference, evidence wise. "I couldn't help asking because you sound so confident." This was her way of putting the ball back in Sally's court.

Bambi glanced at Sally again and wanted to look back at her but didn't.

Sally didn't miss a beat. She wasn't about to let them make her look bad. "I'm pretty sure he was murdered. I'm also pretty sure it wasn't Clarence, nor did he have anything to do with it."

But Clarence had to know who murdered my father, Keisha thought. It was all too closely related. "Do you think I should ask Clarence about the situation to see what he has to say?" Keisha now felt like playing games.

Sally was loving it. Might as well go all out. "Could you tell me again why you weren't in the house?"

"I went to the arcade. That's what I usually do on Sunday mornings." Keisha sensed there was much more to the question than stated.

Sally stood up, "If ya'll have any questions or information please call me." Bambi stood up on that comment.

"Okay," Jessica responded as she started walking toward the door.

"I'll be looking to hear from you about my father soon. " Keisha was standing and walking behind them.

Keisha was glad to get rid of them. She was tired of Sally's bullshit. The visit wasn't a total waste because she was assured that Clarence really did kill her mother. What was good was also bad. Sally visited with the intention and hopes of Keisha giving up information. Since Clarence was the obvious suspect, Keisha felt Sally would interfere with her getting the revenge she wanted. If Sally was smart enough to figure all of that out, Keisha knew she hadn't heard the last of Sally. Keisha planned to keep up with her the same way Sally did with her. Maybe it was a good thing she didn't succeed in her plan.

Before Bambi could crank up the BMW, Sally lit a Black. It was already broken down.

"What was all of that really about? I felt like I was at a tennis match," Bambi said pulling out of the driveway.

"That was a bunch of sistahs going at it when they should have been sharing information." Sally took a long hit.

"Let me get a piece of that," Bambi said eyeing the cigar. Sally passed it. "Damn this tastes good. Keisha was acting like she was tired of us talking about Clarence."

"She was acting like we were saying the wrong things. I know she knows something that she isn't telling us. That girl might be as smart as she is pretty."

"I just think that she's in love with Clarence," Bambi said as she passed the Black back.

"You might as well keep that and buy a few packs." They laughed. "Oh yeah, press the gas a little harder. I have a hot date."

"How old is he?"

"Shit, twenty, or somewhere around there. That's old enough for me."

◆ ◆ ◆ ◆ ◆

8

♦ ♦ ♦ ♦ ♦

Sally had her date in the tub. It was one of her well-hosted evenings. In the past two hours they smoked weed, ate dinner and drank a bottle of Belvedere. Sally met him at the door with a negligee that would have made the sexiest stripper jealous. Tony thought he was in heaven.

The lights in the house were down low and a few candles provided a perfect amount of illumination. Cherry incense had been burning for about five hours. It was a slow burn that kept the atmosphere just right. Slow jams were coming through the sound system through speakers in every room. Marvin Gaye's "Sexual Healing" was on the instrumental version.

Tony never thought that an evening could be so enjoyable without even getting the pussy yet. Sally treated him like a king, leading him to the personally designed antique bathtub she treasured. She was giving him a sponge bath, not that he needed it, but to make him feel good. She washed everything from his asshole to his balls. If the sex was as good as the treatment, he knew that he was about to fall in love and be coming back.

After she made him step out of the tub, she got on her knees and started drying every part of him. She started with his feet and worked her way up. The entire time, she maintained eye contact with him. His dick was standing at full attention as she kept letting her mouth come within inches of the tip, letting his imagination run wild. She wanted him to remain excited. From there she worked her way up to his chest and finished drying him off.

Because he wanted to, they started to kiss each other. It was a long, passionate kiss. She was getting excited because he was. He started kissing her neck and ears, which was right on time because he was hitting the right spots. She stripped off her negligee. All that she was dressed in were stockings, a garter belt, and stilettos. He was impressed with what he saw.

Prince's "Do Me Baby," was just getting to the first verse.

It was time to fulfill her mission. He was in the trap she had set. With a sexy walk, she led him across the hall to her bedroom. Her bed was big enough for five people. All kinds of pillows, in different shapes and sizes, covered it.

She guided him to the bed, and like a true hostess, stacked the pillows so he could be comfortable. With one hand she pulled out a can of whipped cream from behind the pillows. It took a little while for her to find it. To make him feel even more comfortable she placed cylinder-shaped pillows under his legs.

"Just relax baby, Sally is going to give you a night to remember." Going all out wasn't a problem. He had something that she wanted.

"Damn Sally, you got a nigga dick so hard it feels like I might bust any second."

Slowly she sprayed whipped cream all over his dick and

balls. The cool sensation relaxed his dick a little bit. "Damn, that feels good in a weird way. That cream is cold as ice." She laughed a little bit as she was using the coldness of the whipped cream to keep him from busting a nut just yet. She knew exactly what she was doing.

In a seductive manner, she started licking the cream, starting with his balls. She was careful by letting her tongue touch his skin just a little bit.

He was hoping that she would hurry up and suck his dick. Never had he been teased like this before. Every time her tongue brushed up against his tool he wanted to grab her head and make her suck his dick. The way that he was feeling made him know he was about to have a nut that he was going to remember forever.

After she licked off most of the whipped cream, she stood up with a big smile on her face. She had not touched him yet with her hands. She was enjoying keeping him at the edge of climax.

"So are you going to just leave me like this?" He came down from the edge again. He wanted that relief of letting out the load. The roller coaster ride was making him feel good and he didn't mind if she teased him some more.

"Nah baby, I'm about to take you to paradise. This is going to be a night you will never forget." She was standing in a seductive pose, nipples hard, with her hands on her hips. She was waiting for him to come down off the edge just a little bit more. She wanted to make his nut as intense as possible.

Rick James and Tina Marie's "Fire and Desire" started playing.

"If you can suck a dick as well as you do foreplay, I might do whatever you want me to do." If only he knew what he was saying.

It was time for the next move. With warm coconut oil

she moistened her hands and started massaging his nuts. The bottle of oil was placed in the warmer to his left side.

"Oh yes, that feels as good as a motherfucker." She slowly worked her way up to the middle of his shaft and started pumping it back and forth. She could feel the blood inside pulsating. With each pump she slowly worked her hand up to the head of his dick. She pumped a few times without touching the head.

"Sally that feels good as shit." She stopped and moistened her hands again with the oil. He glanced up at her when she let go. The head of his dick was less than half an inch from her tongue so he flexed his dick to make it touch her tongue.

She backed up and smiled. They went through that three times. With her left hand slippery with oil, she grabbed the head of this dick and squeezed as hard as she could while twisting it with an up and down motion. "Oh yes ooh, that feels good. You ain't even sucking my dick yet." It felt like he was about to bust wide open as she kept rotating her hand around the head of his dick with more intensity. "Holy shit," he hollered between the moans and groans. "Damn, Sally."

She climaxed again from hearing him calling her name in such a manner. "Is it good to you, Tony?" She stopped and started playing with his balls.

"You damn right it's good to me." She stopped touching him, again, just in time to keep him from cumming. "You ain't gonna let me bust a nut are you?"

"Yes I am, a big one." At the bottom of his balls she started to lick. She made sure she licked every part at least five times.

Tony was thinking how good it was going to feel to bust off after all the foreplay and being teased. He already had plans of coming back.

After she finished licking his balls she started on his

shaft. When she got to the top she looked up to make eye contact with him while she held the head of his dick on her tongue.

"Tender Love" started playing.

She started licking down the right side of his dick and went back up the left side, making sure she tasted every part. She returned to licking his balls while rotating her hand on the head of his dick. He started moaning and groaning louder. With slight speed she let her hand go and replaced it with her mouth. The moist, warm sensation of her mouth made some of his precum trickle out. She was sucking on his dick like she was sucking on a straw in a milkshake.

It was feeling too good to him, but he didn't want her to stop. Between moans and groans, he could barely catch his breath. "What are you trying to do to me," he whispered softly as he placed his hand on the back of her head.

She was attacking the head of his dick like they were at war. At a furious pace she was pumping his shaft with her left hand. She stopped sucking to rotate her hand around the head then quickly, she put it back in her mouth. She sucked and moved her lips and head to make him feel all the pleasure possible.

"Oh baby, I'm cumming." On that note she moistened her tongue. "Oh shit!" He exploded in her mouth. The power of the release made him put an arch in his back and rise up off the bed. The taste of his cum and hearing him yell out, "Sally, Sally, Sally," made her climax again.

She wouldn't let go until she swallowed every drop. Trying to stop her was pointless. When there was nothing left she swallowed and stood up.

While wiping her mouth, like she just had a good meal, she asked him, "Was that good?"

"You damn right it was good. I'll do anything for you and I mean anything." He was totally drained and had a feeling that he never had before. He could just lie there and relax for days was the way he was feeling.

"Good, I have something for you to do." She bent down and grabbed a revolver from up under the edge of the bed. With it cocked and pointed at him, she said, "Get to telling me about Sherlock."

"What the fuck?" Tony was like the number three man in Cedric's clique.

"You don't think that I'm really attracted to your broke ass, do you? This house costs me money, so get to talking." This wasn't the first time that she pulled this stunt. It never failed.

"Sally you're a cop, what the fuck are you doing?" The surprise made him feel that much weaker. He was already weak from busting the biggest nut that he ever had. With his knees shaking, and being butt naked, this was a secret that he wanted to keep from the streets.

"That should scare you. I can kill you and get away with it and no one would ever know," she said as she extended her arm like she was aiming at his head. "Now tell me what happened to Sherlock."

"Just be cool." He placed his hands in front of him as if to say be calm. He was also saying, with his body language, that he was surrendering. He figured she was crazy enough to put a few holes in him and bury him in the backyard. "What do you want to know about Sherlock?"

"Who killed him and where is his body?" There was a sadistic grin on her face.

He had to admit that he was played well. "How the fuck would I know that?"

Boom. She fired a shot. It landed next to his left knee, making him jump and turn over the warmer and the oil she used to give him pleasure.

"Damn Sally, I'll tell you. Cedric killed him at the skin

game. It happened in the back room. They were arguing about something but I don't know what."

She smiled, "Where is the body?"

"We buried him in the woods just over the Virginia line, by the Arlington Cemetery." He realized that he just ratted on the man who was helping him feed his three children. All that talk about being loyal now meant nothing.

"Okay, that's all I need for right now. There's a tape recorder to your right side." She stopped talking so he could look down. "No, don't touch it."

With what he said being taped, he knew he was trapped. He was played and that was all he could think about. Knowing that she taped him scared him because blackmail was the next step.

"There's no need to be scared, I'm going to protect and pay you. If you change your mind, I'm going to make sure Cedric and many others get a copy of that tape. Do you understand that Tony Wallace?"

He didn't want to answer. His shame was equal to his fear. There was no way he could see to win and he wasn't the kind to die for his honor. He already gave it up.

"Do we have a deal or not?" She held the gun aimed directly to shoot between his eyes.

"Yes, we have a deal," he said in a low tone.

"Good, I promise this is only between us. You are going to be my new confidential informant."

She held the gun on him while he put on his clothes. He had to walk all the way back to the Southeast. Her house was in Georgetown.

It had been a few days since Danny Boy and Clarence had a meeting and Danny Boy was late as usual. When he arrived, he looked like he was up all night. It was ten o'clock, two hours after their scheduled appointment.

"We may have problems," Clarence said to start the meeting.

"Come on Clarence, get to the point." Danny Boy hadn't been over on Pennsylvania Avenue since he started his crack spot.

"Somebody tried to do a hit on me yesterday." If they weren't partners, he wouldn't have felt it necessary to speak with him.

"Who are we supposed to be at war with?" He changed his attitude because war was his department.

"All I can tell you is that they drive a black Escalade. A clean black Escalade." Clean meant that it hadn't been pimped out.

"If we at war, we need to know who with. You got to do better than that, Clarence." It felt good to be able to tell Clarence something.

He didn't appreciate his attitude. "When a vehicle follows you and runs up on your bumper, there's a problem. When I sped up, the Escalade turned around."

Danny Boy took a bit of time to think. "I'm not feeling that Clarence. You sure you ain't paranoid?"

Did he really just ask me that? Clarence thought. "Don't worry about it, let's get down to business. What's up with the fifty grand for the three bricks?" There was tension between them because none of the suppliers wanted to meet with Danny Boy.

"I'll have that by the end of the day. After that, I'm going to need four joints." He already had the money but Danny Boy just wanted to play games.

"So you don't believe me?" Clarence didn't want to argue about drugs and money. So far, all the money had been straight and he was getting his cut. In the back of his mind,

85

he knew there would be a problem sooner or later. For now, their relationship and safety were more important.

"Of course I believe you." This was a lie. "From what you just told me, it sounds like a mistake or something, but I do believe you."

"We've been together too long for this bullshit." Clarence was now standing up.

This was one of the very times that Clarence raised his voice at Danny Boy. "What the fuck is wrong with you? I said I believe you." Though Danny was a little pissed, he was glad to see Clarence lose his cool.

"I'm sorry man, but you don't seem to be taking me seriously. It ain't good for someone to be after a nigga and not know their identity." Clarence wondered if it was a mistake to tell him. The vibe wasn't good.

"Alright, if a cat is after you, then he's after me. We are D & C." Danny took a seat behind his desk.

It was like a moment of silence had been called for. They just sat there, waiting for the other to say something. For at least ten minutes, they looked at opposite walls and out the window and thought. It had been weeks since they were on the same wavelength.

Clarence broke the silence, "I don't know what to do."

"I don't know either. I can't think of a soul that has a plain Escalade." Danny Boy was enjoying that Clarence didn't know what to do.

"Okay, forget about it. Let's talk business."

Danny was getting a good kick out of how Clarence was acting. "Are you sure man?"

"Yeah, I'm sure."

"Tell them people that the loot will be straight today." That meant have the next piece ready. The crack sales were moving faster than the dro sales. Danny liked the idea that he was bringing in more money than Clarence. This sense of power meant a lot.

"Okay, I got my end."

Danny left like he was really in a rush.

Clarence knew that Danny didn't believe him. Things like this didn't happen in the district. The streets always knew who was beefing with whom. Cats in the streets wanted credit for their actions and levels of respect were determined by what kind of work you put in.

Clarence could only figure that it was a vendetta. What bothered him most was not knowing with whom he was dealing.

Just sitting and waiting wasn't his style or appeasing to him. He liked being able to throw punches but punching in the dark wasn't good enough. Other than Danny Boy, Clarence figured it wasn't a good idea to tell anyone else.

Clarence had no choice but to be on guard.

It was ten o'clock at night and Clarence was still inside his office. All day he waited and watched the avenue, hoping to see that black Escalade again. None of the black Escalades that he saw parked across the street from the spot. He continued to send everyone away so he could be alone to think.

"So Clarence, when are you going to let me test what's under your hood? I know you have at least seven inches." Sally snuck up on him.

He didn't even turn his head. Seeing her reflection in the glass was enough. "So you come to harass me?"

She sat down behind Danny Boy's desk and leaned back in the chair. "It's my job to keep up with my number one suspect." She was wearing a three-piece pink skirt outfit, with green pinstripes.

"When do you expect them to show up?" he smirked

Turning to face him, she looked him up and down, "Funny, real funny." Stopping at the wide v-shape between his legs, she wondered how much of a hurtin' he could put on her pussy.

Noticing her stare, "If you mean me, you're wasting your time. Have a nice day." It was one of those days that whatever anybody did or said was irritating.

"Oh shit," she said as she covered her mouth. "The district's newest playa has an attitude, ain't that a bitch." She felt that her timing couldn't have been better.

Clarence turned his head to look at her. His realization that he was out of character made him take a pause. She was the one bitch he couldn't slip with.

"Listen to me good Clarence. I plan to arrest the murderer of Sherlock in the next few days." It was going to take that long to process the paperwork to make Tony an informant for the district. "I just want you to recognize how fast the Pinstriped Bitch is working and moving."

In a cool voice, Clarence said, "It's nice to know you're on the job. I feel much safer."

The sarcasm made her pucker her lips in a manner that said he got in a good one. "That was a real fast change in attitude. I like that in men. Can you use your dick that well?"

"A detective like you is supposed to know these things, along with what I eat for breakfast and even when I shit." Clarence now had a smirk on his face as he grabbed a handful of his dick through his pants.

"At my age, I hate hearsay when it comes to dick. I like to feel it for myself, but if you are scared of some experienced pussy, I understand." The sound of her voice and swinging of her head meant that it was a challenge.

"I'm afraid that if I fucked you, you'd be up here every day spoiling my reputation." He winked his eye at her to make the act complete.

"I like that, Clarence. That gets you ten playa points." She couldn't swing a good enough comeback. "I also think that Keisha's protecting you. I went to see her the other day."

Keisha was an unexpected subject. She was on his mind heavily lately. "That's an interesting theory." The mere sound of Keisha's name threw him off guard, but showing it would be the wrong thing to do.

"Clarence, it's going to hurt me to bust you, especially if I can't get an orgasm beforehand. So, I want to give you a chance to confess."

Clarence laughed and looked back out the window. *This bitch is crazy*, he thought.

"I can get you a lighter sentence."

"That lady was like family to me." The moment he pulled the trigger flashed through his mind. Getting Sally off his back was a must because she kept reminding him of his guilt. "How many people have you heard of killing their future mother-in-law?"

"That's what makes it so interesting. I must admit that you are a genius. Nobody in the streets suspect that you killed her, except for me." Solving this case would really boost her name and put her up there with the best of detectives.

Clarence looked at her with a look of deep intensity. He knew that she was fucking with him to make him slip. There was nothing he could think of to say. Guilt had his brain locked up.

"Clarence, I think she knows you did it. What other reason could there be for her to be mad at you?" With that statement, a small war had been won. She got up and walked out.

Stunned was the only way to describe how Clarence was feeling. Her game was tight. It was tighter than a virgin's pussy. Could it be possible for Keisha to be mad at him because she thought he killed her mother? There couldn't be a way for Keisha to know for sure that he did it. Finding out what was on her mind was a must. What Keisha told Sally, and what she was thinking, were things that he had to find out.

Trying to see through Sally's eyes was a hard thing. There was no doubt that she had one hell of an angle she was working from. She was too sharp and successful at her profession to be ignored. What she had just done was the kind of pressure to make a cat think twice.

The only thing that Clarence could think of was to go see Keisha at Jessica's house. In the meantime, he needed to know why Danny Boy hadn't called him about the fifty grand.

♦ ♦ ♦ ♦ ♦

"Yo, Danny Boy, we must not be going to open shop tomorrow. All we have are two ounces," Skull questioned. He was Danny Boy's main lieutenant. They met in Juvenile. Skull was six four and happy to have his position. It was rumored that he crushed a cat's skull with his bare hands but he never talked about it.

"Yeah man, I'm going to have to see Clarence." His tone said that something was wrong.

"Damn dawg. D & C stands for Danny Boy and Clarence. Danny Boy comes first, so why you always saying you have to see Clarence when it's time to re-up?" Skull had loyalty to Danny Boy. Not that he didn't like Clarence, it was just that his style of doing things was similar to Danny's.

"That's his department, he deals with the suppliers." Danny Boy didn't want to tell his man the truth about why the suppliers wouldn't deal with him although there was very little that they didn't share.

"Hey man, we're bringing in more than thirty grand a

day. Danny Boy isn't the type to answer to another cat." Their spot was on Alabama Avenue. At the time there were only six people in the building and two of them were customers. When one customer stepped out, another stepped in. Nine o'clock was closing time. That would be in fifteen minutes.

"Yeah, I know man. Clarence and I are going to work this out." He and Clarence went through too much together for him to let another cat push his buttons.

"Man, we're being oppressed and held back. When we were in Juvenile, you were always making mad moves. It seems like you done changed." Skull wanted to say that Danny Boy was acting soft. As a big boy, Skull was always taken for granted in the thinking department. It was a simple equation in his eyes. If Danny Boy made more money, he made more money.

Danny had to do some quick thinking. There was no cat in the district that could challenge Clarence's mastermind skills. Clarence kept them alive and made them Ghetto Superstars in a short period of time.

"Clarence and I are going to work this out."

Skull knew by the tone of his voice that he didn't exactly mean that. "Hey man, I'm going to holler at you later. Call me in the morning." Once Skull hit Alabama Avenue, he walked like he owned the block. Only three weeks out of the joint and he was driving a pimped-out Acura Legend. All of this was thanks to Danny Boy putting him down.

So far Danny Boy accepted all of Clarence's decisions. He also had to admit that Clarence had a knack for calling good money. All of this was good while they were laying a foundation but now that they were established, it was time to make some changes.

Danny Boy was also thinking that his man was trippin' about somebody trying to kill him. How Clarence put the situation, it just didn't seem right for the district. He was thinking about it all day.

Who the fuck could there be that wanted to do a hit? It wasn't likely to be a gang banger. Most of them were down with D & C. No other drug dealer's territory had been violated, so it shouldn't be any of them. Since Clarence was running the spot on Pennsylvania, he was only fucking Diamond, so it couldn't be a jealous boyfriend. There just weren't any suspects.

Danny Boy stuck with his first instincts - Clarence was either trippin' or just making it up. Neither was a good thing. For sure though, Danny felt he wasn't making enough money.

The bills started stacking up. Danny purchased a brand new Benz 600 and spent sixty grand pimpin' it out. With a mini mansion, a condo for his mother, a trick bill and a growing gambling bill, the money couldn't come in fast enough. He just dropped twenty thousand dollars at Cedric's skin game over the weekend.

A half an hour later it was time to close up shop. There were no more drugs. After Danny Boy jumped in his Benz and was about two blocks away, he punched in Clarence's digits. As he was doing this, he was feeling like he worked for Clarence.

"Damn it took you long enough to answer the phone. Yeah, I have all the money, and we have to talk. Okay, first thing in the morning, at nine."

Danny felt that this move was more than overdue.

When Clarence put down his cell phone, he was just pulling into Jessica's driveway. The first thing that caught his attention was the plain black Escalade. It had been found. He knew that his instincts led him in the right direction. It was Keisha that was following him.

Jessica nearly jumped out of her skin when she saw

Clarence through the peephole. "Keisha, you won't believe who came to visit us." Keisha was in the living room with James. She couldn't wait to see how Keisha handled this situation.

"Come in Clarence," Jessica said in a polite voice. She was admiring his dark brown Sean John sweatsuit.

"It's nice to see you Jessica," he said, giving her a hug. Can I see Keisha?"

"Sure, follow me." Before they could leave the foyer, Keisha was in Clarence's face with her finger pointing toward the door.

"Why you being so rude?" Jessica asked.

"He's at the wrong place at the wrong time." She was pushing him in the chest, causing him to walk backwards toward the door.

Before his back hit the door, he grabbed her arms and held them up in the air, "What the hell is wrong with you?" Clarence was surprised.

Jessica was wondering what had gotten into her niece. She was standing there thinking that Keisha was making a fool of herself.

"What's going on Keisha?" Jessica heard from behind. James had a puzzled look on his face. "Who's that guy holding your arms? Would you mind letting her go my man?"

Clarence wasn't trying to hear what dude was saying, although the dude was pretty big. He could see that he wasn't a tough guy. "If I let her go, she's going to push me through the door." Keisha was wrestling to get loose but his grip was too strong.

Jessica was using all her strength to keep James from getting by her. No drama was going to go down in her house. At least no more than what already happened, if she could help it. "Be cool, James. They just need to talk."

"When I let you go, don't hit me," Clarence said to

Keisha. He also didn't want to take the chance that James was going to get past Jessica and sucker punch him. Handling James and Keisha at the same time was an impossible challenge. He pushed Keisha back into Jessica. With speed and finesse, he unzipped his jacket and showed James the holster and the butt end of his nine. "This is not the best day for me. I just need to talk to Keisha."

Keisha stopped in motion while Jessica was already holding her to keep her from jumping back at Clarence. Keisha realized, at the sight of the gun, that she was acting foolish and could get someone hurt. She was standing in front of the man who killed her mother. As she turned around to face James she said, "Be cool, I'm going outside with him so we can talk." She could see the confusion in his eyes.

"It'll be okay James, just let them talk." Jessica reassured. She felt like she needed to help out. She felt bad because what she thought would be funny turned into a serious situation.

"Don't make me have to come see you." James felt that he had to say something to save face although there was nothing in his voice that sounded convincing. He never even held a gun before.

"Okay," Clarence said to keep from bruising his ego. He really wanted to laugh.

With an attitude, Keisha motioned for Clarence to go outside. He couldn't take his eyes off the truck. "When did you get the Escalade?"

"What the fuck does that matter to you? You disappointed and lied to me." She wanted to change the subject. She knew that he recognized the Escalade, even if he wasn't certain.

"Sally came to see me. What do you know about that?" The Escalade question could be answered later.

"Clarence, I know you didn't come all the way up here to

talk to me about Sally. I'm not a cop." She was wondering if her heart was beating fast because she just attacked him or because of her feelings for him.

"First, you need to lower your voice." He could tell that she was glad to see him. He was glad to see her also. Her anger was making her that much more attractive.

Her mother's last words flooded her mind again. Slapping him and asking "why" were the instructions from her instincts but her emotions took over. "I hear that you and Diamond are really serious. What's up with that?" She was still talking loud.

"So that was you following me the other day. Few people in the 'hood have plain Escalades." The change in her expression answered his question.

"Why would I follow you, I have a boyfriend. You just saw him." She couldn't believe that he had the nerve to kill her mother then find her to question her.

"Okay, forget about that. Sally says that you think I killed your mother. Tell me about that."

She almost hollered out that he did do it and how she knew but she quickly caught herself. "Well, did you do it?" she asked with sarcasm and disgust in her voice. She didn't care what he said or how he acted.

"That's an insult, she was like a mother to me. So you are trying to put that murder on me. You just need somebody to blame." Clarence planned his response.

It took all of her willpower and strength to stop and think. She made him wait for fifteen seconds for an answer. "No, I don't think that. I'm sorry." She started thinking of how to get him back. There had to be a way, a good, devious way.

"Are you sure?"

"Yes, I'm sure."

"Sally said you think that I did it because you have been

mad at me. I think there's more to it than that." His ego was telling him that Keisha was falling for every word and that he could have her back when he got ready.

"Sally keeps telling me that I'm keeping information from her. Maybe she thinks we did it together." Karyn told her that telling a man what he wanted to hear was an easy way to fool him.

He started shaking his head and started walking off. "The next time you follow me, don't run up on my bumper. I might shoot you." They laughed. He drove off as she stood there and watched. She didn't mind him knowing that she was watching him.

The love was still there. Keisha accepted the reality that her feelings never changed. Jessica didn't lie but still loving him or not, he had to pay.

As angry as she was when she saw his face, she was happy that he came. If he didn't, she wouldn't have known what happened with Sally. As Keisha saw it, Sally was at a dead end. There was nothing that would make her tell Sally what her mother said or what she knew about Clarence and his guns. This information was like a trump card. As good of a detective as Sally was, she wasn't a mind reader.

Sally getting in the way was a possibility. Sooner or later, Sally would find other cases to occupy her time. Since she hadn't figured out how she wanted to get her revenge, Sally wasn't much of a threat at this moment.

By the look in Clarence's eyes, she knew that he still loved her. He made the trip because Sally really had him paranoid. It was understandable. They agreed that Sally was trying to play the both of them. Being able to still get close to Clarence was an advantage that would make getting revenge easier. Clarence left thinking that he knew all the answers, especially after seeing the black Escalade. So what if he knew about being followed. He didn't know that he almost became a victim. "If a man thinks that he's smarter than you, let him think that," her mother told her. Clarence played himself right into her glove. It didn't matter that he knew Keisha still loved him, he took that for granted.

Keisha knew more about his way of thinking than he knew about hers. Still loving him, and being in love with him, were things she felt she could now deal with. All of that was in the open and the element of surprise was on her side.

In a few weeks she'd start college. In the meantime, she planned to keep up with Clarence and make a plan. Her instincts also told her that he would be back to see her. According to Jessica, love makes people do that.

Clarence was feeling like a brand new man the next morning. A lot of tension was released after visiting Keisha, which also led him to the black Escalade. Never would he have thought that she would follow him. It was all good, being that her feelings were apparent. He interpreted her actions as being in love and harmless.

Only one matter remained that was stressin' him - all complications with his man, Danny Boy, had to be avoided.

It was eleven o'clock when Clarence showed up at the Pennsylvania spot. Danny Boy was already in the office waiting for him with seventy-five grand on him.

"Damn Clarence, you ain't never been this late." Danny Boy was pissed because he was missing out on plenty of money.

Carefully choosing his words before he spoke, Clarence said, "I've seen a change in you. We have to make some changes, man." Clarence was throwing words at him as he took a seat at his desk.

Danny Boy was thinking that now wasn't the time.

"What the fuck are you talking about? I'm missing out on some serious paper and I have to blame you."

"You can blame me. Also blame me for getting out of your way. I worked it out so you don't have to call me." Clarence didn't want to be in the middle of money being short and having to go in his pocket. As he thought, Danny Boy was spending as fast as he could make it.

"Okay, who do I call?" He was happy with what he heard. Not having to argue for it made him suspicious, though.

"First, let me get the money for the three bricks and my cut. Then you are free of me."

"What is that supposed to mean? What do you mean that I'm free of you?" Clarence was the one cat Danny Boy never took for granted. He knew Clarence's cold-blooded and calculating side like no other. Others just thought he was a basketball playing pretty boy.

"We do things differently. We both have money. We can just do some things together and other things separately."

"Nah Clarence, you ain't slick. What the fuck are you talking about? What do you know that I don't?" All Danny Boy could think of was being played, in some way. It wasn't going down like that.

"What the fuck is up with the attitude? What the fuck are you yelling at me for? When did we start yelling at each other?" Some people heard them from downstairs, that's how loud they were.

"I think you're trying to play me."

"Listen Danny, I know that you are harboring negative emotions because I've been calling the shots and I'm seeing the suppliers. Your voice and body language say what your mouth isn't saying." No one could have told him that Danny would start tripping. Clarence walked over to the window.

Danny sat at his desk. "Break it down to me." He was prepared to scrutinize every detail.

"First thing's first, let me get the cash." Danny threw it to him. "I want you to keep all the profit from your spot and this spot becomes mine."

Danny wanted to smile because the crack spot was about to explode. Doing four hundred thousand a week, plus weight sales, was a real possibility. He kept his composure. "Shit, I can't complain at all."

"That's basically it. D & C still lives in name, but you do your thing and I do mine on the business level. You still my boy and that won't change." It went over well. Clarence knew there was no way for Danny to say no.

"So this means that I'll be going straight to the supplier without you."

"Yes." A plan came together.

"So how do I do that?"

"You already know him. He'll be at your spot with four bricks." Clarence didn't tell him that a call had to be made beforehand, or it wasn't happening.

They stared at each other for a while. What Clarence was proposing was better than what Danny Boy wanted to propose. "Shit yeah. I'm going over to *my spot*." Danny was so happy that he couldn't conceal his smile. He hollered as he went down the steps.

Clarence wanted to pat himself on the back for being a true playa. The move that he just made with Danny was the only logical thing to do. Their people had already taken sides. When it comes to business, certain styles don't mix. Now they could still remain the best of friends.

With the new resolution, it was time for Clarence to make a few moves of his own. At the top of his agenda was opening a heroin spot. Half of his people would be taken to the new spot. It would be going down in the next few weeks.

To make his life complete, Clarence felt like he needed a queen that totally complemented his style. Diamond could offer sex and good looks, but nothing else. Clarence felt himself becoming bored with her, especially after seeing Keisha last night.

Keisha had brains, beauty, a body, knowledge of the streets and most of all, his respect. Clarence contemplated how to go about getting her back.

Seeing Keisha also made him feel guilty. Shooting Karyn turned into the most regretful thing that he'd ever done. It was hard for him to think about it. Pointing a gun in his direction forced him to pull the trigger. It was like he had a showdown with his own mother. If he had to do it all over again, he wasn't sure of what he would do.

A week never passed that he didn't think about it. So that he could get rid of the thoughts, he blamed Danny Boy. He harbored negative emotions against Danny Boy for the incident. It didn't have to be that house or at that time. They could have waited for another opportunity.

Clarence committed an act of betrayal that he couldn't rid himself of. Telling somebody was out of the question. On several occasions, he thought about telling his mother, but decided against it.

Telling Keisha was out of the question, no matter how much he wanted to make it up to her. She wouldn't understand and he couldn't expect her to. Just facing her was a monumental task. It might be easier in the future. Guilt was the only thing keeping him from going to see her sooner.

Guilt and love just were not mixing. Clarence knew their love for each other was too deep for them to stay apart. The guilt might make it impossible to have a real relationship with her.

◆ ◆ ◆ ◆ ◆

◆ ◆ ◆ ◆ ◆

When Cedric walked into his poolroom, there wasn't a soul in sight, not even his employee that ran the counter. This was totally unusual for an afternoon. The place looked like it was never opened. There was no smell of blunts in the air, all the pool sticks were in the racks and even the pool tables were clean, which seldom happened.

When he saw there were no beer cans in the trash, he figured that his spot hadn't been opened all day. This pissed him off because it meant that he lost money. Losing money to Cedric was as bad as cursin' during a pastor's sermon.

His hired help had some questions to answer. It didn't make sense that she cleaned up when nobody was there to spend money. She was nowhere to be found. This wasn't part of the game plan. Cedric wanted to know what was going on immediately, especially since the front door was left unlocked, even though the sign read "closed."

While mumblin' curse words, he started toward his office. He had plans on giving her more than just a piece of his mind. The closer he got to his office, the louder he became. With his key in his right hand, he grabbed the knob with his left. To his surprise, the knob turned.

"What the fuck," he hollered. His office door was never left unlocked. His temperature and anger went up a few more degrees when he saw her.

"Hello Cedric," Sally said with a smile on her face. She was sitting behind his desk. Her hair was out of its usual ponytail. Its length went past her shoulders, even with the semi-curly style she was wearing. Her black and gray pin-striped two-piece skirt set looked great. It was a perfect match for her skin tone. Her cleavage let the admirers know that she was wearing nothing under her jacket.

"What the fuck are you doing Sally? Where are all of my people?" Cedric blared as he started walking toward his chair.

"When I got here, the doors were open, so I just let myself in." The place was empty because she wanted it that way. "It looks like somebody tried to rob you."

He glanced toward his closet to see if the door was open. There was a safe in there. He couldn't check it while she was there.

"You need to get out of here, I have things to do Sally." He was right at his chair.

She got up and started walking around the desk. She was careful not to let her pocketbook swing too much. "I need to talk to you." She sat her pocketbook back on the desk while still standing. It was great that he was mad.

"Damn Sally, why you want to fuck with me right now?" He slammed himself into his chair. While straightening out her skirt, she sat with him. "My help is missing and I may have been robbed."

"Calm down. You want me to call 911 for you?" she said sarcastically.

He banged his fist on the desk. "Sally, you are the police. Was that a joke? Get the fuck out." His finger was pointing toward the door.

She put her head down in a manner to get his full attention. "Cedric, I'm here because I think your life is in danger. It's my job to protect you." She just thought of this line. It was better than the original plan of arguing with him.

"Nobody in the district is about to fuck with me." He stood up when he said this. "I've been holding it down since back in the day. My work is well-known."

Sally was loving it. Just a little more, she thought. She stood up, "Be cool Cedric. I know these people can easily get at you. We go way back, baby."

"Fuck them people. What they bring, I'll bring. I gets it how I live. I'm a known veteran." He was talking so much shit he had forgot that Sally was a cop.

"Big Cedric, these people are serious about shooting up you and your spot. I heard it from a reliable source." Her source was herself.

"Who the fuck are these people?"

"They say they gon' get you for killing Sherlock."

"Shit, I'll get his people first, just like I got him first."

"Oh yeah, Sherlock tried to kill you?" She said this really fast like they were standing on the block talking shit.

"Yeah, I did him before he could do me."

The door swung open, hitting the back wall with a loud cracking sound. It was the plywood splintering. In a matter of seconds, eight officers in all black gear were in the room. "Get on the floor! Now!"

"You motherfucking bitch," he hollered with a look of disgust.

"Bitch," Sally laughed.

"That's Pinstriped Bitch to you." She thought to herself that was too easy.

His confession to the crime wasn't needed because Tony became a full time confidential informant. With the confession, Tony could be used for other things.

All of what Cedric said was recorded. Sally had a state of the art mini microphone attached to her purse. Everything was a setup. He was just as good as convicted.

Sally was having an excellent day. When she walked out of Cedric's, she started toward her car and partner. Bambi was leaning on the car with a big grin on her face.

"What are you doing?" Sally asked Bambi. Bambi had a Black in between her hands, rubbing it back and forth like she was starting a fire. "Do you know what you're doing?"

"We're about to find out." She stopped rubbing and started pinching the tobacco out of the cigar into the plastic wrapping with her fingers and thumb. "I like the way you got him hyped."

Sally smiled at her work and the compliment. "That was easy, let's get out of here. I'll drive. I can see you're busy."

Bambi smiled as she walked around to the other side of the car and got in. Sally popped in The Game's CD maxi single. "This is How We Do" pumped through the fifteens. She had four of them in the trunk. With the trunk rattlin', they made their way down Pennsylvania Avenue while singing the chorus to their theme song.

Bambi finally removed all of the tobacco out of the Black. Sally was wishing she would hurry up. She planned to clap her hands if Bambi could get the tan wrapper out of the casing without tearing it up.

When Sally stopped at the light, she just watched Bambi struggle. If she laughed, it might hurt her feelings. She almost asked Bambi for the casing but the light turning green stopped her.

Sally turned the music down. "Damn, white girl. I can't get my lungs tight with you. They didn't teach you that shit in college?"

Bambi blushed and handed the casing to Sally.

Sally laughed, she couldn't help it. "When we get to the next light, I'm going to do this in a split second."

"So you showing off. You think a white girl can't break it down, huh?" They both laughed as they stopped at the light.

Sally put her fingernail between the dark casing and the tan paper. With the nail from her thumb, she grasped the tan paper and pulled gently. The tan paper came out of the casing with ease.

"Ding, ding, ding, ding, ding," Sally hummed to the chorus as she flashed the casing in front of Bambi's face. "This is how we do. Here girl, I hope you learned something."

"Fuck you Sally."

"Nah, let Clarence fuck me. I got to get his fine ass next." Handing the casing to Bambi, she noticed his Lexus parked in front of his spot. It was time to go see him again.

"Damn Sally, do you be serious about fucking these young dudes? You old enough to be their mama." Bambi never heard Sally tell her about any of the guys she fucked.

"What makes you think your pussy ain't going to work after you get my age? Most of them think I'm about thirty-five and that they're getting over." Sally knew better than to fuck and tell. Rumors could never get her in trouble. Retirement and a good pension weren't worth the risk.

Bambi was almost finished packing the Black. "How did you get that guy to tell on Cedric? It seems you always have an informant on the inside."

Sally looked at her and smiled. "If I tell you, I'll have to kill you." They both laughed.

"I saw the way Tony was looking at you when we were interrogating him. There was some serious lust in his eyes. I might be white, but I'm not stupid." She was tapping the

Black against the dashboard.

"So you think I gave him some pussy or something?"

Bambi lit the Black, " It's damn sure funny how guys keep coming to the police station to be confidential informants and none of them have cases." Bambi thought to herself that the Black tasted good.

"I think your ass wants to be Black. I can't tell you my secrets, just be a good detective." She checked her lipstick in the rearview mirror. Just thinking about Clarence had her hot.

"Okay, how are we going to bust Clarence?" Sally took a left turn on Anacostia. "Sherlock's murder was easy."

"Girl, you must be reading my mind. Clarence ain't like the average man in the street. But I know that he did it." Sally's entire attitude changed. She hit the CD changer to listen to Sade sing "No Ordinary Love."

"Damn, he got you like that? It takes a treacherous motherfucker to kill someone that close to him." She was really trying to say that she didn't believe that he did it.

"I just have to get in his head and Keisha's head. The answer is between them."

"Damn, you want to get him that bad. Which do you want more, to fuck him or convict him for the murder?" She passed the Black to Sally.

Sally just looked at her and turned up the music.

It came time for Keisha to attend college, as scheduled. It was her second day at Maryland State University and her roommate hadn't shown up yet. She was enjoying the peace and quiet. She spent the afternoon surfing the Internet, searching for ideas for revenge.

When she heard a key in the door she was surprised. "I imagine you're my roommate." The first thing she noticed was that her T-shirt had *"The Clit"* written on the front.

"Hello, my name is Jezebel." She walked across the medium-sized room to shake Keisha's hand.

The second thing she noticed was that Jezebel had on some expensive perfume that smelled great. She stood up to shake her hand. "My name is Keisha and I'm from the district."

"I'm from Queens, born and raised. My peeps and I are going to bring my stuff up."

"Does that say *"The Clit"* on the front of your shirt?" She couldn't help herself.

Jezebel smiled with pride. "Yep, that's what it says. That's the clique I'm in. Look at the back. It says, 'If there ain't no lickin, there ain't no stickin, and if you ain't rich, you can't get shit.'" Jezebel didn't pay any attention to Keisha's facial expressions. "I'll tell you about me when I get back."

Jezebel was a twenty-two year old stripper/high-priced call girl. Since she ran away from home at the age of eleven, she learned to use her feminine treasures to survive. She learned the ways of the streets the hard way. It took a few years to get off drugs and start making things happen for her. When she met her partner, Cleopatra, things started to change. They called themselves "The Clit." At that time, she was sixteen, and Cleopatra was twenty-five. By making love to each other, they grew stronger and wiser. At age eighteen, she changed her name from Maria Jenkins to Jezebel, to make a brand new start.

Jezebel wasn't just some young, black chick with good looks, she was intelligent and talented. Just from natural ability, she could sing in five octaves and comprehend everything that she read. On a daily basis, she read and wrote for three hours, religiously. Cleopatra taught her that in order to get respect she had to do things that demanded respect. This became her motto to live by.

Getting an education was the first thing on her agenda and what she desired the most. Telling people that she had a degree in this or that would get her lots of respect. Getting a G.E.D. was an easy way out because it only took six months at a community college.

Years of pain from being on the streets, especially dealing with an abusive pimp and an abusive father, became her motivation and driving force. She never learned to love herself until Cleopatra taught her. Her only desire for a man was to use him to fulfill her financial needs and wants. Making men lust after her was her biggest source of power, although she did it effortlessly. She studied every facet of seducing men; she became so good that she was able to get money from them just for letting them eat her pussy. That's how they got the name *The Clit*.

Jezebel transformed herself into a goddess. All things she did pertained to being sexy or looking sexy. From her fingernails to her hair, to the way she walked, represented feminine sexiness. Whenever she went out, everything had to be perfect.

When she wasn't being seen, she was tightening up her game by reading *The Art of Seduction*. She knew that getting to a man meant getting to his dick but the best way to get to his dick, and get something in return, was through his ego. She used her looks to attract a man then used his imagination to take him to the next level. By that time, she would already have what she wanted. A lot of times, men couldn't contain themselves after eating her pussy. It was that good. She didn't care though because she had Cleopatra to pick up where they left off.

Keisha was checking out the eight piece Louis Vuitton luggage. She was surprised that her roomie could afford something like that. Cleopatra had on the same kind of T-shirt. Her instincts told her that they were lesbians.

"Hey Keisha," Cleopatra said when she first came in the room.

"Hi, you must be part of Jezebel's clique." She couldn't bring herself to say the word "clit" out loud.

"Yes, I am. I started *The Clit*. It's about Black women empowering themselves." Cleopatra had a beautiful smile and sweet sounding voice. Her head wrap made her look like an African queen.

Jezebel and Cleopatra hugged each other and started kissing like they wouldn't see each other for years. Keisha didn't know what to say or do.

"Bye Clee," Jezebel said as she was closing the door.

"Bye Jezzie. I'll call as soon as I get back to New York." They waved one last time before Cleopatra walked down the hall.

"So, who is that, really?" Keisha asked while she closed her laptop. She had to get to know her roommate and lay down the law.

"That's my everything." Jezebel opened her trunk and started putting her clothes on the bed. They had a cozy room that was just big enough to hold two people and have a little space in the middle. "She's been so good to me."

"I don't mean to be in your business, but you look like you could have any man that you want." She wanted to say that she looked better than most of the video girls. "So, why are you gay?" The last part was said with bluntness.

Jezebel was that fine. Her skin was such a bright tone of light brown that she almost looked like she was glowing. With dark black, wavy hair, like an Indian, her complexion stood out that much more. It was plain to see that she had a bit of Latino in her also. With a cute nose, almond shaped eyes, a sexy set of lips, and naturally arched eyebrows, she had the makings of an ethnic angel. At five-ten, she had an ass just big enough for her to shake a man out of a coma and put him right back in it. Her modest set of tits and shapely curves made her *that* girl.

"Thank you Keisha, you're very beautiful too." She held up a black Versace blouse made out of chiffon. "You like it? This guy named Eric bought it for me."

Keisha thought to herself that the blouse did look good. "So, you like guys also?"

"Well, since we're talking, I'll break it down." She threw the blouse to Keisha. "I hate men and only love one woman, and she just left. I use men to get what I want. It's the code of *The Clit*."

Keisha liked the part about hating men. "So that means I'm not going to catch you up here getting your freak on with another woman, right?" Keisha was spoiled all her life, always went for what she wanted and spoke her mind.

Jezebel giggled at the statement. "Nah girl, but would it matter if I had a guy up here licking my clit? We always say 'licking the clit.'"

Keisha never experienced having her clit licked. "Well, I just want you to know that I'm not gay. So what's up with the blouse?"

"Cleopatra taught me that respect comes first. We won't have any sexin' in the room until you change your mind, and I'm not trying to get at your pussy. The only female that I fuck with is my Cleopatra." Jezebel liked Keisha being straightforward and speaking her mind. Because of her looks, it was tough for her to have relationships with most females. They were insecure around her.

Keisha was admiring Jezebel's style. "That sounds good." They shook on it. "Now what's up with the blouse?"

"You can wear whatever I have. I'm just a little taller than you."

That sounded good. Keisha was really thinking about having Jezebel helping her get her wardrobe together.

"Damn, you're sweet. Tell me something, your parents really didn't name you Jezebel, did they?"

"Sit down little sister." They sat in the chairs that went with their desks. "My father mistreated me. A pimp mistreated me, along with a lot of other men. I hate men and use them to the limit, and not for small shit. Since I'm that bad, I changed my name to Jezebel Delicious. I'm bad as hell, and delicious." She put some of her hair behind her ear with her finger. "Can you feel me?"

Keisha was smiling from ear to ear. She was totally astonished by Jezebel's attitude and gangsta demeanor. She was not sure of what to ask next.

Jezebel crossed her left leg over her right. "Little sister, I'll make a man do whatever I want him to do. Every man, since I was seventeen, that put dick in the pussy has ate me out and paid out. This pussy is so good that one guy tried to sue me for brainwashing him. He said that the only thing that he could think about was my pussy. Girl, I put the clamps on the chump." They laughed and high-fived each other. What men have done in the past to get the pussy again was pretty close to what she said.

"Stop lying Jezebel, yo' pussy can't be that good. What you got, multi flavors or something." They laughed again.

"Okay, I put some butter on it. But I got all these clothes, my Jag, and my phat bank account from men that I put this pussy on." Jezebel was feeling a good vibe with Keisha.

"You can really get men open like that?" Her sexual experiences with James weren't that exciting, and he never licked her clit or talked about it.

"Girl, I can do any man that I put my eyes on. Men are weak."

"What if you wanted to make a man hurt, could you do that?" The excitement in her voice was immeasurable.

"When I break a man's heart, he hurts deeply. I mean it's

the kinda shit he never forgets and the next woman, unfortunately, has to pay the price. That's why they spend big, thinking that will keep me around. Sometimes, when I get bored with them, I don't even let them touch me anymore. They'll pay just to be in my presence."

"What if you wanted a man to jump off a building, could you do it?" The question almost sounded like a challenge.

"Girl, I ain't never tried that, but I'm pretty sure I can. If you'd like, I can teach you some of my game."

"Yeah, it's all good. I got a dude I want to make suffer, suffer so much that he would wish he were dead."

"That shit sounds good to me. Girl, we'll get him back and make him wish his Daddy never had that nut."

Keisha was so excited that she had to take a walk. Having Jezebel teach her how to make a man go crazy was exactly what she needed. Having Clarence going out of his mind would be perfect. After that, she could just kill him. There was also Danny Boy who would be an easy sucker for Jezebel. Just getting Clarence would satisfy but if Danny Boy got in the way, then he'd have to pay as well.

A night didn't go by that Keisha didn't think about her parents, especially her mother. Most of these nights she cried herself to sleep. She and her mother were just like sisters. There was absolutely nothing they couldn't talk about. Sherlock was really cool and understanding when he was around. She was closer to Clarence than she was to her father. That's one of the reasons the betrayal hurt so much.

Keisha wanted to be just like her mother, by dedicating her life to her man. She bragged to her friends that Clarence would be all hers in the end. There was truth in that. She planned to see him pay, at the hands of a woman. Her plan was formulating in her mind. Payback's a bitch.

◆　◆　◆　◆　◆

11

◆ ◆ ◆ ◆ ◆

"This coke is the fucking bomb. Put some more in that pipe." Skull tricked Danny Boy into getting high with him. First, he got him to smoke blunts laced with crack. The more he could get Danny Boy to do, the easier his life would be. Skull was Danny Boy's bodyguard and confidant.

"You right man. We've made fifty grand just today off this shit. At this rate, I'll be a millionaire in a few weeks. It's going to take Clarence a few months selling dro to even come close to where we are." Danny Boy started smoking an ounce a day with Skull.

"Man, fuck Clarence. If it weren't for the respect you started getting in the streets, he wouldn't be where he is now." All day they would drink, smoke and talk about Clarence. He passed the pipe to Danny Boy.

He lit the lighter as he placed the pipe in his mouth. Smoke from the crack pipe filled Danny's lungs as he sucked as hard as he could. There was an instant rush that left him feeling like life was perfect. It felt good, though the rush was nothing in comparison to the first rush. That was hours ago.

"Clarence would have taken over if I hadn't said something. I started D & C." He put the pipe in the ashtray. "I brought that nigga into the game and look what he tried to do to me." It had only been a week that Danny was dealing directly with the suppliers, and so far, he hadn't missed paying off. But much of his profit was going up in smoke and toward gambling.

"Clarence owes you. He should be paying you a cut of what he sells in dro." If Skull could manage to get Clarence out of the way, he and Danny Boy could be partners.

"You right." Danny Boy took a drink of his Barcardi Rum. "He owes me, but he acts like I owe him." Deep in his heart, he knew that he needed Clarence's thinking to be able to handle being a major playa, but his pride was making him say other things.

"Clarence hasn't done a bid like us. When the heat comes down, he ain't going to be able to handle it." Skull only talked to him a few times and there was only so much that he could say bad. Most of what he heard was good. His name was ringing all over town.

"That's my man, but he needs to be brought down a notch or two." Danny needed something to make him feel that he had something on Clarence, even if it were just a small thing.

"Hey man, I'm going to holla at you later." Skull was heading to another spot to smoke coke. He could see that Danny Boy zoned out. "I'll see you first thing in the morning."

"Yeah, my nigga."

Danny Boy was always intimidated by Clarence's intelligence. At times, it seemed that Clarence knew more about the streets than he did. This bothered the hell out of him.

Clarence kept him from robbing a lot of people because he kept telling him about the bigger picture.

All of the things that Clarence said made them the force that they had become. Danny Boy would never deny him that or try to steal his credit for being brilliant. It was Clarence's role to set the guidelines and his to pick the moves. After he didn't show any hesitation on taking out Sherlock, there was nothing more he could ask. Clarence also killed Sherlock's wife as if he didn't have any remorse or feelings. He never even talked about it. He stuck to the guidelines they set. For that move, and style of handling the situation, Danny Boy had the utmost respect for Clarence.

Even with all of that and its value, Danny Boy felt that he was living in Clarence's shadow. His pride was the reason for this. His ego told him that Clarence should be the one living in his shadow. Danny Boy couldn't be that major dude until he surpassed his own partner.

It was that bad in Danny Boy's mind and he didn't doubt that Clarence knew what he was feeling. When Clarence told him about the hit, he felt he was testing his loyalty. Danny Boy even wondered what things would be like if were dead. He had no shame in thinking these thoughts: Trying to get ahead of Clarence was going to be a hell of a task because keeping up with him was already hard enough.

Danny Boy even thought about robbing and killing the supplier. It was just in his nature. If Clarence weren't a part of the picture, he would have already done it. He would definitely have something to say about him messing up the hand that was feeding them. Those would be his exact words. Hearing Clarence talk that talk would be that much more torture and make him more powerful. He knew the streets would be talking about how Clarence carried him for years, they were already saying it.

If it were anybody else, he would just start a war. Danny Boy knew he had to come up with something else. No matter how much money he made, it wouldn't satisfy his feeling of inferiority. He had to have something to satisfy him, mentally.

◆ ◆ ◆ ◆ ◆

Jezebel was the talk of the Maryland State campus and Keisha was stunned. All she did was wear her pink *The Clit* T-shirt and a pair of sexy J-Lo jeans. It had to be the T-shirt because everybody was talking about what was written on the back.

"Damn Jezebel, everywhere I went today, they were talking about you and your T-shirt." They were also talking about how good she looked. In high school, Keisha was used to getting the majority of the attention so there was a bit of envy there.

Jezebel just sat on her bed and put her book bag on the floor. "Keisha, I'm tired, I haven't even got my reading in for today." She knew that she would have the campus drooling. Intentionally, she made all of her conversations short and sweet. She spent her day getting signed up for classes, getting books and getting to know the campus and the surrounding area.

Keisha already figured that Jezebel liked to read because she had a bunch of business books. "How are you going to get in all this reading with all the attention you're getting?"

"As a Black woman, I have to get, and keep, my head right. *The Clit* is about empowering the Black woman. Didn't you hear what Cleopatra said?" She got up and started stripping down to her underwear and put on a beautiful pink robe. "Oh yeah, I'm used to the attention, I used to be a stripper," she said matter-of-factly.

Keisha was beginning to believe that Jezebel really knew some serious shit. "Damn girl, you act like the attention ain't shit. There are other girls on this campus that look just as good as you." Keisha was sitting on the edge of her bed.

"What are you talking about? It ain't like I'm Janet Jackson or something. It ain't all that big a deal." Jezebel was going through her things, getting ready to take a shower.

"Girl, you got to teach me all you know. I'm your student." Admiration was all in her voice.

Jezebel sat on the edge of her bed, facing Keisha. "Keisha, I like you, and I want us to be great friends, so you need to tell me about that *demon*."

"What are you talking about?" Keisha thought she was about to start talking some crazy shit.

"You had a real bad dream last night. You were tossing and turning and saying a lot of things. I wanted to wake you up." She left out the part about the names.

Keisha remembered having the dream. It was the same dream she had for weeks. She started playing with her fingers like she had been caught. "It's about this guy that hurt me really bad. I keep having dreams about him."

"I can relate, I used to have nightmares about all the terrible men in my life. I don't have them anymore. What did he do to you?" Jezebel could tell by Keisha's expression that it was really bad.

"I can't tell you. It isn't that I don't trust you, I just got to get myself together to be able to talk about it." If Jezebel pushed her she would tell her everything. She sensed that Jezebel understood her reluctance to talk about it and felt she really wanted to help. Plus, Keisha needed to be understood concerning what happened.

Jezebel put her left hand on Keisha's right knee. "Little sister, we're going to get him and he will hurt. No man will be able to hurt you again. I have to take a shower. Later."

Jezebel gave her a smile that said everything would be alright.

Sally was waiting for Clarence to come outside. His Lexus was parked in front of his new heroin spot on Wheeler Road. She was sitting on his hood with her legs crossed, smoking a Black. Her purple two-piece pants set with pink pinstripes was looking good on her.

"Sally, is this really necessary? People are beginning to think that we're lovers and shit." Clarence saw her earlier but made her wait for an hour. He figured if she would wait that long, then he would talk to her, especially since her presence wasn't stopping business. There was a line around the block and getting longer by the minute. All of the dope fiends knew what Sally was all about.

"So, do you always make the ladies wait on you? I've been out here for a while. That can really damage a female's ego." She didn't mean a word. She was enjoying chasing Clarence as a murderer and sizing him up as a future lover.

"You didn't have to let me know that Cedric pleaded guilty. I watch the news." Clarence wanted to get rid of her as fast as possible. "Would you mind getting off my car, or do I have to call the police?"

She laughed. "My bad young thang." She put her feet on the ground and stood in front of him. Looking up into his eyes was enjoyable. "You know I can't stay away from you for too long."

Clarence looked at her with a blank expression on his face. It was a few weeks since she ran up on him and he expected it to happen earlier. At Sherlock's funeral is where he actually expected to see her.

"You know they have escort services for what you need.

I'm not available. Diamond and I are getting married." Clarence was just making things up to say.

"You got game Clarence, real good game. At times you are quiet, other times, you real slick. Then you can talk without saying much, and that's what you're doing right now." She was shaking her head and wondering why he was still with a dumb ass bitch like Diamond.

"Thank you Sally, I appreciate the comment," he said sarcastically. "You know what, my fiancé can get real jealous so unless you plan on getting into a match with her, you need to split."

"Clarence, I came to tell you that I figured it all out." She pressed Cedric to the point that he told her Danny Boy, and a few others, were at the spot when Sherlock was killed. It was all the same info that she got from Tony. Since Danny Boy didn't see the murder go down, she couldn't charge him. Once she was satisfied, she went and got Sherlock's body.

Clarence rolled his eyes and looked up at the sun.

She liked his reaction. "It was Danny Boy's idea to rob Sherlock's house. Naturally, he called you to go with him. Somehow, Karyn got a gun and started shooting, that's when you ended up shooting her." She needed one more piece of evidence to make a case against him.

"So, did you come to arrest me? It sounds like that's your intention but the shit you sayin' just sounds like a theory." Clarence pretty much knew what she was coming to tell him. One of Cedric's people talked. That's the only way he figured she got Cedric for Sherlock's murder.

"Keisha knows that you killed her mother, don't you feel guilty about that?" She already knew she wasn't going to get anything out of him. The look on his face said that he knew her persistence all too well. Still, she enjoyed fucking with him.

"Clarence, you can relax, I'm not going to be at the

funeral tomorrow to see how you interact with Keisha. Just don't slip baby boy, I'm watching you and when you least expect it, I'm gonna swoop down on you and get that ass." Winking her eye, she sashayed off.

They both knew she was lying.

Clarence wanted to warn Danny Boy about Sally. This was a matter they really had to talk about, no matter how he might react. Shit might really get hectic.

Sherlock's funeral was like a major event. Everybody from DC was there, including the media. Sherlock was forty-five years old when he was killed. He started in the numbers business when he was thirteen. There was nobody that could say a bad thing about him. Even a few men cried.

Keisha broke down at the sight of seeing him in the casket. Jessica and Jezebel gave her moral support and strength. The mortician used a lot of makeup to make his face look like it should. Quite a bit of the makeup got on Keisha's clothes.

Keisha regained her composure by the time they got to the cemetery. They were going to bury Sherlock right next to Karyn. Sally and Bambi watched the funeral and burial from a distance. What they saw surprised them. "Excuse me," Keisha said to Jessica. "This just wouldn't be right if I didn't have Clarence up here."

Keisha stopped the proceedings and walked toward Clarence and his posse. They were about thirty yards away and Diamond was by his side. Keisha motioned for Clarence to come to her. When he saw the gesture, he made sure that she meant him. Once it was established she meant him, he began to walk toward her with a confused look on his face.

Diamond was fuming so she left and sat in the car.

Danny Boy wondered what the fuck was going on. When he saw Keisha, he thought she was really looking good in her black dress. He noticed the girl she was with was also looking good. As a matter of fact, his dick got hard looking at both of them together.

"Clarence, I'm still mad at you for standing me up the morning my mother died, but my father would want you to be one of the first to throw dirt in his grave. Would you please?" She was thinking to herself that she could get hypnotized just looking into his eyes.

"There's no way I could tell you no. Let's go." He offered his arm and they headed back to the gravesite and took care of business. All eyes were on them. Everybody felt that it was his place to be by her side during this time.

"I don't believe it, Keisha has lost her mind or something." Sally was smoking a Black and listening to a jazz CD.

Bambi wasn't sure of what to say. "I don't think it's what it looks like. Many people feel that Clarence should have inherited Sherlock's throne."

"I know that. Keisha's up to something. Even that other girl doesn't belong with them. She isn't from the district. You see that dress she has on? It's a Vera Wang and runs around five grand." She passed the Black to Bambi.

Bambi took a long drag. "Maybe they're going to get back together." What Bambi really wanted to say was that Sally was trippin'.

"You might have a point there. They have serious feelings for each other." Sally hit the CD changer, wanting to hear something more aggressive. NWA's "Fuck the Police" came through the system.

"I think you have too much of a thing for Clarence. One minute you want to fuck him, the next minute you want to arrest him. What type of shit is that?" Bambi still didn't believe that he murdered Karyn.

"It's an older woman thing. Sex gets better as you get older."

"It might be an 'I'm jealous of Keisha' thing."

Sally put her binoculars down. "That was fucked up. Imagine Sally jealous." They both laughed. "I'm jealous, you better believe it. He's an exceptional young buck. I know he can fuck, I feel it in my bones." Sally sounded like she had an inside scoop.

"If he fucked you, and fucked you well, would you let him get away with murder?" Bambi was having fun. The Black she was smoking tasted good as a motherfucker.

"Let me get some of that, you got some in your purse. Only if he let me get it on the regular. He ain't gonna fuck me right then stay in jail." They laughed so hard, they had tears running down their faces. It was about ten minutes before they stopped laughing.

"Stop laughing Bambi, I know Keisha is up to something. We have to start concentrating on her." Her new angle was to treat Keisha like she was a suspect.

"We still have some of her stuff." Bambi was the kind that made suspects out of all parties until there was evidence that said otherwise. That's how she was taught in school.

"We're going to act like we are her and do the things we think she ought to do. We're going to get in her head." She was still going to see Danny Boy. There was no telling what she might come up with.

"That makes a lot of sense. It looks like Danny Boy and Clarence are about to have a meeting. They are like the last ones to leave. Word on the streets is they have separated."

"I guess it's true. Why would they have a meeting at a time and place like this?" Sally suspected that their street problems might be the wedge she needed. If they were against one another, she might get one to tell on the other. There was a lot of tension between them.

"Word is that they're both trying to out-do each other. Danny Boy is supposed to be very jealous of Clarence."

"Let's just watch them to see what happens."

Other than by phone and e-mail, Clarence and Danny Boy hadn't made contact with each other, even when they were in the same club at the same time.

It was strange to see two different sets of cats all wearing the same colored jackets. Clarence and Danny Boy were the only ones who had on suits. They waited until the rest of the crowd left and decided to talk in the middle of the parking lot. Clarence thought they were alone, until two others appeared and stood nearby.

"What's up Danny Boy? It's just supposed to be you and me at this meeting." Clarence was in an eye lock with Skull.

"Skull and I don't have any secrets." Danny Boy wanted Skull there for support. His feelings of inferiority were that serious. It was to the point that he had his people ready to start a war. "I want you to treat him as my equal."

Clarence looked around the cemetery to get his thoughts together. He noticed Sally's BMW then looked at Danny Boy. "Our business isn't his business."

Clarence wanted to get deeper into the issue. There was really no way to do that without increasing the tension. On general principle, he wasn't going to just let it pass without saying something.

"He's my advisor and won't say a word. Let's get this over with." Skull smiled on that comment.

Like a true strategist, Clarence went on with what he called the meeting for. "Sally is going to be coming at you. How are you going to handle it?" Clarence had his chin cupped in his left hand. They were standing just far enough apart that no one could make contact without taking a step.

"Dealing with her is going to be real easy, ain't a damn thing changed. I have nothing to tell that bitch. That's the shit you wanted to talk about?" A tape recording of his last sentence would have made Danny Boy feel better than the best hit of cocaine.

The response was taken personally, just the way it was meant, but Clarence knew better than to show that he was insulted. "That bitch gotta be slicker than that. We can't get rocked to sleep." There would be a time and place. *The Art of War* let him know that it's hard to fight on two fronts at the same time. Danny Boy winning a battle was far from him winning the war.

"Man, I can handle her. She's on you harder than she's on me." All of their people were staring at them, ready to do each other. "Word on the street is ya'll fucking."

"Whatever you mad at me about is going to get in the way of your judgment. When does it stop Danny Boy? You know the 'C' doesn't do anything that's questionable, so let's call a truce."

As usual, Clarence was two steps ahead of Danny Boy. Many told him that on his word, Danny Boy and Skull would be history. It was tempting but they had gone through too much together and he really didn't want to see Danny Boy hurt, or even worse, dead.

Danny Boy was feeling chumped. There was no good way to answer. In his heart he had mad love for Clarence. In front of Skull, after all that he said, there was no way that he would let that show. Agreeing to a truce was admitting that he was the only one at war. Not agreeing would make him look less of a man and that was something he couldn't do.

He just stood there, staring into Clarence's eyes studying his facial expression. Neither of them was blinking. It was all on Danny Boy. He began to feel himself sweat. A bead gathered on his stomach and started running down to his crotch. He knew the longer he took the weaker it made him look.

"We don't need a truce, there ain't a war. I never declared a war."

Clarence refrained his desire to call Danny Boy a dumb rock smoking motherfucker. He would have to kill him on the spot, and under no circumstances, would he place himself in that position. Playas don't do that. Playas have patience.

Danny Boy and Skull felt like they won a major battle against Clarence. No matter what Clarence said, they planned to oppose him. Sally and her reputation meant little to them, though Cedric warned them how deadly she could be. Cedric had yet to figure out whom the informant was in his crew. All Danny Boy and Skull cared about was making money, spending money, getting high and trying to assassinate Clarence's character. They were feeling like they were on easy street. Before they pulled out of the parking lot, Danny Boy and Skull had their whole crew laughing at Clarence. They told a version of what went down that held no resemblance to the truth.

Clarence made a decision before the meeting started that it was time to change the name of his crew. People were urging him to separate his name from Danny's. Many of the people that worked for him wanted the same thing. From then forward, his crew would be called "LCP"- -Little Clarence Playas. By the end of the week, all of his people would have new jackets and hats with the new colors, green and gold. One way or the other, Clarence was going to end the trivial shit. The money was getting too good for distractions.

◆ ◆ ◆ ◆ ◆

Jezebel and Keisha were on their way back to school, in Jezebel's 2003 Jaguar.

"When are you going to tell me what Clarence did to you? I know it was more than just cheat on you." Jezebel was feeling Clarence because of the way he handled himself with Danny Boy and Skull. She could tell that they were against him from a distance. Keisha filled her in about their beef.

"On the day that my mother was murdered, he stood me up. We met at the arcade for the longest time on the weekends, always early in the morning. We were supposed to meet that morning, but for some reason, he never came. I tried calling him, but he never answered or returned my calls. This was the only time that he lied to me and said he was going to be somewhere and wasn't." Keisha was making it sound the best she could.

"Say what?" She looked at Keisha like she said something incredible. "That's it?"

"There's much more to it." Keisha already worked out a

lie. "Clarence and I were together for five years, but we never had sex."

"Ya'll never had sex?" Being in love with a man was a foreign thing to Jezebel, let alone without having sex.

"Nah, James was my first. I planned on having sex with Clarence after we got married and that was supposed to happen in the summer." She could see that Jezebel wasn't exactly buying the story yet.

"So, did he call you the day after your mother was killed?" So far Jezebel was thinking that Keisha was a little crazy.

"They took my phone and computers for the investigation. But he tried to call me at Jessica's. That isn't what matters though."

"Well, what matters?"

"I know that Clarence was having sex with a lot of girls because I wouldn't. I learned to accept that until we got married."

Jezebel thought to herself that she would never agree to that if she decided to have a serious relationship with a man, unless the money was right, like millions. She wasn't going to say anything at the moment. "I hope there's more to it than that." She was in a rush to hear the good part. They just crossed the Maryland line.

"I decided to deal with it as long as they knew he belonged to me. Of course he had to call me every day and come when I called, even if that meant leaving someone he was with at that moment."

"So you laid down some serious law." She liked that.

"Also, he had to leave someone alone if I felt they were seeing too much of each other."

"Go on." Shit was getting interesting.

"I told him twice to leave Diamond alone. That's who he was with that Sunday morning."

"Mind telling me how you knew that?"

"I had pictures on my e-mail of them at a hotel in the Northeast. I have a lot of friends and I had plenty of pictures. I planned to ask him about it." Keisha knew that she had her.

Jezebel touched her on the arm. "We got to get that chump. I'll enjoy making him endure the pain and embarrassment you went through." She was thinking of what to do to get his attention.

"I have a good plan."

"Hold up, tell me something."

"Okay, what's up?"

"If you feel the way you do, why did you call him over at the funeral?" Jezebel wanted to know if Keisha was confused.

"I still love him and want him back. I was testing him to see if he still has feelings for me." She remembered what Jessica told her about the possibility of him still loving her.

"So you just want to teach him a lesson."

"Yeah. After you put that charm on him and break his heart, I'll pick up the pieces, then he'll be all mine. Oh yeah, drop me off at Jessica's."

"That sounds simple enough. When do we start?" She liked the idea, but even more, she liked the challenge of conquering a guy that had many women after him.

"It ain't that simple, there are a few more details."

"Like what?"

"While you are going after Clarence, I'll be going after Danny Boy." This was the part of the plan Keisha loved the most. What she saw happen between them gave her the idea.

"So, you want to make him jealous while I'm baiting him. They do seem to be enemies. That's *nasty*." Jezebel gave her a high-five.

"Yep. So that means that you also have to show me how

to dance. I want to do this thing really big."

"Let me get this straight." They pulled into Jessica's driveway. "You want me to go after Clarence while you go after Danny Boy. You also want me to teach you how to dance." This sounded like a rather big plan but Jezebel was down for it, maybe too much.

"That's what I like about you. You're always on point."

"What if one of them decides to kill the other? They seem to be beefin'." Jezebel was the kind to avoid unneeded drama; life was already hard enough.

"That isn't going to happen. I'll be controlling Danny Boy and you'll be controlling Clarence."

"Okay, more power to the Black woman. I'll see you tomorrow." They kissed cheeks.

"Jessica," Keisha hollered when she unlocked the front door.

"I'm in the living room." She was watching one of the family reunions on her plasma television.

"I need your help." Keisha sat down next to Jessica on the couch. "Cut that off, we need to talk."

Jessica complied. "Now what?" She wasn't in the mood to talk. All she could think about was her brother, Sherlock.

"I have to tell you a real big secret. Will you promise not to tell?"

"If you're pregnant, who am I going to tell? But I can keep a secret." There was a little edge in her voice. Sherlock took care of her all her life. He was the one that paid for her master's in accounting and nobody ever knew.

"Will you promise not to tell?" Keisha turned to the left to face her.

"I told you I can keep a secret. You sure sound like your Daddy, 'Don't tell this, don't tell that.'"

"I said do you promise? I can't tell you unless you promise. Believe me, you want to know." It didn't surprise

Keisha that it wasn't easy telling Jessica.

"I promise not to tell," she said in an emotionless manner.

"I need you to help me get revenge on somebody. I want to make them suffer as much as I have, but I'm going to need your help." Telling her from the top would have pissed off without thinking.

"What the hell are you talking about? Who is fucking with you? Girl, you need to stop playing games."

Sherlock taught his little sister to be tough although she was born with an attitude. Seldom did her grittiness come out and she learned to be a professional. No matter how somebody changes, there are just some things that can't be removed and will come out in a given situation. One of those things is a violent nature when it comes down to someone you love being done wrong.

"Be cool. I need the side of you that can think. I still remember what you did to your last boyfriend who you thought was cheating." Bringing back those memories may not have been a good idea. She wanted her to be mad after she convinced her.

"Oh boy, I was sitting here enjoying a tape, but you want to play games. So you miss Sherlock that much, I miss him too. I'd rather read a book than figure you out." She figured that Keisha was going to start talking about Clarence again so she stood up and was about to walk away.

"This is really serious. I know who killed Mama," she blurted out. Keisha was looking up at Jessica with a look that said, "Please sit back down."

Jessica turned toward her and crossed her arms in front of her. "Did you just say what I think you just said? Gir-r-r-l!" She was shaking her head back and forth.

This wasn't going to be easy at all. "Be cool Jessica, remember she was my mother. Sit down, we have a lot to talk about."

"You got my attention, but first, let me get this straight." She was sitting and waving her finger at Keisha. "All this time, you've known who the murderer was, and you've been —"

"Damn Jessica." She touched her forearm and kicked of her shoes to get comfortable. Quickly she got into a kneeling position on the couch. "I need you to calm down. I need the rational side of you."

"To do what?" She folded her arms again. "You should have just told Sally and let her do her job." As soon as she said, "tell Sally," she knew what Keisha was going to say.

"Jessica, you're making this hard. I'm Sherlock's daughter and I couldn't just tell the police. Plus, I didn't *want* to tell the them."

"So because you have a gun or two, you want to bust a cap and do some time." Jessica didn't agree with many of Sherlock's rules, especially when dealing with people that weren't street.

"Can you just listen? Listen now, talk later. *Okay?*"

"Okay, tell me who killed her." She wracked her brains trying to put it all together but was also trying to stay calm. Karyn was like a sister to her.

"Don't say a word." Jessica nodded her head and put on a calm look to agree. "Clarence killed my mother."

Jessica just sat on the couch. She looked all around the room before she looked back into Keisha's eyes. She was being quiet for three reasons: one, she promised, two, she didn't know if she should believe her and three, she wasn't sure of how to react.

Jessica let out a breath. "Clarence didn't kill Karyn, I don't believe that. What's wrong with you?" Of all people, she wasn't prepared to hear that Clarence did it.

"I'm dead serious." She stood up. "I didn't want to

believe it either. Mama said it before she died." Jessica not believing her was unexpected.

Jessica looked up at her with a funny look. She decided to skip the subject by cutting the television back on.

Keisha snatched the remote out of her hand. "I'm telling you the truth. Let me explain."

"Okay, go ahead." She was thinking to herself that her niece had gone crazy.

"When Mama told me, I didn't want to believe her. When Sally told me that a 10-millimeter was used, I knew it was true. Clarence is the only one in the district that has a 10-millimeter and he did it on purpose."

"Nah, that isn't enough to go on. Clarence isn't like that, I can't believe it." She talked so good about him that it was ridiculous. She couldn't believe that she was having this conversation.

"Listen, I wasn't in the house because he told me to meet him at the arcade. He wanted me to take Mama with me but she didn't want to go. I wish I tried harder to convince her." The phone call was playing over and over in her head. "Is that enough?"

"*No!* That isn't enough. You're saying all of this to make yourself hate Clarence. I understand." In the morning she was planning on calling a shrink for her niece.

"They took over two hundred thousand out of my room. Where do you think they got the money to start all those drug spots?" Keisha was hoping this would convince her because there were no more details to bring up.

"I was wondering where they got the money to get those cars and things. All he and Danny Boy did was rob and bang." Jessica knew that Danny Boy's Benz set him back at least one hundred and fifty grand. They didn't have that kind of money until a few months ago.

"That's why I was mad at Clarence. He betrayed all of us

to be loyal to Danny Boy. I bet Danny Boy found out that Sherlock was killed at Cedric's and decided to make a move." Keisha knew of their plans of making a big lick and becoming drug dealers. She couldn't convince Clarence to work for Sherlock no matter how hard she tried.

"Okay, I believe you. So why did you call him over at the funeral?" She was not fully convinced.

"I remember you telling me that he probably still loves me as much as I still love him. It was a test. I could see it in his eyes." Keisha was glad to be over the hump. "I got a great plan for payback."

"Hold on, so why did he come to see you?"

"He wanted to know what I told Sally. Knowing her, she's been pressin' him, just like she did Cedric." She was keeping all of this information to herself and it felt good to finally let it out.

Jessica did too much thinking and talking to be upset. "So why not tell Sally and let him go to jail? If you kill him, then you're going to jail."

"That ain't good enough. I want him to *suffer*. I want him to feel what my mother did before and after he shot her. You should have seen how she looked. She died in my arms." Tears came to her eyes. "That bitch-ass-nigga betrayed us. Mama treated him like a son."

Jessica was now fully convinced. She knew that what she just saw wasn't an act. She never saw her niece act like that.

"Calm down Keisha, I believe you but I'm not going to help you kill him. That's out of the question. I wouldn't go to jail for Sherlock and I damn sure ain't going to jail for you." Her instincts were telling her to call Sally to save Keisha.

"Well, we can start by taking all of his money. Maybe we could shoot him up with AIDS or something. I know you have some ideas." Keisha knew exactly what she planned to do but she was just blurting out anything that came to mind.

"Keisha, I think you need help. Maybe you need some rest."

"I just need you to do the same setup for Clarence that you did for my Daddy." This is where Jessica's CPA skills came into play.

"How are you going to get that close to Clarence, and what about Danny Boy? I know you ain't going to let him off the hook." Her wheels started turning.

"I'm going to have Clarence in the palm of my hand. He'll want me bad as hell when he sees me with Danny Boy." This would also spark off a serious beef.

"That's real trifling isn't it?" She wanted to argue that jail was better for them but Keisha had too much fire in her. This girl was on a mission. She was truly Sherlock's daughter.

"What they did was way past trifling, I just want my revenge. Clarence has to get his." She was talking a bit loud, loud enough to wake people up.

"I got your back, just calm down. If you fuck Danny Boy, what makes you think Clarence is going to take you back? You just told me that they're beefin'." Jessica was convinced that her niece had lost her mind.

"I got this. I'm staying with you tonight, I need some rest." Enough had been said.

"That's a good idea. You get some rest because you're not thinking clearly right now." Jessica tried to reason.

It took long enough. Keisha was able to set aside enough of her feelings for Clarence to come up with a plan. She recruited two of the most reliable and closest people she could trust. Her plan was based on the things they could do. Most of what she was feeling for Clarence was contempt. Her mind was made up that she would do anything to hurt Clarence. Danny Boy was first base. If Jezebel were able to get close to him, she would use her to get his money and goods. She wanted him to lose it all. Danny Boy was no problem; he would be the easiest part of her plan. The streets said he was feeling inferior to Clarence and Keisha was ready to be the equalizer. Giving him some pussy was a sacrifice she didn't mind making.

Since that terrible Sunday, it was the first night Keisha slept without having a nightmare. She had an inner peace and a sense of purpose that gave her strength to execute her plan. Like the calm before the storm, it was time to put in work for her peeps. She had big plans for Clarence and each idea was bigger than the next. Watching while Clarence fell deeper and deeper would be the ultimate for her. The first part of her plan came to her quickly, but it needed to be carefully rolled out. She didn't want to fuck up because she was too anxious.

Jessica thought about it all that night. There were doubts that made her want to call Clarence and question him. Imagining him shooting Karyn was hard for her. Was the money that important? Had he gone crazy? Did Danny Boy push him to do it? Or, was it her niece who was crazy? Keisha sounded very convincing as she presented the facts. In the morning she told her niece that she was down for whatever, as long as she wasn't involved with a murder. Keisha assured her that wouldn't be a problem.

Sally arrived at her office at ten thirty in the morning after entertaining Tony all night. She felt he deserved to be rewarded for the information he was providing. The reward, she told him, was to make him feel good but admitting that she needed and wanted the dick was out of the question.

"What do you have for me Bambi? You had all morning." She didn't even think about saying hello.

"Hello to you too. I bet we partied all night." Bambi just returned to the office from handling the investigation. She was sitting at her desk, smoking a Black while listening to Brooke Valentine's "Girl Fight" on the radio.

"Girl, you know the Pinstriped Bitch had to get her groove on. I can't step out the house until all things are tight." She was thinking that she shouldn't have made him wait that long, as good as he was.

"Okay, let's get down to business, you're going to love this." Sally walked over to her desk and sat on the edge. "Keisha got two calls to her cell just before she left her house. They were about a half hour apart."

"Were they from the same number?"

"Yes, they were."

"Now do you know who called her?" This is what mattered the most. It needed to be Clarence.

"We'll have to get that information later. But about fifteen minutes after she got a call, she made a call to the same number, twice, about ten minutes apart." Bambi was pointing to the telephone records.

"Oh yes, the last call she made was just before she left the arcade." Sally walked back over to her own desk. It was time to smoke a Black. "Candy Shop" by Fifty Cent was pumpin'. She sat down and crossed her legs.

"I have more for you."

"Spit girl, spit. It ain't time for foreplay."

"Chill, and let me get some of that Black." She had just finished hers and walked over to Sally's desk. "I talked to the manager at the arcade. He recognized Keisha and Clarence and said that they came in on the weekends, in the mornings, all the time."

"Oh yeah!" This was the best news that she heard. "So she went to meet him. She didn't tell us that. Why in the hell is she protecting him?"

Bambi still wasn't convinced. "We are going to have to ask her. Or, we could start out by finding out if that phone number belongs to him." She tried it and found it to be disconnected. She passed the Black back.

"I know that number belongs to him. I'm willing to bet it's a burnout." Sally was thinking of how she wanted to approach Keisha while she took a drag on the Black.

"What if that number doesn't belong to him?" She was playing her role as the devil's advocate.

"Keisha has a reason for not telling us that she was supposed to meet somebody, and that somebody being Clarence. I'll bet anything on it." Sally chose to think like people who were having a relationship.

"Let me hit that Black first." Sally gave it to her as she stood up.

"I bet that number is listed at least a hundred times on those phone records. Let's see." They walked back over to Bambi's desk.

Bambi mentally beat herself up for not digging that deep. She started looking through the phone records. "Damn Sally, you're right. She was talking to that person a lot. I mean a lot, like several times a day, every day."

"Let me lay this out. Clarence called her to get her out of the house and he called back again to make sure she was gone. After that, he got with Danny Boy. While they're in the house, Keisha calls him to see where he was." Bambi was taking in all the details. "Let's see if the last two calls lasted longer than a minute."

Bambi looked. "Both calls are a minute a piece."

"Oh yeah, we got this thing on lock. She either left a message or asked him where he was. So they leave before she gets back to the house." She had to give Clarence his props, he did it right up under everybody's noses with no real evidence to link him to the murder or robbery. That gangsta shit was turning her on.

"Yeah, I can feel it. So we need him to confess, or for Keisha to confirm what we know." There were no more doubts in her mind.

"That's where we have our problem. Without her assistance, he's going to beat the case. We need her to help us." There had to be a good reason she wasn't coming forward. Sally determined whatever the reason was, was the key.

"This shit is deep. I can't believe we have a daughter that refuses to help convict her mother's murderer. It doesn't seem right." Throughout her schooling she never heard of such.

"I know that we have to press her a little bit harder. Besides her, we only have Clarence and Danny Boy." Danny Boy might have another piece to the puzzle. Word on the street was that he was losing his cool by the day. He just might be the one who would slip.

"Do you think she loves him that much?" What she saw at the funeral was a sign that Keisha might be trying to get Clarence back.

"She acts like she hates him but her actions say otherwise. It doesn't really make sense."

"We need to go see her. Maybe if we threaten to arrest her, she'll tell us what's on her mind." Curiosity piqued her interest.

"Clarence must be a bad motherfucker. If the dick is that good I better leave him alone." They laughed as they high-fived each other and said, "Not!"

Jezebel became the most sought after female on campus. In men's eyes, she could do no wrong, but it meant little to her. She perfected her game at the age of eighteen.

On a daily basis she would eat lunch on the campus' main square. Guys would hold a table just for her so they could be in her presence.

"Hello fellas, sorry I'm late." She brought her own lunch as usual, a fruit salad and a tall glass of orange juice.

"Baby, you're so fine, you could never be late, just as long as you get here," Todd said, sitting on her left. He had a little money and was the captain of the football team.

"Thank you Todd," she purred in a sexy tone.

Jermaine was not the type to be outdone. "I'd wait forever for you to show up."

"Would you wait for us to get married before we had sex?" She took a sip of her juice. She was wearing all black with a black headband. From a distance she resembled a cross between Amerie and Vanessa Williams.

"I'll wait," Calvin busted in, "as long as you want me to, if the pussy is as good as you say it is." Calvin had rich parents that were into real estate development. He was making sure he got a seat with Jezebel everyday. He was paying other students to hold his spots, starting at six o'clock in the morning.

She laughed. "You got to know how to lick before you stick." She knew she was going to get the most out of Calvin. He already financed a couple of shopping sprees. This meant she had to call him back whenever he called.

"I can lick you dry," they all chimed together.

Jermaine hollered, "I have the most experience," hoping she would take him up on it. He was a dog and wanted to score just for the record.

"Let me tell you something Calvin." She was using a semi-aggressive tone to play like she was displeased. "I have to warn you that I might drive you up the wall. Are you willing to take that risk?" She knew that Calvin just wanted her on his arm to show off and impress people. That fit her plans.

Todd and Jermaine looked at Calvin like he did something dirty. There was no surprise, everybody knew Calvin had plenty of money. On many days he came to school in a limousine, but still, they had to try.

"I'm willing to do anything and I do mean anything." He practically begged her the night before. When she checked her e-mail, she found that he sent her a copy of his checking account and a statement for his Gold American Express card. She picked him and broke down all the rules. All he could do was say yes, the Jezebel bug bit him hard.

While she finished eating her last two pieces of fruit, she made them wait for her reply. "Well fellas I've appreciated all of the attention but Calvin has played the game the best." She smiled at Calvin. "I'll call you tonight for our date. Be ready and waiting by seven thirty."

Calvin smiled like he won a championship. He was a senior and being groomed to take over his father's vast empire. In his mind he thought that he chose and won her over but it was the other way around. When she saw the limousine she started investigating. Intelligent he was when it came to the books. This made him more than just a good-looking black dude that had too much money. Not only did she plan to get paid, she planned to get educated about real estate development. She told him that it was all business to her, nothing more, nothing less. He readily agreed to all of her demands, without hesitation. She warned him that she was about to take him on the ride of his life. She pussy whipped him before they even kissed.

As Jezebel got up to leave, Calvin grabbed her plate and cup to throw them away. When Calvin held his head up, she kissed him on the forehead. All eyes were on her as she walked away. Calvin could barely wait for that evening.

Jezebel was glad to catch her new partner in the room. Keisha smiled when she saw her. "I saw you down there doing your thing. Those guys treat you like royalty." She intended to learn everything from Jezebel that she could.

"It ain't nothing. Once I teach you, you're going to be laughing because it's so easy." She was thinking Keisha could be a part of *The Clit*, whether she got to lick her clit or not. That would be left up to Cleopatra.

"Tell me something."

"What do you want to know?" Jezebel loved to answer questions. It made her feel powerful.

Keisha turned her chair around to face her. "You can have any man that you want." Jezebel nodded her head. "And you can make a man give you all things you want." Jezebel was still nodding her head. "So why do you study so hard? Why do you read so much? You read the *Wall Street Journal* and *Black Enterprise*. All of that don't mix."

"Yes it does."

"No it doesn't."

"The Black woman has to be strong because so many of our men aren't handling their business, then they abuse us. We got to be all that we can be." It was only three years ago when Cleopatra started teaching her about business.

Keisha sat there with a look of puzzlement on her face. Jezebel continued. "I'm trying to break into the corporate world and be successful with my talents and knowledge, not my looks nor sex. So I came to college and I read a lot. *The greatest hustle is knowledge.* Ultimately, I want to create and run my own corporation." This was a subject that she seldom discussed. It terrified people that she could be so sexy and intelligent. She took a chance on Keisha because of all the positive vibes.

"Jezebel you have never talked to me about these things." She thought Jezebel read certain things to make herself seem intelligent to men. She was mistaken, she was intelligent. "Damn girl, you serious."

"Black women need to learn to be entrepreneurs. Our men aren't trying to do it like they should. Well, a few of them are, but the majority of them aren't. There are men who will do anything for a pretty face and a chance at some pussy and those are the ones that will have to lick the clit." Jezebel's face started beaming. Her instincts told her that Keisha was ready for the trip.

"I've never heard anything like that. So that's why you don't respect most men." It was really making sense. Destiny provided her with the right roommate.

"Girl you've got to read more books, like *The Mis-Education of the Negro* by Carter G. Woodson. Oh yeah, Bob Johnson and Reginald F. Lewis get all of my respect and can have the pussy without having to lick the clit."

"What's up with them? Bob Johnson runs BET and he's old." She knew he was rich, but didn't see what Jezebel truly respected about him.

"No girl, Bob Johnson started BET from scratch. BET was the first black owned company to go public. He and his wife became *billionaires* before Oprah Winfrey." As of yet she hadn't discussed these things with a man, only Cleopatra. There was too much risk.

"I have a lot to learn. Do you talk to men about these things?"

"Hell no, they're too fucking insecure. I haven't met one that I felt could deal with it. So I just use my charms and make them pay my way."

"Well we'll have to start my lessons today. I don't know how to dance like a stripper." Becoming a stripper in the district was the first part of her plan to hurt Clarence.

"I have to tell you some really good news first."

"Okay, what's that?"

"Calvin is about to burn up plenty of cash. He'll be licking the clit soon."

"I knew it." She jumped up in the air. "He has plenty of money. He has told people that you are all he thinks about. What did you do to him?"

"It's all in the presentation and his fantasies. I'm just going to get paid to entertain him. I'll teach you." With Keisha's looks, body and desire she would learn quick.

"What's the first thing that you are going to teach me? I want to be just like you." Keisha knew that she looked just as good as Jezebel and was just as smart. It would be a matter of learning to work her assets.

"We'll start in the morning. We'll be running three miles a day, three times a week." Keisha's mouth popped open. "A Black woman has to be in shape – mind, body and spirit." The first thing was to teach her to love herself. When she was content with herself the rest would be easy. *The Art of Seduction* taught that a content person couldn't be seduced - not easily.

Keisha wasn't athletic, all she ever did was hit the bag in her basement and cheerlead. She never cared for playing sports and cheerleading didn't require that much. "Oh well. That's what I have to do. So how are you going to handle Calvin tonight?"

"When I get through with him, he'll never want another woman." The last guy she seduced ended up mentally damaged when she told him that she was bored with him. Cleopatra was the only one that could satisfy her needs.

"What are you going to do to him?

"I already did it. He thinks he has the woman of his dreams but it's all in his mind. Girl I have to get some sleep. I'm going to make him wait forever to satisfy his fantasy."

Keeping him wanting more and more was the key. Just stay a little outside of his control while teasing him.

13

◆ ◆ ◆ ◆ ◆

"Where the fuck is my money?" Danny Boy hollered as he kicked the kid in the head as Skull kicked him in the legs and ribs. They had him on the floor in the back room of their spot. "I got your money Danny." It had been three weeks since they'd seen him. Some of Danny's soldiers found him at his girl's house.

"Bullshit." Danny Boy picked him up and body slammed him. At least twice a week Danny Boy had to beat up one of his workers or people that he was frontin'. Many of them started smoking crack and gambling too much, trying to be like him. Most of them started smoking crack with marijuana, then they graduated.

The kid was begging Danny Boy to let him live. He begged him to front him a quarter of a kilo and before he knew it, he smoked too much to pay off after going on a seven day binge. If he worked at the spot, he wouldn't have smoked while he was supposed to have been hustling. A female fiend tricked him into testing the pipe.

"Don't kill him," Skull told him. Things were already too far out of hand. They were spending too much time getting high.

"Get this piece of shit out of here." Skull grabbed the kid by his jacket and dragged him to the front of the spot. Skull kept Danny Boy from going over the edge.

"I got him, just relax Danny Boy."

Danny Boy smoked a Newport to calm down. Before long he was going to have another body. It had been a long time.

Skull came back in rubbing his hands together like he just finished taking out the trash. He left the kid on the sidewalk, right in front of the spot. "Hey man we got to get it together."

"You right." Instead of becoming a millionaire like he thought, Danny was barely treading water. His supplier wouldn't front him any more because he continued to be short. To keep things going, Danny would pawn his Benz or truck. There was close to one hundred fifty thousand dollars in the Benz. After getting the Benz back he would go on another binge. On many days they wouldn't have any drugs.

"Word on the street is that Clarence is just waiting to take this spot." Skull wasn't just using Clarence's name to get close to Danny Boy, he needed to save the machine that was keeping him high and paying his bills. When he said they needed to get it together, he meant it.

"Clarence ain't getting shit." When he gave up the D & C title Danny Boy thought a major battle was won and that he would be able to outsell Clarence. Clarence was taking in one hundred grand a day from both spots and getting heavier into the weight game. "You right as a motherfucker. This up and down shit ain't going to do it."

"Shit was good as a bitch could be when we started. We got to get back to that."

"I'm getting ready to get back to that. Yo' ass is fired." Smoking was the problem that had to be solved. Skull was smoking just as much as he was and was the one who got him started. Once, he and Skull and a bunch of bitches stayed up in a hotel for four days until they smoked up two kilos of crack. After that it was all downhill. That was right after the funeral.

"What the fuck is wrong with you? I'm the one that helped you put this shit together." Skull was blindsided.

"I really want to kick your ass. You tricked me into smoking that shit." Though he would never admit it, Clarence would have never let him get on that path. The cat who was making Clarence out to be the enemy was the enemy.

A lump formed in Skull's throat. "After all the loyalty that I've shown to you, this is how you do me?" Without his position, Skull would be nothing but a crack head. A broke crack head at that.

"Get the fuck out."

Skull could see that Danny Boy was dead serious. With his head hanging low, he left.

Picking up the cell to call Clarence is what his instincts told him to do but pride wouldn't let him. All he had to do was apologize but his ego got in the way. That made him hate Clarence even more. It wasn't the kind of "I hate you because you offended me" hate. It was that "I hate you because I have to admit you are the better playa and I need you" hate.

Clarence could have put him back on and in a big way. All he had to do was stick with his man and they would be on top together. These thoughts plagued him everyday. Now he was going broke.

"Snap out of it Danny Boy," Sally said when she walked in the room.

He would have felt better if it were Clarence. Coming

back to the present, he remembered that Clarence told him a few weeks ago that she would be dropping in on him. It was a good thing he didn't kill that kid.

"I don't sell Blacks, so what do you want?"

"Don't be so mean Danny Boy, Sally isn't here to hurt you. I just want to talk." She could tell that he was having a bad day, the entire place was messed up. What caught her eye first was the blood on the floor. Some of it looked fresh but most of it looked like it was dry for a few days.

How would Clarence handle this? he asked himself. He remembered Clarence saying something about not making her mad because she could cause problems. "I'm getting ready to go somewhere so you got to make it quick."

She already knew the angle she wanted to use on him. "I came to let you know that I got some good evidence on Clarence. That gun of his is going to bring ya'll down." The squinting of his eyes told her she sparked his interest.

"Danny Boy does Danny Boy and Clarence does Clarence." He was getting tired of shit coming back to him, Clarence is doing this, why ya'll fall out? It was getting old and fast. Now Sally was all on him.

"When we pick up Clarence and question him, do you really think he's going to remain loyal to you? He's been saying some pretty bad things about you." She lit up a Black. She was telling straight lies.

Danny didn't automatically respond. His eyes looked at the floor. When they were rolling together there was no doubt in his mind about Clarence's loyalty. Now that they were separated and he was making tons of loot, Danny Boy didn't know if he could trust him.

"Listen Danny, you can save yourself and I'll make it so that you can keep hustling without the police fucking with you." It was like hitting a matchstick from a hundred yards away. Bull's eye. She found a weak link.

Danny looked up at her and remained silent. What she put in his mind was not there before. Would his ex-partner do him and what should he do about it? He leaned back and looked at her.

"I know you were in house when Clarence shot Keisha's mother. I can put you in jail later or save you now. What's it going to be?" His look, silence and facial expressions told her that he was definitely with Clarence. His reaction also said there was the possibility of singing.

All of his errors with Clarence came flooding back to his mind. If he weren't trippin' he wouldn't have to be thinking that it might be necessary to go for self.

"He didn't do that Sally. He would have never kill her, they were almost family." He still had to represent.

Sally just shook her head and walked out. The dirty seed started taking root in his mind and once it started growing, she would return, in due time.

They knew each other for far too long and did too much together for Danny Boy to doubt Clarence. It was he, not Clarence, who showed many signs of weakness. Danny Boy felt like a sucker for hesitating to represent him when it came to the police.

Still, Danny Boy didn't know what to do, what to think, or what to feel. For sure though, he knew that he had to stop sinking.

That day finally came for Calvin to see if Jezebel was all that he dreamed and hoped for. It was an entire two weeks of dating and shopping and he didn't allow her to ask for a thing. He took her to the finest of restaurants and exquisite events like operas and art exhibits. She even made him rent a condo for her.

Jezebel prepared her bedroom for this special night. The bed was covered with black satin sheets to match her outfit. For two days she told him exactly what she was going to do, and what she wanted him to do, even down to the time she wanted him to arrive so the festivities could begin.

The entire place was lit with nothing but candles. Cinnamon incense, with a touch of musk oil, burned for a beautiful aroma.

Looking at the clock, it was time for him to arrive. She met him at the door wearing a black see-through negligee. Underneath she had on a Victoria's Secret bra and a black thong. Her hair was fixed in a way to show off her beautiful neck and shoulders. She had him sippin' Cristal from the moment he walked in.

"My Boo" by Usher and Alicia Keys was playing in the background while Jezebel did a seductive dance for him. He was sitting in a chair, enjoying the show. With every twist, turn and shake he became more excited and hypnotized.

Though he had seen plenty of strippers dance, none captivated him like she did. He couldn't take his eyes off of her and his dick was about to bust out his pants. He was impressed. Not only was her body beautiful, she knew how to dance and entice with it.

When she took off her bra what he saw made him want to jump out of his seat. They were firm and rounded, like a sculptor carefully hand carved them, with nipples that looked like small missiles.

With her clothes on she was attractive and stunning. With her clothes off she was irresistible and intoxicating. No other woman that he had been with had him this open.

In a seductive voice she said, "Are you ready for this Calvin?"

"Yeah I'm ready." He stood up and took off his jacket. Taking a big step when he stood up, he was standing in front of her.

"Slow down baby, we have all night." She helped him with his shirt. When that was done, she took his hands in both of hers, raised them over his head and kissed him passionately. All of her movements were extra feminine.

"Your body is beautiful, I almost can't believe it." He pulled her closer to him by grabbing her ass with both hands. It was as firm as it looked and felt just as good.

She turned him so that her back was to the bed. Gently she rubbed his shoulders while kissing his chest. She kissed and rubbed her way to his pants.

While on her knees she opened his pants and pulled them down to his knees. With the same care she helped him out of his satin boxers. He thought to himself that a woman never paid this much attention to details.

Prince's "Adore" was about to go off, and next would be her favorite song.

As she stood back up, she cupped his balls in her left hand. While caressing his dick, she put her right hand behind his neck and started kissing him. Their tongues danced in the heat of passion. He wrapped his arms around her as her breasts rubbed up against him making him feel like they belonged together.

He kissed her neck. Gently his hands came up her sides toward her breasts until he had them cupped in his hands.

The look on his face, and the way he was caressing her breasts, let her know her

game was being put down perfectly. She jumped on him so he could suck on them while he was standing up. She was smiling at her new capture.

She took her legs from around his back after he sucked on her titties long enough. It was time to move on. With him ready, and standing at attention, it was time for him to pay his dues. Slowly she crawled to the head of the bed, letting him see all of her ass and pussy lips.

A camcorder would be the only way to make the night better. *It was definitely a night to remember*, he thought.

"You're on Calvin," she said while motioning with her finger for him to come to her. With her legs wide open, Babyface's "Soon As I Get Home" complemented the atmosphere. It was perfect timing.

Calvin climbed onto the bed with a bit of fear in his heart. This was the most sophisticated woman he had ever experienced. So far she talked the talk and walked the walk.

She was holding her pussy lips open as wide as they would go. "Are you ready Calvin? It's your time to shine."

"Yeah I'm ready."

The chorus to the song played "I give good love, I'll buy your clothes, I'll cook your dinner too, soon as I get home from work, I'll pay your rent ..." Jezebel closed her eyes after that last statement because she had Calvin doing everything she wanted him to do, including paying her rent.

He started to lick slowly and gently, with long strokes, just the way she instructed. On the third lick, he concentrated on her clit, and a surge went through her body. "That's it Calvin, lick the clit just like that." He started licking faster. She let go of her pussy, but his hands replaced hers to keep her flower open. Her hands caressed the side of his face and played with his head.

"Yes Calvin, it belongs to you. I didn't think you could lick so good." Her screams of passion were getting deeper, along with her breathing getting faster. Intentionally, she was calling his name to stroke his ego. Getting her pussy eaten out was good, but not as good as she was acting like it was.

"That's it Calvin, don't stop. Make me cum. Yes, your tongue is good." Power over him was what it was all about. She intended to make him feel like he conquered the world.

It was almost too easy.

"Yes Calvin. Yes Calvin. Yes Calvin. You made me cum." She shouted, and started breaking away from him to make him feel like he was in control.

"Where are you going?" he asked as he grabbed her by the thighs and pulled her pussy back close to his mouth.

"You're about to make me short-circuit baby. You don't want me to go crazy do you?" Her hand was covering her clit. Having her clit licked all night by a person that she respected was a beautiful thing but he wasn't on that list.

"Let me taste you for a few more minutes." This was the first time he felt he was making decisions on what they did, outside of spending money.

"No baby, I'm ready to let you have all of this good pussy. I need to feel you deep inside of me." She was showering him with kisses as she talked to him.

He didn't give it a second thought. "I'm ready to make love to you." From the moment he set eyes on her, he made plans to get her. Her holding out, and so many cats chasing her, made her much more attractive.

As she laid back she pulled him toward her by holding onto his neck. He put up no resistance. There was a gigantic smile on his face as she wrapped her legs around his waist and back. With her left hand she guided the head of his dick toward her love entrance. Their eyes were locked.

"Take your time, I've been saving this pussy just for you." She let out an "ooh" and arched her back as he entered.

He loved how wet and warm her pussy felt. He pushed up in her as far as his four inches would go.

"Oh Calvin, your dick feels better than your tongue." She was lying. She could barely feel him, though she hadn't had sex with a man in months.

He was stroking at a medium speed. "Your pussy is as good as you said it would be." He could feel himself getting that explosive feeling. The pussy was that good.

"Oh Calvin I'm cumming again. I think I'm going to fall in love with you." On that note he stopped stroking. He heaved a few times, and then rolled over.

She was wishing for Cleopatra and a dildo.

Sally tried to meet with Keisha on several occasions but she just wanted to talk over the
phone. Sally's purpose couldn't be accomplished over the phone. Baltimore City wasn't too far of a distance.

When Keisha opened her dorm room door, she was surprised. There Sally was, in the flesh, wearing a three piece black pants suit with gray pinstripes.

"How are you Sally?"

"I'm fine, thanks. May I come in?"

"Sure, come on in, " she said as she stepped to the side allowing Sally entrance. She immediately started looking around the room. "I'm sorry I can't provide refreshments."

"That's okay Keisha. I won't be here long."

"Okay because I'm in the middle of studying for a Marketing exam."

"Mind if I take a seat?" Sally didn't wait for an answer.

Keisha sat on her bed. "So what's up? What's so important that you couldn't tell me over the phone?" Keisha knew that Sally just wanted to rattle her some more.

"Funny that you say phone. I have your phone records from the day your mother was killed."

"I don't get it, what do my phone records have to do with my mother's death?" Keisha's look was saying that the question had to be really stupid.

"We looked at the calls you made that morning." Sally was taking the slow route to make sure she was using the right approach.

"Okay, would you mind getting to the point?"

Sally was glad to hear hastiness. "It seems that you left your house just in time and got back to your house just in time." Sally decided to go for the bluff move, with a little pressure.

"So are you saying that I sent somebody to kill my Mama?" Wrinkles were showing on her forehead as she took in what Sally was implying.

"That's not what I'm saying. A prosecutor could easily say you conspired with the killer but the evidence says you are protecting the killer." She could see what she said was getting to her.

"Listen Sally, what are you trying to do? I can't believe you just said that. Maybe I should just get a lawyer." Keisha didn't give herself time to think if Sally was bluffing.

"I know that Clarence called you just before you left your house. Then you called him right before you went back to the house. I have the phone records that show it." She took some papers out of her purse and slid them on the desk.

Keisha couldn't figure out why Sally would get her phone records. She couldn't bluff. Keisha was getting pissed because Sally was trying too hard to spoil her plans. Meeting her head on was the only thing to do.

"Who's going to believe that I killed my Mama just because I called Clarence? He was my boyfriend." She was about to start yelling at Sally but something inside her told her to calm down.

"A jury just might believe it. With all of the evidence we have on Clarence, we won't lose this case. You should just give him up for your own good before fingers start pointing at you too. We both know that he did it, and so does he."

"I don't know that he did anything." Keisha walked over to her window. The right moves had to be made because

Sally was really bringing the heat.

A little bit further, Sally thought. "Why are you protecting him? You don't have to go to jail for him. I bet he wouldn't go to jail for you."

Keisha turned around in a slow manner. "So, what you're saying is, if I don't lie on Clarence, you are going to send me to jail?" Sherlock taught her to think and act like she was innocent.

"Yes, pretty much. If that's what I have to do, then that's what I'm going to do." Sally didn't want to take it that far but she had no choice but to be blunt.

"I'm not going to lie on Clarence, my Daddy didn't raise me like that." Fierceness was in her eyes.

"Okay, be ready to make bail." Sally walked out the door.

Keisha felt that she was blindsided. What she was threatened with was totally unexpected. Just the thought of going to jail, let alone for something that she didn't do, kept her distracted. Not only could she end up in jail for her mother's murder, Clarence and Danny Boy could end up getting away with it. Trying to beat the case would be one hell of a chance to take. There was too much at stake for Keisha to think straight. She needed to talk to Jezebel but she wouldn't be back until the morning.

A decision had to be made and it had to be the right one.

♦ ♦ ♦ ♦ ♦

Clarence and his people were partying all night. They were having a private party at *Dreams*, and only a select few were invited. He was celebrating making his first million. He told everybody that it was just an appreciation party for his top people and all of them got big bonuses.

"Yo Kevin, we got a move to make." Clarence made Kevin one of his closest people. "Get three of our soldiers, we got to go see an old friend."

"Okay boss." When Clarence said move, they always moved, no questions asked. "Meet us out front in five minutes."

Clarence's journey to the top happened faster than he could have ever imagined. Everybody was riding him. They all wanted him to be down with whatever they were doing. Clarence was considered to be the nigga with the platinum touch. With all of his success and money, he never changed. He still acted and dressed the same. The biggest piece of jewelry he owned was a plain platinum chain with a pendant that said "Lil' Clarence." People loved that he was modest and humble. With all that he had, he was still lonely.

"Where are we going boss? They're going to miss us at the party." In a few weeks, Kevin would be turning eighteen, and he was looking for Clarence to bless him with his own spot. Clarence was the blueprint that he planned to follow. Kevin put the Suburban in motion.

"Chill, it's only eleven o'clock. There is one last dude I need to bless with a gift."

"Okay. Who is it that we fuck with on Alabama Avenue?" Kevin questioned as he drove. His surroundings told him he was not on their territory.

"Danny Boy."

Kevin thought about hitting the brakes. Many people in the streets were saying they were bitter enemies. "What's up with that?"

"I got to bless him because he helped me start this. He also helped me get away from him." Since Clarence changed his name, and the name of his crew, shit had skyrocketed. Money was coming faster than he could count. One supplier was trying to give him a hundred bricks of cocaine. It was only a matter of time before Clarence took it. For now, he was moving all the heroin he could get his hands on. The dro took him to the half million mark. Heroin put him past fifth gear.

"You a better playa than me. After all that shit he's been talkin', I'd be giving him something else."

"I feel what you're saying. If we were still bangers it would be a totally different level, but we ain't beefin', he's just mad that I made some really great decisions." It wasn't that Clarence didn't want to kill him, he didn't want to kill anybody else that he had feelings for. Guilt made him swear that he would only kill again if he had to. Killing someone that was close to him, and losing someone that was even dearer, kept him up many nights.

"So how are you going to bless him?"

"Just a little something to pick up his spirits. Ever since we changed the crew's name he's been having ups and downs." They just stopped in front of Danny's spot.

For a Wednesday, Danny Boy was having a rather decent night. He used to close his spot at six o'clock but due to his irregularities and debt, he stayed open as much as possible. He needed all the money he could make. He needed to get his Benz back ASAP.

Not having his Benz was right up there with not having his Mama. His determination came out. Being one of those cats "that used to be a playa" was the last thing that he would let happen. Before it would even get to that point, he would put a bullet in his own head. Clarence was also part of the equation.

Danny Boy was in the back and two of his workers were up front handling business. One was pitching while the other was on guard and kept the pitcher supplied. The other two workers were at home resting. He went from having ten workers to having four. His name in the street turned to nearly nothing. Vultures were waiting to claim his spot.

"Hey man, that's LCP out there. Yo Danny Boy, LCP is on the block." Danny Boy ran to the front with a nine in his hand. He looked out the window to see if his worker was correct. There were about ten crack heads trying to cop. At the end of the line he saw Kevin in a green and gold jacket.

"You out of bounds LCP," Danny Boy told Kevin when he got to the front of the line.

"I got orders to come in peace. Just be cool." Kevin was sent in first because Danny Boy already personally knew him. "Get them crack heads out of here."

"Yeah you crack heads hurry the fuck up." Business with them was handled quickly. Danny was holding his gun toward the floor, with his finger on the trigger, ready to blast. It was the work of Clarence. What could he want?

When the last crack head walked out Kevin went to the next step. "Listen Danny Boy, we are coming in peace. I'm calling my peeps and Clarence. We can do this with or without pieces. It's your choice." Kevin didn't have a gun. He knew Clarence would retaliate if anything happened to him.

"We'll keep them out." Danny didn't doubt that Clarence was coming in peace. In front of his boys he couldn't do anything that looked sloppy. The pitcher was the last one to pull his piece out. Danny got behind his workers and the table.

"Remember, we come in peace." Kevin pulled out his Nextel and pressed the side button to use the walkie-talkie. "They say with them out." Two more LCPs came through the door with their weapons out. Kevin waited for them to get in place. "It's all straight."

Clarence slowly walked in. Kevin faded to the back to let him in the front. "We have to talk Danny, without the weapons, I'm clean." Clarence held up his jacket to show that his waist was clear.

There was nothing to stop Danny Boy from blowing Clarence away at that very moment. There was also no getting away with it. It was unlikely that any of them would survive. Clarence was just as good as armed. It was a thought, not a desire.

"What do we have to talk about?"

"I still got love for you. And you the one that said there isn't a war." It was nice to be able to put those words back on the table. The situation was just perfect. "Let's put the heat away."

Danny Boy calmed his senses and blood. When he saw Kevin he knew they had come in peace. He put his joint on the table but his boys didn't move.

"Now tell your peeps to put theirs up," Danny Boy suggested.

"I'm not feeling that," Clarence stated. "How about all at the same time?" Clarence wouldn't take the risk if he thought Danny Boy wanted to have a shoot out. The weapons were put away slowly.

Clarence assessed that Danny Boy's people felt trapped. They had no way of telling if there were more LCPs outside or not. "Let's talk in your office."

"Just you and me," Danny Boy commanded. It was his spot. "Nobody in, nobody out."

Danny called himself being smart. He intentionally left his gun on the table so his peeps could grab it if necessary.

"One thing first." Clarence walked up to the table. "Take the clip out the gun and empty the chamber. Your peeps might get fidgety and get trigger happy." Clarence had his hands on the table.

Both crews put their hands back on their weapons. Each side was waiting for the other to pull out. If that happened there would be a blood bath. Each side knew what the other was thinking, by instinct. It was a situation that none had prepared for or imagined.

Clarence didn't want to offend Danny Boy by picking up the gun because it might start a shoot out. Also, there was no way he would let anybody have the ups on his peeps so it was a request that he had to make.

Danny Boy thought to himself that Clarence was still on point as ever. "My bad, I didn't mean any offense." He walked back over to the table and offered Clarence a pound to show sincerity. They dapped. Danny Boy lifted the gun up just enough to let out the clip. With similar motions he emptied the chamber. Clarence was rubbing his hands together, just in case Danny Boy tried something.

Danny Boy laid the gun back down after he clicked the

safety. Though there was no need for that, he wanted to show Clarence that he was keeping it real. "I even put on the safety."

"Thank you, now let's talk."

"In the back." Danny Boy led the way. He wanted to get it over with as fast as possible because there was money to be made. He hadn't seen a fifty thousand dollar day in a while.

Danny Boy offered Clarence a seat when they got in the office. "So what's on your mind Lil' Clarence?" Clarence was shining. He had to admit to himself.

Clarence knew what he wanted to do, but he didn't want to say the wrong thing. "My man, I still have crazy love and respect for you. I need to pay my respects to you." Clarence was holding his fingertips together.

"Yeah man, I feel the same way about you." Danny wasn't about to say a word about respect and love, though he felt the same. "So what is this really about? You ain't come over here just to talk."

"I want things to be different between us, not as a team, but as two playas that respect each other." Clarence wanted to bring up all the things that Danny said about him. Instead, Clarence let it all go for the future benefits.

"Come on Clarence, I think you're being just a little bit too nice. I mean, what is your motive?" Danny was feeling a little guilty, he said many things that he would not say to Clarence's face.

"Man, we're just like brothers. If you have pain I hurt. I want to see you back on top of your game. No more, no less."

"So you want me to start working for you?" Danny would rather go broke before he started working for Clarence.

Clarence sucked his teeth, "Nah man, I said together. My game is truly sincere. I've been blessin' all my people and I got to pay my respects to you too." Clarence would never let a cat like Danny Boy work for him. There were too many negative emotions in his heart. Pride and jealousy aren't good combinations. As a matter of fact, it was combustible.

"So break it down for me, I'm not going to be part of LCP or under LCP."

"Right."

"So what are you offering?"

"Without you, I wouldn't be where I am at right now. Plus I want us to have a better relationship, like we used to have, and stop hearing all the bullshit on the streets. I got three bricks of snowflake to give you, no strings attached." It was interesting to Clarence that people said something like this would happen. Here he was saving the man that used to be his partner.

"No, I don't want it." It just didn't seem right. Clarence had no good reason to look out for him. He was only down, not out. Pity was something that he would never accept, especially from Clarence.

"Is it that bad between us? I just want to see you back at the top of your game. You can pay me back if that makes you feel better. I'll even let you get it for what I'm getting it for." Clarence figured that this was all he could do.

"I'll be back on top in a few weeks." These were just words, he was still smoking coke, just not as much and not as often.

"Look Danny Boy, I hear about the deals you've been making. We don't have to speak after this. It's our secret." He ran out of things to say. "I'm going to leave it out front. It's up to you to pick it up." Clarence stood up and walked out. True to his word, he left a leather bag in front of the spot.

Danny Boy didn't have to think that long. It was the lick

that he needed. His mind was made up on whom he was going to rob. With three bricks, for almost free, he could be back on top in a few weeks. "Go get that bag before one of those crack heads steals it. Clarence just paid a debt to me." His workers would never know the difference.

◆　◆　◆　◆　◆

"Damn Jezebel, it's about time yo' ass got in." It was one o'clock in the morning.

She had a big grin on her face but the sound of Keisha's voice took it away. "What's wrong with you? You act like you just lost yo' best friend." Jezebel was hoping to share her night with Keisha. She had Calvin thinking he could walk on water.

"I got a big problem and I don't know what to do." Keisha was getting out of the bed.

Jezebel was putting her bag in the closet. "What could be that wrong."

"Sally is talking about sending me to jail for my mother's murder." Keisha didn't realize how loud she was speaking.

Jezebel sat on the end of her bed. "No she ain't. What makes you think that?" She was trying her best to take what she just heard seriously.

"She came here tonight accusing me of protecting Clarence. She knows he's the killer." It slipped, she put her hands in front of her mouth.

"What did you just say?" Jezebel thought for a second to run the words back through her mind. "You just said that Clarence is the killer. That was a Freudian slip." Sigmund Freud had a theory that the truth slips out of people's mouths when they are under stress.

There was no way for her to take it back. "Let me explain."

"What the fuck is there to explain?" Her hatred for men took over.

Keisha could see Jezebel going into a mode. "Listen to me, let me tell you what happened." Keisha was afraid that Jezebel was about to be mad at her.

Jezebel was only half listening. "Are you sure that he killed your mother."

"Yes, she told me before she died. Sally confirmed it when she told me about bullet casings found at the scene." She wanted Jezebel to know that she wasn't tripping. She still needed her, even if she were angry with her.

"We got to make that nigga pay. Are you *sure* he killed her? This shit is serious." Jezebel was thinking how her pimp used to beat her and treat her like trash. Her entire persona was about having power over men and making them pay.

Keisha saw that Jezebel wasn't angry with her. That was a relief. She ran the whole story down as Jezebel took it all in.

"So why don't you just tell all of this to Sally and let pretty boy go to jail for a long time." She wanted to call Sally herself.

"That's too damn good for that motherfucker. I want that nigga to pay for what he's done to my mother, my family, to *me*. I was his girl." Keisha started pacing. "I want him and Danny Boy to lose sleep just like I've been doing. I don't care if I have to go to jail, as long as they get theirs." There was relief in expressing her thoughts to someone else.

"We have to think about Sally first. We have to find out what we can do about her." She almost forgot about Sally trying to charge Keisha.

"She said she could charge me with murder for hire, accessory after the fact and conspiracy to commit a crime. She said I'd never see the daylight again." Keisha never thought about it being a bluff.

"Damn that's grimey!" Jezebel was respecting Sally's style.

"If I have to go to jail, then so be it, but I won't go before I get mines. My Daddy would turn over in his grave if I tell on Clarence. I'll tell Sherlock's people before I tell the police about Clarence. That's how I was taught."

"I respect that girl, that's how Cleopatra taught me." Cleopatra was on her mind all night. Calvin got her started but she needed someone to finish.

"So I need to get Clarence and Danny Boy before she gets me. I want to do this myself."

"I have a good idea, we have to figure out what Sally can and cannot do. Believe me, police officers love to bluff so they can see a person sweat." She had male admirers that could point her in the right direction.

"When do we do that?"

"In the morning. You need to get some sleep and I need to get some rest also." What she just heard turned her on. It wasn't her beef, that didn't matter, Keisha put her on the squad. Betrayal was at the top of the list of things not to do. A violation of that nature against a sister had to be repaid with lots of interest, on top of interest. Jezebel chose her job as the one to make sure all things went well. Getting revenge on Clarence was now part of her top priorities. If necessary, the rest of *The Clit* would be called.

"So why don't you just kick me to the curb?" Diamond was up waiting for Clarence to get in. With no clothes on, except a fur coat, she was sitting in the living room. She cut the DVD player off when she heard his key in the door.

"It's a little early in the morning to be acting all stank."

It just came to him that he hadn't given her a thing as a reward. The thought never entered his mind.

"I heard your party was really nice. Why did I have to hear about it from one of my girls?" She thought about making a scene at the club but that wasn't her style.

"I guess I forgot to tell you." He put his keys on the dining room table and proceeded to the kitchen. His tone was less than unemotional.

"Clarence," she hollered. "I want to talk to you." She was right behind him when he opened the fridge. "Who's the bitch you been fucking cuz you sure ain't been fucking me." She wanted to smell him to see if he smelled like another woman's perfume.

For the past few days she was spazzin' off at him about any and everything. He reached in the fridge to get some apple juice. "No I haven't been with another bitch. I've been with my boys." When he turned around, she reached to touch him, but he pushed her back a little.

"So I can't touch you anymore?" She let her fur coat open and asked him, "So you don't want this anymore?" He looked at her after he took a large swallow of apple juice. She looked deep into his eyes to see his feelings and soul. No man ever had the will to resist her.

"I'm tired Diamond, maybe in the morning." He walked past her, heading into the living room.

She was behind him, step for step. "Hell no motherfucker, you ain't gon' keep disrespectin' me."

He stopped at the couch and tried to pick up the remote but she snatched it up. Slapping her in the mouth went through his mind. "Give me that and sit the fuck down." He pushed her into the love seat.

She wanted to jump up and fight him. Getting an ass whooping appealed to her more than being ignored. "Ever since that day at the funeral you've been treating me like I don't exist. Do you still love Keisha?" Until the party, their problems were just between them. Not being at the party was an embarrassment to her. She was sure people would start talking.

"Sometimes a man needs his space. That's all there is to that." Admitting she was on point was out of the question. His chances of getting Keisha back in his life were slim to none. She was in Baltimore City and had a boyfriend, plus, she was still mad at him for standing her up.

"That's bullshit Clarence!" The anger in her voice revealed that she was about to cry.

He turned to look at her. "You're going to wake the building. Just give me some time." At the moment his mind was on Danny Boy and his spots. Diamond was a minor matter. There were too many other women that he started seeing, on the low.

"I don't care if you fuck ten women and Keisha, as long as I get mine and I'm the one seen with you." Losing Clarence would mean that her status would drop, big time.

"So you mad because I didn't take you to the club. Damn, it was a surprise party for my clique. They didn't know about it." He questioned himself for arguing with her. He was hoping that his lack of interest in her would change but his love for Keisha was just too strong.

She stood up. "I'm supposed to be your woman. Why couldn't you tell me?" Her voice was raised again.

"You're right Diamond, I'm sorry. I'll make it up to you." His mind went straight to Keisha when he thought about sex or romance. There was also some guilt mixed up in all that.

"You need to start now. If I can't get no dick tonight, I'll be gone tomorrow. No man resists Diamond and this good lovin." She walked down the hall and slammed the door when she went into the bedroom. She wanted to bring up the idea of marriage but there wasn't enough leverage to do that.

He wanted to explain to her that it wasn't her fault that he had other things on his mind. She was right about Keisha though. He wanted her back in the worst way. If he could turn back the hands of time he would have told Danny Boy that he wasn't going up in that house. At that time, the idea to rob Sherlock seemed simple, but the fallout afterwards made their lives miserable. At least, he figured he might as well get Keisha back since she stayed on his mind all day. Real love can ride a man like a monkey.

♦ ♦ ♦ ♦ ♦

It took two days to find the crack head she was looking for. "I've been looking for you, Skull."

Skull was living in an abandoned building with other crack heads. His parole officer put a warrant out for his arrest. None of his relatives wanted him around because he borrowed and stole all that he could. Skull kept silent, he only heard about Sally and never encountered her, until now.

"I need some information on Danny Boy." Getting an instant headache as she got close to him, she moved back because the stench. She was about ten feet away from him and his smell was still that appalling. There were other crack heads there that also added to the smell of the place. If it hadn't been the middle of the day she wouldn't have been found in that building, under any circumstances.

"What are you a cop? Get lost." It was his instinct talking.

"I got a little present for you. It's white and it's hard."

She was wearing a dark gray pants suit, with black pinstripes. She was watching Skull for three days.

"Oh yeah, so you peddling soap?" His tone changed. He needed her to be a little more specific.

"Nah, Sally don't play games. She pays for what she wants and I got a gram of rock." Addicts were the easiest to get info from, especially the ones that used to sell drugs.

He came closer, the only light came from a distant window. "Let me see what you have." He was kneeling so he wouldn't be seen through the window. At night he would go out and rob cats that didn't have the heart to hunt him down. The police were also looking for him. Sally was the least of his worries.

She pulled her gun from up under her jacket. "I ain't playing games." She nearly had the gun in his mouth and the other crack heads scrambled away. "If I like what you say, I'll let you get high. If I don't like what you say, I'll make you high forever."

He was looking up at her, and the gun, with pity in her eyes. He started to think about the times that he never got caught slippin'. "Sally, be cool. I don't know anything about no murders."

"Maybe you do, maybe you don't. Let me be the judge of that. Tell me about Danny Boy and Clarence." Sally worked overtime on this case, keeping up with all the details of their drug operations. Her obsessiveness pushed many of her other cases on the back burner.

What Danny Boy did to him came to his mind. "They ain't that cool. He wanted to put Clarence back in his place."

Progress was being made. "After Sherlock's funeral what did ya'll talk about? I saw you with them."

That gram was going to be some real good smoking. "Clarence was telling Danny Boy that you would be seeing him. Danny Boy said he wouldn't be giving any information."

"Information about what?"

"Danny never told me."

"Are you sure about that?" The other crack heads were scared that some shit was about to pop off, making the spot hot. She slapped him across the head with the butt of the gun.

"Damn Sally, that hurt." He shook it off by rubbing his head. "He used to say that Clarence might start feeling guilty and break down for something they did." He kept his hand up to his head to keep from getting hit again.

"That's it?" She faked like she was about to hit him again and he jumped back. "There's got to be more than that."

He kept his hands up. "He didn't tell me much more about what happened. He just kept saying that Clarence's guilt might fuck them up." She felt that he was now entitled to the gram.

"Here." She threw the five rocks at him. Sally turned around and started walking out as the other crack heads gathered around Skull. They knew he had that thing.

All she got out of him was confirmation. There was a good chance that she could get one to turn on the other, she thought, as Bambi picked her up in the BMW.

Destiny Child's "Survivor" was pumping in the system.

"So was going up in there worth it?" Bambi asked as she was pulling off.

"I didn't get much out of him. He basically let me know that they are worried about me pressin' them." Sally started breaking down a Black. She was thinking about going to see Danny Boy again.

"That isn't enough information for us to close the case. One of them needs to talk, or she needs to talk." Bambi felt it was best to lay low for a minute to let them all relax.

"I think she's almost ready to crack. I had her really

scared. I still can't figure why she's protecting him." She felt that if she could figure out why then she would be able to get in Keisha's head.

"I got it! It's been right in our face this entire time." The idea popped into Bambi's head a few days ago but it started making sense to her as she drove.

"Go on white girl, spit game."

"She wants to get revenge herself."

Sally simmered the idea in her head for a few minutes. At first she wanted to say that wasn't Keisha's style. Less intense people kill people everyday. Keisha's facial expression on the day of the murder came to her. "I'm not sure if I'm feeling that. I think that if she wanted to kill him, she would have done it already. Plus, she ain't a street chic."

"Just imagine if your mother was killed by the man that you loved, you would feel more than hurt, you'd feel betrayed. Would killing him be enough?" Bambi was eyeing how Sally was breaking down the Black. She still wasn't able to pull that tan paper out.

"Girl you must have gotten some really good dick last night." They both laughed.

"You might be right," Sally continued. "She probably can't even get close to Clarence. I can't imagine him being that stupid." Sally was thinking to herself there was nothing Keisha could really do to get good revenge on Clarence.

"I'm thinking that she won't be satisfied with just seeing him go to jail or murdered on the streets. If the man I'm supposed to marry killed my mother, there would be all hell to pay." Bambi wished that she had something to say about Keisha to validate her theory.

"Bambi, I hate to tell you this, but I know more about Clarence than anybody in the city. Clarence is too smart to be got like that." She was getting ready to pull the paper out of the cigar casing.

Bambi was glad they stopped at a red light. Sally was moving too fast. "Maybe if we press her she'll change her mind and tell us what she knows." Before Sally started packing her Black, she hit the CD changer. It was time for some Keith Sweat to help her get in the mood for her date.

"I'm with you Sally. Let's tell her that we know her motive for covering for Clarence is revenge. It can't hurt, plus it would be good to see her expression and what she may do afterwards." Her gut instincts wouldn't let her dismiss the idea.

"That sounds good." It was a good distraction, and reason, to go see Keisha again. This time, she just may crack.

"Oh yes, Mr. Big Dick lick this pussy!" Sally was trying to make him suffocate in her crotch. She was getting with Kevin two or three times a week, depending on the urge. "Oh that feels good." She felt sweat building up on the back of her knees. "Damn, you good pussy eating motherfucker." She started gasping for air. She just couldn't get enough of Kevin.

Spasms of joy went through her body as sexual tension was being released. Not the built up kind. It was the smooth feeling that comes with having sex on the regular. Her pussy was pulsating with each spasm. The intensity caused her to arch her back and throw her head back. "Oh, oh, oh," was all she could holler. With all her strength she grabbed at the sheets. "Oh, oh, oh," she was still hollering, at a slower pace. That orgasm was enough to last for weeks, but why settle for that, when she could get it on the regular.

"Fuck me Mr. Big Dick," she demanded, "before I find a reason to arrest you. Put me in the buck."

"You got that." Kevin, without hesitation, placed her knees up to her shoulders and mounted her. From the orgasm she just had she was wet to the max.

"That's right motherfucker." Kevin started pounding her. "That's it, fuck me hard like you hate the police." She reached her hand underneath her to play with his balls.

"Fuck me faster than that. Is that all you got Mr. Big Dick?" she challenged. Her pussy was used to taking all of him in. Making love wasn't her thing, she liked to fuck, and be fucked, hard.

It was starting to get good to her after about fifteen minutes as she started to wiggle and throw it back at him. "That's it Mr. Big Dick, don't stop. Please don't stop." Kevin was getting tired.

"Boy, you better not slow down on me. Bang this pussy young buck. I'll fuck you to death." He sped back up. "Yeah that's right!" She started moaning and groaning. Kevin was sweating and almost out of breath. With every thrust he was putting all of himself inside of her. The harder he fucked her the more she wanted it.

"Oh yes," she screamed. The high-pitched sound of her voice made him start to cum. She started having her second orgasm just after he started. They were both exhausted.

After they slept for a few hours, Sally woke up and started massaging his back. She figured the liquor and all the sex had set in and relaxed him. "So what's up with Clarence and Danny Boy these days?"

"Ain't shit really. Danny Boy is doing his thing, thanks to Clarence. They've even been partying a little bit together."

"I thought they had problems." The last few times she questioned Kevin, she was under the impression that they hated each other.

"I forgot to tell you that Clarence blessed Danny Boy when he blessed the rest of the crew." This wasn't something he thought was really important.

"So what do you think Clarence is up to?" There had to be more to it than that.

"I've been trying to figure that shit out also. I would have never given a cat three bricks of coke who talks about me like a dog. Danny Boy won't even admit that Clarence helped him." Kevin was thinking that Clarence was trying to trick Danny Boy into working for LCP but he managed to make Danny Boy stronger and stop talking about him.

"Maybe they go so far back that he had to help him out." She wanted to say Clarence was making sure that Danny Boy didn't tell any of their secrets.

"Danny Boy had the same opportunities as Clarence but Clarence is just a better playa at the game. If I were Clarence, I'd kill Danny Boy. They have a serious history together."

Sally kept throwing around ideas. Clarence was keeping Danny Boy happy to keep his mouth shout. Danny Boy could take Clarence out whenever he wanted by telling about the Sherlock murder/robbery. If Clarence got Danny Boy hit everybody would be looking at him, so it was best to keep him happy.

If she ever caught Danny Boy in a weak position she would press him with a proposition. For now she kept her eyes and ears open for a weak spot to appear. Opportunities always had a way of presenting themselves.

Bambi's revenge theory was making more sense as time went on. For Keisha to get revenge in a sophisticated manner she would have to come back to the district. It would surprise her to see Keisha move back. Keisha getting close to Clarence could only be accomplished if she and Clarence were together. Keisha didn't exactly seem like the kind to inflict extensive punishment on a person. Sally was just trying to keep an open mind and be reasonable.

Keisha's dance lessons started to show significant results. She learned many things from Jezebel and everything about her changed, in a matter of weeks. She dressed, acted, talked, walked and thought differently. The campus men were showing her just as much attention as they did Jezebel. It was a week since she and Jezebel talked about the plot for revenge. Jezebel had to do some research first.

Jezebel was waiting for Keisha at the Baltimore Law Library. "Damn girl. What took you so long?

"You know how it is, I can't step out until I'm looking as tight as my sister." Keisha became addicted to the attention that men were giving her.

"Remember I told you that knowledge is the greatest hustle." Jezebel had that extra glow about herself.

"Yeah, you tell me that all the time." When Jezebel spoke Keisha hung onto every word.

"I've been reading these law books and cases for the past few days. It looks like that lady cop can only get you for one of three things."

"When did you start studying the law and reading law books?"

"I've done this for a while. Cleopatra is a certified par-alegal, she taught me. She said that the Black woman has to always be one step ahead of everybody, so we studied the law for all things that interest us." Everybody in *The Clit* started out as a prostitute. They felt it was in their best interest to know how not to get caught, and if necessary, what to do if they were. Jezebel got with a guy that was familiar with the DC law to put her in the right direction.

"Knowing the law really empowers a Black woman." Keisha was thinking it would be hard to catch up with Jezebel's brain.

"That's right little sister." It was a must that Keisha be put in *The Clit*, in time.

"So put the cake on the table, what can she do to me?"

"She can't do shit because she doesn't know if you know anything. She doesn't know what your mother told you, nor does she know that you know about Clarence carrying tens. Basically, she doesn't know shit."

"But she knows about the phone calls that were made."

"Clarence was your man. Ya'll talk, that doesn't mean that you took part in a conspiracy. She can't prove that ya'll had an agreement. She can't prove that you did a murder –for hire. She can't prove a motive. She can't prove accessory after the fact. And most of all, she can't prove that you are trying to cover up the murder."

"But what about me not telling her what I know?" This was a good question.

"We ain't going to tell her what you know. If she knew all that she claims to know, she would have already arrested Clarence and Danny Boy." Jezebel respected that she asked a good question. "They can never assume what is told, or not told to them, unless they see it. That's why they ask so many questions."

"So that means that Sally can just kiss my ass." They high-fived each other.

"I got a plan that will throw everybody off. You said ya'll were eventually going to get married. So, instead of me getting Clarence, you need to go through with that." Her wheels were turning non-stop. She wanted everything to be airtight.

"So what's up with that?" She was wondering what the real reason was behind the change. She had to admit that she did the things that Jezebel respected and didn't mind Jezebel suggesting the change.

"I want to just coach and have your back. I need to watch

Sally while you do your thing. Plus, Clarence loves you. He'll kill to get you back once we make our first move. I'll just play Danny Boy a little bit. I can see he'll be easy."

All night long they exchanged ideas. Keisha was feeling like she met the sister she never had. Jezebel loved Keisha just as much and loved teaching her things. It was right up Jezebel's alley, helping her get revenge on Clarence and Danny Boy more than anything else. She made sure every detail would be covered. This one would go down in the books as one for the empowerment of Black women. Clarence and Danny Boy were representatives of men that mistreated and abused Black women and the goal was to make them suffer as much as possible, with Clarence being the main target. They changed plans three or four times before they were satisfied. In the days to come they would continue to discuss and refine the plan. It was on and poppin'.

◆ ◆ ◆ ◆ ◆

16

◆ ◆ ◆ ◆ ◆

It had been three months since Danny Boy climbed back up the ladder. To show his appreciation, and to make himself look good, he hosted Clarence's twentieth birthday party at Insomnia.

"I propose a toast to our first year of getting money," Danny Boy commented, with a grin on his face. He and Clarence toasted their glasses of Cristal.

"Yeah man, it'll be a year next month that we made that major move." Clarence would not have said a thing like that if he and Danny Boy weren't alone in the VIP.

Danny Boy had his eyes on one of the strippers. "Yeah man, I think about that all the time. You really made me have major respect for you after that." All the booze made him relax. It was almost a year since they had a real heart to heart talk.

"We had to do what we had to do. " Telling Danny Boy that he felt guilty about killing Keisha's mother was out of the question. Nothing, ever again, would let him trust

Danny Boy. Negative feelings just don't go away like that.

"So what happened to you and Diamond? She ain't even stripping anymore."

"I got tired of her. She didn't have shit on her mind." Diamond gave him an ultimatum about getting married. When he didn't go along with it, she called herself walking out on him.

"Tell me something, my man. I know you fucked Keisha at least one time. You can tell me the truth."

Clarence laughed and smiled. "I'm going to tell you the truth. She wasn't going to let me get it until she graduated or we got married." Her name alone brought back many memories.

"Man stop bullshitting, you ain't never get the pussy?" They never talked about Keisha much. Danny Boy was really talking about her because of how loyal Clarence was to him. He wondered if Keisha had the power to make him choose.

"I'm serious man, I wanted to marry her. I still do." It was the first time he slipped and said this to anyone.

"I didn't know that." Clarence always kept it moving. This was the first time Danny Boy saw a chink in the armor.

"It ain't your fault. The game, and my crew, comes before any female. Ain't that right?" Clarence meant to say that he'd give up all of his wealth to have her back, especially to bring her mother back.

"I just mentioned her name because I saw a flier in the front of the club showcasing a new stripper named Keisha who starts next week."

Danny Boy and Clarence made real good peace with each other in the past few weeks. Danny Boy didn't want Clarence to think that he was trying to be funny. Soon, he was planning to start copping from him, if the price was still right. Mad respect in the streets for his comeback had softened his pride although he still had certain negative desires.

"I can't imagine her doing the stripper thing. She's got plenty of her own money. I don't think it'll be her." Rumors said that it would be her but Clarence just laughed when he heard them.

"Yeah, she didn't even hang out. Is she still mad at you?"

Clarence told Danny Boy that she was mad at him because he was with the wrong girl that morning.

"Last time I saw her, she had a man. He seemed to be really going for her." Their dates came back to the table and took their respective seats.

Clarence and Danny Boy never talked about a woman in that manner. "Fuck it and keep 'em moving," was their motto for all females, no matter how good they looked or how good the pussy was. Danny Boy really took good notes about Clarence's feelings for Keisha. She definitely looked good, but she didn't seem like the kind to be able to keep a hustler's attention. Danny Boy sort of saw her as a prize because of her father. He always figured Clarence felt the same way or he was using her to get closer to Sherlock since they talked about the numbers game on several occasions.

Danny Boy still had the desire to be on top of Clarence, in the game, or any given situation. He decided to be patient and not appear to be the enemy.

Although he changed his style, he still got high, but only on the low. He picked workers that didn't get high and were all about getting money. He had a few guys that were truly dependable and with that, learned to be more cunning and more of a playa. There was no need in destroying himself because of his desire to top another nigga.

Clarence couldn't take it any longer, he had to see Keisha. He paid Jessica five bills to tell where she was but had no idea that Keisha expected his visit and planned accordingly. She didn't know it would be on a Thursday. When she heard the knock at the door, she and Jezebel figured it was either James or Calvin.

"Who is it?" Keisha asked in a sexy voice as she sauntered toward the door. She and Jezebel were listening to a Luther Vandross CD.

"Open the door, it's Clarence," a deep voice said from the other side.

Keisha looked back at Jezebel with a look that said, "What should I do?"

Jezebel made a silly face and told her in a low tone. "Handle him like a seductress would. Open the door."

Keisha put her left hand on the doorknob and put her head down. She wanted to prepare herself to look at him, face to face. He knocked again, harder than he did the first time. This made Keisha feel better. She was trying to figure out how to handle him.

"What are you waiting for?" Jezebel said in a voice that was just loud enough for Keisha to hear.

Keisha motioned at her with her right hand to be cool.

"Damn Keisha, open –" he hollered, as he continued to bang on the door.

Keisha was looking dead in his eyes. She had a desire to jump on him and kiss him until he couldn't take any more. And just like an Amazon, kill him after she was satisfied. Just as Jezebel taught her, she kept her emotions in check as she sought the weak spot to his heart. She also couldn't help but to recognize how good he was looking in his black turtleneck.

Clarence was speechless. She was already a natural beauty, but there was something different about her. She was now wearing makeup and provocative clothes, she was stunning. It was like the new and improved Keisha and all he could do was stare. His head told him that he was making the right move.

She knew she still had him. "What are you doing here Clarence? This isn't the district." The look in his eyes told her that she could drive him into a light pole if she played her cards right. She placed her hands on her hips.

"I need to talk to you. Can we talk in private?" He waved at Jezebel to be polite. She waved back.

Keisha said, "Yeah, wait for me in the lobby. I need to freshen up first." She needed a small break from him to catch her second wind.

Clarence did as he was asked. Keisha took thirty minutes to change her clothes, freshen up her make-up and change her hairstyle. She and Jezebel went over the plans.

When Keisha got in the lobby she ignored the girl that was holding a conversation with Clarence. She just walked past as she said, "Let's go." Clarence was right behind her when she walked out the door. She could not have asked for a better situation to scope his feelings.

"Why you walking so fast Keisha? Slow down." She didn't stop until she got to a bench to sit down. It was a spot that would make them be noticed by all.

"I'm not walking that fast. I just needed to get some air." He took a seat beside her. Jezebel was watching from the room window. "Sally hasn't been back to see me, so what do you want?"

"I need you back in my life." There was a humble look on his face. He was admiring the slit in her leather skirt.

"I'm still mad at you for letting me down." What he said was music to her ears.

"That was a year ago, what about forgiveness? What about all the love we had." With the way that she was carrying it now they would look great together at the club. He was feeling her gangsta.

"If I were at the house I could have saved my mother, but I was out waiting on you." She looked away.

"So what do you want me to do Keisha? I can't bring her back." What she said was just as good as accusing him of the crime.

She looked back at him. "What can you do? What are my options? Show me how good your game is." She planned to play him as long as she could.

"I can make you happy for the rest of your life, like we planned." The question was like the opening that she needed.

"A lot of things have happened in the last year. You may not be up to the challenge anymore."

He took the bait. It was a fight to get his woman back. "So that means you need a square nigga in your life, like your James."

"I have to admit, he's really good to me." She wouldn't have gone there if he didn't open the door. It was like he had shown a sign of weakness.

"I can tell by the looks that you give me that you still have feelings for me."

She didn't expect him to have that kind of comeback. "You sound real confident Clarence. What makes you so sure?" Her question was outside of the plan.

"When you called me over at the funeral, we did have some serious chemistry. People are still talking about that." Clarence knew that he was on the right course.

"I'm not sure Clarence. They say that you are one of those people in the district. You might neglect me again and that'll make me want to kill you." She wasn't quite back on track. Her feelings for him were running interference. She couldn't even look at him.

He put his finger on her chin to turn her face. She wanted to resist but his touch, in such a compassionate way, made her feel like her chemistry on the inside was changing. She put up no resistance, as he inched closer to her, while he turned her face to him.

He waited for their eyes to meet. "I need you in my life, Keisha." Their lips were less than a quarter of an inch apart. When her bottom lip and his upper lip touched she jumped from the bench.

She took three steps and stopped. Her body was telling her to kiss and hold him tight. These emotions were stronger than her desire for revenge. She couldn't call out for Jezebel like she wanted to. Jumping up was the only reasonable thing that she could think of doing. Running away would have called her bluff.

Clarence wasn't sure of what to do. He was certain that she still had mad love for him. That was enough for him to know that she would soon be his, again. It would just be a matter of time.

Slowly, he walked up behind her and placed his hands on her shoulders. His touch brought her back to reality. Her heart started racing when his lips touched her neck. It sent waves of joy throughout her entire body.

"I love you and want you back, Keisha," he whispered in her left ear.

She turned around while waving her left arm to make him release her. "We might not be that good for each other, Clarence. I have to think about it. Give me your cell number so I can call you." The first part of the mission was completed: Clarence had his nose wide open. Talking to him any longer might defeat the purpose and she was close to giving in to her desires. A vision of her mother put her back on track.

Clarence pulled out a piece of paper and an ink pen. As he was writing down the number she admired his style. She also liked how other females were peeping him.

"So wassup, you gonna call me?" Clarence asked as he extended the piece of paper to her.

"I don't know, I have to think about it. I don't need you coming up here because my boyfriend shows up a lot." She was lying. She knew she had James in full check.

He gave her the number without teasing her, like he wanted to. She looked him in the eye and started walking back to the dorm. He was so confident she would call that he didn't ask her for her cell.

She was happy as hell to get back to her room. "Tell me what happened girl. I could tell that you had him begging."

"Yeah girl, I got him mad open. He gave me his cell and promised
me the world." They hugged each other. Keisha didn't want to tell her girl that she was nervous.

"He thinks he's a playa, but he's about to get played." Jezebel loved the progress of her student.

Keisha jumped on her bed. Her mother was still on her mind. Her entire expression changed. Jezebel sat on the end of her bed.

"What's wrong Keisha?" Jezebel asked with a sympathetic voice. "We have a better start than we wanted."

"Damn girl, I was just thinking about my mother. We used to be really close and I really miss her."

Jezebel touched her on her knee. "It's going to be okay. I got you girl. I also have something for you, we're going to be sisters forever." Jezebel got up and reached in her drawer.

Keisha was wondering what Jezebel had for her. She was better to her than any blood sister that she could have asked for. "Haven't you done enough for me?"

Jezebel held up a black *The Clit* T-shirt with white letters. "I got one for you and me. It's all about the Black woman."

Keisha wasn't exactly sure about joining *The Clit*. "I don't know about that, Jezebel."

"When we get finished, there isn't going to be a thing here for you." She sat back on Keisha's bed and started stroking her hair. "Look how beautiful you've become since you started loving yourself." There was lust in Jezebel's eyes.

"I'm not sure about that, being in *The Clit* may not be for me."

"What the hell is there for you? After we get finished, who will be able to keep you growing?"

She almost hollered out Clarence but stopped herself. All the things she and Clarence talked about flooded her mind. "Thanks for the t-shirt but let me think about it." They kissed cheeks before they went to sleep.

It was Friday afternoon and Alabama Avenue was full of people. There was a line leading into Danny Boy's spot that ended around the block. He was in the back, counting the dough as it came in, and giving orders.

"Excuse me," Jezebel said as she made it to the front of the line. "My man runs this spot." As good as she was looking, no one dared to question her.

Jezebel had on her black and white *The Clit* t-shirt. It was cut off to show her well-toned midsection. Her white shorts were so tight, they looked like they were painted on. Showing off her sexy and tanned thighs, her shorts were just long enough not to show any of her butt cheeks. With calf-high stiletto boots, she knew she was the street's main attraction.

When she got the crack sellers' attention, she struck a sexy pose before she spoke. "I need to see Danny Boy, tell him the woman of his dreams is here."

They didn't know what to think or do. The room was stuck on pause and all eyes were glued on her.

"Do I have to go back there and get him myself?" she asked as she shifted her weight to the other hip.

"Danny Boy is here." Danny was curious because of how silent the place seemed to be. A few of his dudes were behind him. He started grinning as he checked her out. She was looking good. "What's up lady? Have we met?" He was in cool acting mode.

"We can meet if you follow me outside."

"Nah, you might be trying to get me shot, come in the back." She was too much of a stranger.

"I ain't feeling that. Meet me at the *Platinum*, I'll be stripping tonight and drinks are on me." She wasn't about to let a group of men trap her. There was too much lust in their eyes. "You can bring your boys." She walked out without hearing his response.

Danny Boy was totally thrown for a loop. Fo' sho' he was going to be at the club with his boys. Although she was fine, he didn't want her distracting his spot anymore. She should have never gotten into the building.

Still, she turned him on and had his full attention. He certainly wasn't going to miss her stripping. She was looking so good that he was hardly able to remain focused. The way she acted, the pussy had to be good. All day he tried to figure out where he knew her from. He only knew that she wasn't from the district.

17

◆ ◆ ◆ ◆ ◆

"Mama, I miss you," Keisha said as she placed flowers on her mother's grave, removing the ones she brought last month. "I came to tell you some really good news." Tears started running down her cheeks.

"I finally came up with a plan to make Clarence and Danny Boy pay for what they did to our family. I guess it took me a long time to put the pieces together because I still have love for Clarence. My love for him is making it that much harder but it also makes me feel like punishing him that much more. I feel like he betrayed us. He did betray us. He betrayed all the things that he talked about.

"Oh yeah, Mama, I have a great friend that's helping me get revenge. She belongs to a group called *The Clit*. I know you wouldn't approve, just because of the name but her name is Jezebel, and she's trying to get an education, just like you talked about me getting. The girl reads three hours a day and really has it all together. She has helped me put the plan together. At times she acts like she hates what Clarence did more than I do."

Jezebel was standing in the background waiting on her partner.

"Maybe it's because of how some men have treated her in the past. She plays men better than any woman I've ever met. She says she's trying to break into corporate America by owning her own business. She's the kind of woman that I want to be like." Keisha always took her time when she visited her mother. She was at the graveyard for about half an hour.

She was silent for ten minutes. "What we have planned for Clarence is going to rock his entire world. Jessica has a small role to play in the thing too. I could only get her to do so much. You know how much she cares about her career. Her part is important, so I can't argue with her. It took a big argument for me to convince her that Clarence did it.

"Oh yeah, Danny Boy is going to get his also. Jezebel is going to set him up good. He'll pay the price, but not like Clarence will. I love you Mama, I have to go." Keisha wiped her eyes and got up off the ground. Her knees had gotten dirty, but that was okay.

Looking over to the next grave, she walked and took up the old flowers and put down fresh ones. "Daddy, I got everything in order. You'll be proud of me. I love you."

When she started walking toward her Escalade, she noticed Jezebel and smiled. She was happy to see her girl. Jezebel's Jag was parked next to her truck.

"I thought you were going to see Danny Boy," Keisha stated in an inquisitive voice. She still had her mind on her parents.

"That was a piece of cake, I got him where I want him." Jezebel caught some tears off Keisha's cheeks. As an act of love, she sucked the tears off her fingers. "Your tears are my tears little sister."

They hugged and held each other for a few moments. "It hurts so much Jezebel, they didn't have to kill her." She placed her head on Jezebel's shoulder.

"Let it all out, I got you. I'll always be there for you." Jezebel was waiting for this moment of weakness for a long time. She was about to certify herself as Keisha's moving force. "I love you too much to let you down. It's time to be strong my sister."

Keisha let her go. The look on her face was one of embarrassment. They stepped back from each other, like the moment became too intense, too deep. "Without you I wouldn't be able to pull this off. I love you for that. Why are you crying?"

"I told you that your tears are my tears." Jezebel didn't wipe away the tears so Keisha could see them. It was better that she knew.

Keisha started smiling because she didn't think that anything could make Jezebel cry. Jezebel wiped the tears from her cheeks.

"I'm sorry, I guess I got caught up in the moment, let's go. We have things to do." She knew that Keisha wasn't ready to take the next step she was thinking about.

"So what happened with Danny Boy?" Keisha had no idea what Jezebel was showing her. She saw it all as sisterly love.

"He'll be at the spot. I made him an offer he couldn't refuse, right in front of all his boys. You know how I do."

"I'm ready to do my thing."

"I'm ready too."

As usual, on a Friday night, Club Platinum was on and poppin by one o'clock. Danny Boy just came through the door with his crew. He was trying his best to make Jezebel wait as long as possible. He already sent a few of his soldiers inside to see if she was there. She was there, at a table by the stage, with a girl who looked familiar. His boys said that they knew her from somewhere, but they just couldn't place her. Danny Boy and his boys were talking about Jezebel all day. He felt it was time to make his move.

When Danny Boy came to the door, he and his crew were let in for free. He was instructed to go to the table with the ladies. His boys were sent to two other tables nearby with two free-flowing bottles of Cristal.

A bottle of Cristal was brought to the ladies' table when Danny Boy took his seat.

"You did say you were the woman of my dreams," Danny Boy commented as he was sitting down. So far he hadn't seen Keisha's face, just the back of her hair.

"I think you might know my friend," Jezebel commented, as he was getting comfortable.

Danny Boy hadn't recognized her presence because he was staring at Jezebel. His eyes opened wide and almost jumped out of his seat when he looked. "Keisha!" he hollered with a tone of familiarity to hide that he was surprised.

"Hi Danny Boy," she said in a voice just loud enough for her to be heard. Her hands were up under her chin and she was wearing a smile that said "whatever, whenever."

"So you know my girl, huh? She didn't tell me that she knew the district's hottest hustler." She thought to herself that he was just too damn easy. He couldn't even hide the fact that he was drooling.

"Well, she hasn't been in the district in a minute and we used to go to school together." Danny was thinking that he was really the shit because everybody in the club was checking them out. Before Danny Boy arrived, half the cats in the club approached the table trying to holla at Jezebel and Keisha, but they didn't get no play.

"I've heard some really good things about you Danny Boy so I had to come back and check it out myself. Know what I mean?" Keisha was just saying whatever she thought would go to his head. The way that he was smiling and drinking, she knew that he was easy to manipulate.

"Yeah. Fo sho," Danny Boy said as he slouched down in his chair. His mind went straight to wanting Clarence to see him. "The wall says Keisha's supposed to be dancing tonight. There's also a Jezebel, is that supposed to be ya'll?" He was feeling smart for asking this question. He felt like they were doing it just for him.

Keisha stuck her finger in her mouth and licked it like it was a tasty lollipop. "I'll do that in a few minutes Danny Boy, but we got something just for you."

"It must be my birthday or something." Danny Boy downed his glass. Keisha dancing was a sight he was willing to pay major bank to see. Where the hell was Clarence? This just might be what he prayed for.

Jezebel stood up and caressed the side of his face. "This night is the beginning of many nights to come." Keisha stood up and threw a kiss at Danny Boy. "We'll be right back," she said in a sexy voice.

Danny Boy was feeling himself. His mind was on fucking Keisha. That would make him feel like he had something up on Clarence. Doing Jezebel was also on his mind but doing the both of them would make him the talk of the district for the longest.

A waitress put another bottle on his table. He looked over at his boys and saw they were also being kept happy. None of them considered that Danny Boy was being setup. The way they saw it, they were getting free drinks and enjoying it. They planned to get their brag on for D & C for the longest because their man was holding it down with two of the finest honeys in the club.

Keisha and Jezebel spent over five grand to make this night happen. It was now time to put the icing on the cake.

The deejay stopped the music. "Ladies and gentlemen, we have the pleasure of holding the premiere show of two of our finest, new dancers. They're going to put on a show that none of ya'll will forget. Ya'll give a round of applause for *Jezebel*."

"In Between the Sheets" by the Isley Brothers started playing. All eyes were on the stage and Danny Boy. He felt privileged to have a seat right up front.

Jezebel walked on the stage in step with the beat. Her legs were looking great. The black suit jacket that she was wearing made her legs stand out. When she got in front of Danny Boy, she seductively took the jacket off. Danny Boy grabbed the bottle of Cristal and a glass and got closer to the stage. His boys were calling out his name and hollering "D & C."

She gyrated her hips and threw her pussy directly at Danny Boy. She was wearing a purple nurse's uniform with high heels to match.

Slowly she turned around so he could check out her shapely ass. Nobody approached the stage for the sake of looking lame and getting embarrassed. After she was fully turned around, she bent all the way over, shaking her legs, thighs and ass. The crowd went wild as they saw a thong underneath.

Danny Boy felt shivers run through his body. He had to shift his hard dick to see if he was dreaming.

When she turned back around, she slowly unbuttoned her uniform. She continued to dance with the beat, seductively, while shaking her hips, teasingly peeling the uniform away from her shoulders. When she made eye contact with

Danny Boy, after spinning around twice, she pulled her costume down slowly, revealing her titties. She had Danny Boy captivated, and she knew it. She leaned back a few degrees to shake her perky titties at him.

Danny Boy shook his head.

Then she just stopped. She stood there to enjoy the energy she was receiving from the crowd. All of the attention was getting her close to an orgasm.

To keep them going, as well as herself, she started rubbing all over her body. She was acting like she was having sex with herself but this was nothing new to her. She was just showing the crowd how she pleased herself when she was alone. She appeared to have gone into her own world. The song ended just as she completely removed her costume, revealing her thong.

The crowd gave her a standing ovation as she left the stage. They wanted an encore.

"Okay Keisha, it's all on you. We got his head all blown up, both of them." Jezebel was hoping that Keisha would be able to handle it. She did a great job when they auditioned for the club's owner.

"I can handle it but I wish that I went before you. You really did the damn thing." These weren't just words.

"Just let the music guide you. I'll be at the table." She was putting her jacket back on.

"Ladies and gentlemen, it isn't over. We have another great dancer from the district. Ya'll know her as Sherlock's daughter, Keisha. Yes, it's young Keisha, but she's all grown up now. Ya'll give her a round of applause."

The crowd clapped and people came closer to the stage. They had to see this up close. A few cats tried to get Clarence on his cell phone.

Keisha bit her lower lip when she saw them running toward the stage. She took a big swallow of her drink and said, "Fuck it."

"Fire and Desire" by Rick James and Teena Marie came through the sound system as she sauntered onto the stage. She had on a white robe that reached her knees and a white baseball cap on her head. It was pulled down over her eyes.

When she got in front of Danny Boy, she took her hat off and threw her hair around like Ashanti does in her videos. She stopped to make eye contact with Danny Boy. The crowd knew for sure that it was Sherlock's Keisha. Slowly she untied the belt to her robe. Danny and the crowd couldn't wait to see what was underneath.

Her tongue seductively licked her lips. She tossed the belt of her robe to Danny Boy, which landed on his shoulder. She strutted up and down the stage, teasing the crowd with peeps of what was underneath her robe. When she got back in front of Danny Boy, she took the robe off and tossed it at him. He quickly grabbed it to keep from missing anything just as Jezebel sat down at the table.

Keisha was wearing a black leather policewoman outfit with black stilettos. She got into character, letting loose any inhibitions she may have had, sort of in an animalistic way. She didn't give a fuck anymore. With her arms above her head, she started shaking her ass to the ground in a slow manner meant to tease. At one point she bent over to let Danny Boy see the space between her titties. The crowd was mesmerized. Soon her ass was touching the floor. Her legs were spread wide enough for Danny Boy to let his imagination run wild.

When she came back up, she had already had some of the snaps undone, but she was about to take it to the next level. Lil Jon's "Get Low" started playing and the crowd started hollering, "Three-six-nine, three-six-nine." She was moving with the tempo of the song. She tore away at her costume and threw it at Danny Boy. All she had on was a sequined thong and pasties on her nipples. She broke it down to the floor right in front of Danny Boy. He couldn't believe what he was seeing.

All the lights went out but her thong kept the stage lit up. The crowd was chanting with the song, "To the window, to the wall. Get low, get low."

When the lights came back on, she worked the pole like she was an experienced dancer. Before ending her dance, she pulled off her pasties and threw them into the audience. She sauntered right in front of Danny Boy and ended her dance with a split.

Jezebel was proud. The crowd was hollerin' and screamin' for more. Keisha couldn't believe that she went through with it. Danny Boy jumped up on the stage with her robe to cover her. He felt a need to be her protector. When she looked up into his eyes, she knew that she had him, she just needed to remove a bit of apprehension. Danny Boy coming on the stage couldn't have been a better thing.

She wrapped her arms around his neck and aimed her lips directly at his.

"Were you ready for that?" He was surprised, it all happened so fast that he didn't know what to do. He wasn't in a rush after all that excitement.

"You have to ask?" She was wishing that Clarence were at the club watching. She grabbed the back of his head, putting all of her tongue into his mouth. She put her all into it.

Danny Boy had no choice but to kiss her back. Backing up from her was out of the question. This is something that couldn't be explained to his boys. None of him desired to back up.

Jezebel was saying to herself, "Go girl, go girl."

It seemed like they kissed forever. Even after the deejay started playing music people still had their eyes on them.

While she was kissing him she kept thinking about how the news was going to make Clarence feel.

"Let's go Danny Boy, we have a limousine waiting for us outside." He was speechless as she led him off the stage with Jezebel right behind them. People were staring and getting out of the way. Keisha had a tight grip on Danny Boy's hand as she made her way out of the club. She gave some heads-up to a few people that made eye contact with her.

She couldn't believe what she was doing. This adventure was like losing her virginity all over again. Before she got on stage, she didn't think that she had the will power to dance in front of all those people. Without the alcohol in her system, she figured she couldn't have done it. Once she started, she felt powerful and her pussy stayed wet. With Jezebel by her side, she felt that she would be able to do anything. What she was afraid of gave her a rush that she wanted to feel again. Plus, the night wasn't over.

Just as planned, the limousine was waiting, and they had their prisoner. The first part of the plan was complete. Danny Boy's head was blown way out of proportion. It could be seen in his expressions. Still, they wanted him so deep in the web that there was no possible way for him to get out. With the completion of the next phase, he would have more to brag to his boys about.

Once they were seated in the limousine, Jezebel told the driver to head toward Danny Boy's crib. She and Keisha were sitting with their backs to the driver with Danny Boy sitting opposite them. The limousine was pulling up to the corner just as they all got comfortable. Danny Boy was grinning at the crowd through the tinted windows.

"It isn't over yet Danny Boy," Jezebel said as she took off her coat.

"That's right Danny," Keisha added as she was pulling her thong to the bottom of her legs.

Danny Boy was looking at Keisha with a look of awe. Never had he felt so good. He started taking off his D & C jacket.

Jezebel removed her thong and held it up in the air. "I hope you know how to eat pussy cuz if there ain't no lickin', there ain't no stickin'." She and Keisha high-fived each other.

Keisha crossed her right leg over the left and slowly slid her robe up to reveal her thighs.

"Yeah, I know how to eat pussy," he said hungrily. He and his boys talked all day about what she had written on her shirt. Though he wanted to bury his dick up to his balls in some pussy, he was willing to eat some first. The thought was already in his mind. With Jezebel butt-ass naked before him, and Keisha just wearing a robe, there was no way he was going to pass up the chance to do both of them. Plus, his dick was hard enough for him to break down a wall.

"Do you really know how to eat pussy?" Keisha challenged.

"I can eat you as long as you can take it." Jezebel smiled at his cocky response.

Keisha, looking deeply into his eyes, opened her legs wide and told him, "Bring it on. Show me what you can do." She had a virgin clit and only had sex with one other man. Jezebel built her up for this moment.

"Ain't nothing but a word." Danny Boy got on his knees. He didn't care about the floor being hard and getting his brand new jeans dirty. Eating Keisha out would put him one up over Clarence.

Jezebel took off her heels and took a kneeling position on the seat. She was enjoying her work.

Keisha tensed her body as Danny's face and hands got closer. It was too late to turn around. When he spread open her clit, she thought about calling the whole thing off.

"Just relax, this is the revenge you want," Jezebel whispered in her ear as she gently held Keisha's shoulders.

The first three licks made her eyes roll back in her head. "Umm," she moaned. She spread her legs wider and pushed her pussy toward Danny Boy. She didn't believe Jezebel when she told her how good having her clit licked would feel. "That feels good," she stated with an out of breath voice. She grabbed the side of the seat to regain some kind of control. It wasn't supposed to feel this good. Regaining control wasn't possible. Sensations of joy were running through her body.

Danny Boy was licking as fast as he could. Her screams were turning him on. On the strength that it was Keisha he was doing, he started cumming in his pants.

"Just enjoy it Keisha," Jezebel whispered in her ear. "Enjoy all the sensations." Jezebel started playing with her titties by cupping them from the bottom.

Before Keisha realized it, Jezebel was sucking on her titties and it felt good to her. Her breathing was out of control and all she could do was scream, "ooh" and "ahh". The more Jezebel sucked, the more she liked it. She didn't have any control and it felt good. It wasn't a weak feeling, it was powerful, because they were serving her.

Keisha screamed as loud as she could when her legs started to tremble. Her pussy started pulsating and letting out her cream. She never thought that an orgasm could feel so good.

Jezebel kissed her in the mouth, "That was beautiful Keisha. I know it felt good. Your screams made me cum too." She pulled Danny up. "That's all you get for now." The limo stopped in front of his house just as she was speaking.

Danny Boy was satisfied. Putting up an argument after all that wasn't in him. What mattered most to him was that he had one up on Clarence, he could get the pussy later. He figured they wanted him to spend some money before they gave up the pussy.

"You know you got to spend before you get in." Jezebel stuck her fingers in her pussy. Keisha wrapped herself up in her robe. "I'll find you tomorrow."

"A'ight, bet." He got out of the limo a satisfied man. The limo driver pulled off.

Keisha didn't know what to think. She did know that she was feeling better than she felt in a long time. The orgasm left her feeling flushed, yet powerful. What Jezebel did seemed like a natural thing and she even felt closer to her because of it. Keisha was welcoming the change and excitement and couldn't wait to see Clarence.

They hugged and kissed when the limo pulled off. Jezebel pulled out a big black rubber dick. They needed to satisfy their lust in a way that made them independent of men. More power to the sisters. They licked and played with each other as the limo rode all over the district.

Jezebel had herself a brand new sister and a half-completed mission. She had two more things to do: complete their plan and make Keisha a member of *The Clit*.

18

◆ ◆ ◆ ◆ ◆

Clarence met Kevin at the Pennsylvania Avenue spot at eleven o'clock. He just needed somebody to talk to. "Yo, Kev, what the fuck is going on?"

"It's the only thing the streets are talking about." Kevin saw a few pictures that were taken.

When Clarence woke up his e-mail was full of pictures. His cell and two-way were full of messages about the episode. "I can't believe Danny Boy did me like this. He knows how I feel about Keisha." He slammed his fist on the desk.

Kevin could only think of a few occasions that he saw Clarence mad. "What's up with you and Keisha? You feelin' her like that?"

Clarence put his nine on his desk. "Yeah man, it's that serious." Though he treated Kevin like his brother, he couldn't tell him the real deal. Clarence was pacing back and forth.

Kevin didn't know what to say, think or do. He never saw

his man act this way. Pain was written all over his face. He knew that Clarence had feelings for Keisha, but nobody knew just how deep they ran. All anyone knew was they were just cool in school.

"That motherfucka betrayed me after all I did for him. I even let him get away with talking about me like a bitch ass nigga, but I don't play this kinda shit."

"Damn Clarence, what the hell is wrong with you?" Kevin got in his path to make him get back in character. He could see that he wasn't about to calm down on his own.

"It's this simple." Clarence pulled a ring box out of his pocket and opened it. Kevin never saw a diamond that big up close. "Danny Boy knows that it's this serious. I told him last week."

Kevin knew what it all meant. All he could say was, "Damn, that's fucked up."

"I'm going to talk to him first when I see him at the club tonight." There wasn't a lot to it. "Danny Boy just crossed the line."

Clarence left, he had to get out of the city. He passed word to all that he would be at Club Platinum to see Danny Boy but first, he had to see Keisha. It was a good idea that he got out of the city to let himself cool off. He knew that no matter where he went that day, cats would be talking about what happened.

"I told you Keisha was coming back," Bambi hollered when she got in the BMW. Usually they didn't get together on Saturdays.

They met at a Hardee's restaurant parking lot. "The entire city is talking about it." Sally lit up a Black. "They say she and this other girl put on one hell of a show. What do you think it all means?" She wanted to hear the educated theory.

"Sally, let me hit that Black first."

"Is that why you didn't want to meet at your house? Does your husband know that you smoke Blacks?" Sally wanted Bambi to start keeping up on the buying tip because she was always leaving hers at the office. She handed her the Black.

Bambi took a small drag and let the smoke out. "Now I can really think. She's trying to make one of them kill the other."

"That's interesting. Her real beef is with Clarence, so if Danny Boy kills him, what does she do? If Clarence kills Danny Boy, what does she do?" She really knew the most logical answer; still, what would happen when it all came to a head, was no simple guess.

"She left the club with Danny Boy. She probably will get him to kill Clarence, since he is the one who betrayed her." She took her third drag off the Black and passed it back.

"So what happens next?"

Bambi stammered a bit, she was really caught up in the situation. "She'll probably get Danny Boy to rat him out. She might even just let him be." It was really a tough one.

"Now your educated ass can't think. You the one that said she would come back to get revenge." Sally just didn't know what to do.

"So what did you hear through the grapevine? What did your private snitches tell you?" She had her own privates as well.

"Word is that Clarence is mad as hell. He's going out to look for Danny Boy and they're supposed to meet at Club Platinum tonight. We have to be there."

This was the same thing she heard. "I don't think one of them is going to do the other with all of those witnesses. Clarence is definitely smarter than that." She figured that

Clarence was too smart to let Danny Boy get at him easily. This also provoked other thoughts.

"Well, it seems that Clarence has some serious feelings for Keisha after all. Clarence has to know that Keisha is playing him." They were just tossing around ideas.

"You know what, we're overlooking something. Keisha couldn't have pulled off that stunt last night by herself. That other chick, Jezebel, has something to do with this too."

"We have nothing on her but I did hear that she made a hell of an entrance at Danny Boy's spot yesterday." Sally hadn't given Jezebel much thought.

"So that means she's down with whatever Keisha is trying to do." This, Bambi was pretty sure of, it was obvious.

Sally came up with a conclusion. "Aw shit," she said while she banged her steering wheel. "This isn't good. Clarence is mad at Danny Boy, who at this moment has to be happier than Osama Bin Laden was on 9/11. Keisha is out to get the both of them, without pulling a trigger. She's turned into a scandalous bitch with a mission, and won't stop until it's accomplished. I like that girl. If she gets them they deserve it, but I have to try to stop her."

"So what can we do?"

"Club Platinum is going to be under heavy surveillance tonight so we'll be on the inside watching. All of the district is going to be there for the show."

Realistically, they didn't know what to do or think. It was going to be really hard to make the next call. Sally came up with one good idea that she could put into effect that might help.

Clarence called Keisha's dorm before he left the district. She told him what time to show up. He still had to wait until four o'clock, two hours later, to speak with her. James had to leave first.

When she got in his Suburban, she had a serious look on her face. She was acting like she didn't know that he was coming. She looked at him and said with an unexpressive manner, "What's up Clarence?"

Clarence pulled out the three pictures, one was of her dancing on the pole, one was of her doing a split and the last one was of her kissing Danny Boy.

"Like I said, what's up Clarence." It was a statement not a question. Her voice had a tone that said, "why are you asking me this."

This was a new attitude to him. "I want to know why you did all of that. Why did you do it with him?" He couldn't believe that she was acting like she didn't care.

"What does it matter Clarence?" she asked nonchalantly, looking at her fingernails.

He looked at her like she lost her mind.

"Payback's a bitch, ain't it?"

"So is all that he's saying true? He's telling the district that he ate your pussy." As cool as he was acting, his voice revealed that he was sincerely angry.

His pain started, her pain was ending and healing was beginning. "Yeah, he ate my pussy." Saying that he did a damn good job would be taking it a little too far.

He placed his left hand over his mouth as intense pain was running through him. In his arms, legs and chest he was experiencing a feeling that he never thought was possible. She was watching him from the corner of her eye and couldn't wait to tell Jezebel.

Pride made him close his eyes and internalize. He had a million questions and a million choices. Just letting the situation be wasn't one of them. What would a true playa do in a situation like this? He did all that he could do in the past not to battle with Danny Boy. For the same reason that he was truly loyal to Danny Boy, was the same reason that he felt like killing him. Going after Danny Boy would bring him down a few levels and he would still lose. His brain wasn't functioning. There was too much tension, too many emotions, too much crowding his mind, too many people knew, and there was too much love for Keisha.

Keisha let him think for about three minutes then she reached over and tugged on his jacket. "Look at me Clarence." He pulled his hand from over his face. She waited for him to make eye contact. He was holding his head sideways, toward the floor.

"Clarence, the only man that I love and want is you." It was a simple matter of pointing him in the right direction. It was a simple sentence that could do big things.

He straightened his head up. "Why did you do what you did?" His voice was low. He was also thinking that he really didn't have to kill her mother, there had to have been another way. He wanted to say this but there was no way, not now.

She was loving it. "I had to do it because of what you did. It's about respect."

"What the *fuck* did I do?" His eyes were watering; it was the anger that he couldn't hold anymore.

"You let me down Clarence, and it got my mother murdered. She was like a mother to you too." She said exactly what was on her mind.

"Maybe I saved your life." He said this on instinct because he didn't expect her to go there. The pain of guilt was coupled with the hurt he was already feeling.

"Maybe you did, maybe you didn't. You said you'd never to let me down but then you went and did it at the wrong time," she screamed back.

Clarence put his head back down on the steering wheel. In slow motion a vision of Karyn hitting the wall was going over and over. There wasn't any time for him to think, she was shooting at him, and he had to shoot back. From the moment they entered the house, he prayed for a way to keep from killing her. On many nights, he thought to himself that it would have been better to shoot Danny Boy before they got in the house but he wasn't able to force himself to do that. His loyalty was in the way.

"You still didn't have to do what you did. You put me out there in front of the whole district." He still had his head down.

"What about all the tricks you were with? I swallowed that shit. I was even cool with a few of them." She lied about the last part to stop him from saying that Danny Boy was his boy.

He couldn't argue, nor could he make a decision. She was absolutely on point.

"This is the new me, Clarence. Take it or leave it. If you can't handle it, it's best you step." She opened the door and started to get out.

"Hold up," he hollered before he even realized what he was saying. The gateway to his heart and soul was fully opened.

"I'm not going to listen to you and watch you act weak."

Acting like none of his buttons were pushed wasn't in him at the moment. She just hit him with a jab and an upper-cut. Too much happened for him to lose Keisha, again, especially to Danny Boy.

"Girl, you really gangsta. You win. Remember when we talked about getting married? Let's do the damn thing. That's all there is to that." He thought that he was fighting her back. Making her all his would be the only way to solve the problem and allow him to keep his respect in the streets.

"Save the bullshit Clarence!" Her feelings for him still had some strength but she had to will herself to stay on point and not allow herself to get hurt again. "I'm gone Clarence."

He grabbed her before she got a chance to get her body out of the door. Her right leg was in midair. "I got you a ring. Here, look." He reached in his pocket and showed her the box.

She got back in and closed the door. "So open it up. It better be tight or I'll never speak to you again." She leaned her back up against the door.

"It's the tightest one that they had in the store." He popped the box and she leaned toward him. His suspenseful expression didn't register any of the conversation that they just had.

Inside she was blown away. She planned to see if she could push him toward a marriage just as they talked about before. It was another part of the plan that worked itself out. She thought to herself that the rest of her plan would be easy.

She still had her back up against the door, acting like she was half interested. She wanted to ask him when he had purchased it but it really didn't matter.

She put her left hand out. "It's tight, put it on." Those words were a relief to him. He put the ring on her finger before she changed her mind and he sat back in his seat to relax. "I think you forgot something Clarence," she said with her hand dangling.

"Oh yeah." He grabbed her hand and kissed it. "Will you marry me Keisha?"

Her smile said that she couldn't have been any more content. Playing with him came to mind, just to see what he would do. "Ain't no sex until we get married Clarence." She just had to throw that in there.

"We get married in two weeks, at the club."

"We are partners in all your endeavors, just like we talked about." This was a major part of her plan.

"I love and trust you." He didn't know what he was saying. "No problem."

"Yes, I'll marry you Clarence." She leaned toward him and they kissed each other. She put all her energy into the kiss to make him feel like she belonged to him. It was easy. She let Jezebel become her strength and support system. She knew for sure that she was a new woman and that her feelings for him were in check. She kissed him passionately.

"I love you Clarence."

"What about ole boy?"

"Let me see your cell." He was all smiles. "Hey James, I have something to tell you. I'm getting married to Clarence. Yes, that's right, Clarence. He gave me a ring today. I'm sorry. Bye James. Don't come by anymore or call me. Remember, he has a gun." *Click.* She felt bad for a minute because James was truly a nice guy, but Clarence was where her heart was.

Clarence was really feeling what he had done but couldn't help but feel like he was played just a little bit. It wasn't like she cheated on him. To him, however, it was like he won the war to have the woman that he gave his heart to. He blamed himself for their breakup. The pain that he felt that day helped him to feel less guilty about killing her mother. It was a matter of damage control. With her as his wife, all would be all good especially because Danny Boy hadn't fucked her. He planned to say that she used Danny Boy to get him back in her life.

To Keisha, it was all just a matter of time. She got out of the truck with a fresh feeling. She had confidence that Jezebel and Jessica would play their parts. Once she and Clarence were married, the foundation would be complete. Revenge would only be a matter of making him do a few things.

The sophistication of the trap that Clarence entered into

had him totally fooled. There wasn't a soul on the planet that could have warned him. He felt that he knew Keisha and that she totally belonged to him. A man loving a woman that he had done wrong was a lesson that was about to be put on him. What's obvious is hard for many to see, especially when love is involved. He was too close to Keisha to see her real intentions.

"What's up big sister? I got that ass," Keisha hollered as she came in the room.

Jezebel put the *Wall Street Journal* down to hear what she had to say. "You got to tell me every detail. Don't leave out a thing."

Keisha kicked off her sneakers and jumped on Jezebel's bed. "Clarence was so hurt that he was about to cry. He had pictures from last night." Digital pictures travel fast in the information age. This was something she didn't think would happen but it was a beautiful thing. She kind of liked the pictures. They would be great in her photo album.

"I saw you about to get out of the truck twice." This was how she knew her student was playing him real good.

"You know I had to put the bluff down. I had to make him talk to me. And get this, he already bought a ring and proposed." She couldn't help but to wonder what he would have done if last night never happened. She showed Jezebel the ring.

"So, when is the wedding?" Deep down, Jezebel didn't think that Keisha was going to be able to make him go that far, but she was impressed. The ring was all that by any standard.

"It's a week after we take exams. He wants to get married at the club, right on the stage. He's really trying to make a statement." She couldn't stop staring at the ring. She was imagining how nice it would be if all the negatives never happened.

"Girl, it's going to be a hot ass summer. I'm gonna have Danny Boy pick me up tonight. It should take me about a week to have him in position." She planned to only tell him that she was a student. She was using the spot that Calvin rented for her as an address. She wasn't worried about him showing up because she had him right where she wanted. He wouldn't breathe without her telling him he could so popping up, unexpectedly, was a definite no-no.

"When they meet up at the club tonight, all hell is going to break loose. So neither of us is going to catch a stray bullet because they can't have guns in the club."

They high-fived each other followed with a big kiss. One thing led to another. Keisha was practically a member of *The Clit*.

♦ ♦ ♦ ♦ ♦

Danny Boy was feeling himself so much that he celebrated all night and into the next day. He was on
such a high since Jezebel and Keisha dropped him off. It was
over thirty hours since he slept. He was drinking and smoking coke, which had him wired to the max. He told all his
boys how he ate Keisha's pussy and how she got freaked.
They wanted to know all the details because they followed
the limo and only could imagine what was happening after
the performance they gave. It was eleven o'clock at night
when he got to Jezebel's condo.

"Hi Danny Boy. It took you long enough to get here."
She couldn't let Danny Boy meet her at school, or let him
know that she roomed with Keisha. To him, they were just
strippers.

Danny Boy slowly walked in the door. "You look good
enough to eat." Jezebel smiled and closed the door.

She was wearing a tight, white leather cat suit. Very little was left to the imagination. Her fresh shoulder length

micro braids made her appearance complete – she looked enticing.

"Don't you have something for me? You know I got to have mines." When she spoke to him on the phone, she sent him to a jeweler to pick up a bracelet she picked out. She made him do it just because she knew that she could and he would. She also told him about Clarence and Keisha showing up at the club together.

He reached in his pocket. The piece set him back about four stacks. He felt it was worth it. He had the district screaming his name. Plus, she spent big money on him last night. "How can you afford this spot? This motherfucker is full of good shit."

"It's simple, good pussy ain't cheap, and cheap pussy ain't good. I'm a hustler baby, just like you." She could see he was tired.

He sat down in her loveseat. He would have been in the bed, asleep, if he didn't have to show up at the club. Clarence putting out the word that he was bringing Keisha to the club was a direct challenge.

She sat down next to him. "When we get to the club, I need you to be on your best behavior. Clarence is probably going to start something." She took the bracelet out of his hand and put it on.

"Fuck Clarence." He wanted to see the look on Clarence's face. It was about time that he was pulled down a notch or two.

She wrapped her arms around his neck and kissed his cheek. "Thank you for the bracelet, I love it. I can't wait to repay you."

"I can't wait either but right now we have to get to the club. Let's go. All of my people are waiting." He would have tried to fuck her on the spot if he could have focused but Clarence was heavy on his mind. His entire body was numb from all the cocaine in his system and there was no way he was getting it up.

Danny Boy felt like he was about to become the playa he envisioned. With his newfound respect, he felt invincible. He even thought about robbing a few suppliers that would- n't deal with him directly. His true self wanted to emerge because he felt he had an edge on Clarence. Now, no matter what he did, people wouldn't compare him to Clarence. By eating Keisha, and bragging about it, he'd disrespected Clarence. Even if he married her, people would always say that Danny Boy ate the pussy. This feeling he had was worth plenty.

Sally wouldn't say it was her, though she knocked on the door about ten times, really hard. She was in that kind of mood.

"This better be good," Keisha hollered before she answered the door. "What are you doing here Sally? I'm try- ing to get dressed. I'm sorry." She just remembered her manners. "Please come in." Sally was the last person she wanted to see.

Sally walked in slowly. Looking around the room, as she usually did, the first thing she noticed was the change in Keisha's demeanor and appearance. She turned toward her when she got in the middle of the floor.

"What's going on Keisha? When did you start strippin'?" She was admiring her tight pink mini-skirt.

Keisha closed the door. "You don't act like you came to tell me something about my mother's killer or is this purely a pleasure call?" She made her way to where Sally was.

Sally was feeling Keisha's way of changing the subject. For now it was good. "We both know that Clarence killed your mother."

Keisha showed her the ring. "You keep saying that, but if he murdered her, do you really think I'd marry him?"

"I'm still thinking about charging you with accessory after the fact for protecting Clarence from prosecution."

"If that makes you feel good, then go ahead, but I know better Sally. If you could prove that I knew he did it, you would have already arrested him. You can stop bluffin'." Keisha's voice was telling her to leave.

Sally's temperature went up a little. "Since you think I'm bluffin', I plan to arrest you if one of them kills the other." Her precinct two-way started buzzing.

"I'm not going to let Clarence kill Danny Boy, and I sure ain't going to let Danny Boy catch Clarence slippin'."

"Did I hear my name being called?" Clarence walked through the door without knocking. Keisha walked over to him like he was her savior and they kissed like they were newlyweds.

Sally said to herself, "Ain't this a bitch."

"Dag Sally, you all over the place, aren't you." Clarence was feeling that good.

Sally started walking toward the door. They stepped out of the way while they were giggling. "No, I just wanted to let her know the progress of her mother's murder investigation."

"Bye Sally," Keisha commented with sarcasm in her voice.

Sally was almost to the door. "By the way, is Danny Boy's tongue worth my time?" She shut the door before they could speak.

Clarence prepared himself for that comment. He wasn't expecting to hear it from Sally, nor see her.

Keisha hugged Clarence around his neck. "Don't worry about that, baby." She kissed him on his lips. "I belong to you." She was holding him tightly. "Let me finish my make-up, baby." She let him go.

He took a rest on Keisha's bed. To amuse himself, he started looking through *Stacy*, from Triple Crown Publications. "What was that all about?"

"She wants to arrest all of us for my mother's murder." He looked up at her. "She says she'll be at the club so you can't act up. Plus, if anything kicks off, there will be plenty of witnesses, so just be cool." She was checking his facial expressions in her mirror.

"I just want him to know who's the man." He started pacing. "I also want him, and the district, to know that you belong to me." He was doing his best to act like the situation wasn't bothering him. He told all that he would be the one getting the pussy, keeping it, and marrying it.

"I think we should live together Clarence."

"You know we can do that when you get ready. We can do that tomorrow if you want to."

"No, not that fast. We'll be busy making love tonight and tomorrow. I need to feel you up in me Clarence. My pussy has been calling your name for awhile." She changed her plans because things were going too good.

He stopped pacing. "What's up with all of that?" They talked about waiting for sex, now she changed her mind.

She got out of her chair. With her hands on his chest, she put in work. "I need you to forgive me for what I did. I would have never fucked him. This pussy is just for you. I also forgive you." Halle Berry couldn't have acted out the part any better.

"I forgive you, boo, but all that ain't necessary." What she was saying, doing and how she was acting was exactly what he needed to make him feel that he was making the right moves.

"I want us to get off to a great start, just like we used to talk about. I'm your down-ass chick, no matter what happens." She got on her tippy-toes to kiss him. "I love you Clarence."

"I love you too Keisha. It's almost twelve o'clock and we have to hit the club." He was anxious and impatient.

Just before Sally arrived, Keisha received a call from Jezebel. She knew that they were already at the club. It would look like each one was supporting her man. So far, their plan was going perfectly; however, they weren't certain there weren't going to be any guns in the club. Whatever else went down, they felt they could deal with, since they both had control of their peeps.

"Damn, damn, damn," Sally hollered as she banged her hands against the dashboard. "Drive, Bambi we have to get to the club."

"What's wrong? I two-wayed you about Clarence."

"I had her going, then he came through the door. That ain't the same Keisha we met a year ago." Sally hated that she wasn't able to get in Keisha's head.

"So what did she tell you?"

"She told me she has a plan."

"That's what she said?" Bambi didn't think about what she asked.

"Not in so many words. She's setting them up to turn against each other. It's the ultimate revenge. Start driving." She lit up a Black.

"I told you." She started giggling.

"Since you know everything, tell me what's going to happen." Sally looked at her with a smirk on her face.

"My bad, but you ain't got to act all stank." She forgot about the mission at hand.

"We got to figure out what she's trying to make happen before it goes down. She must want Danny Boy to kill Clarence."

"If you wanted that, wouldn't you be with the killer so you won't catch a bullet?" Bambi figured there was more to it because of the show last night.

"So maybe she's going to be with the both of them. That will definitely turn them against each other, cause one to kill the other." Sally thought for a second. "Then one would be living."

"Then she could kill the last one living. But she might as well kill both of them herself without even being seen." Bambi took the Black out of Sally's hand. They would be at the club in a few minutes.

"We have to remember that Jezebel has a part in this. They have plotted something really good. Plus, they know the police are watching so they're being overly cautious. Keisha told me that I was bluffing about arresting her." This was the first time a person had the balls to tell her that. "Keisha seems to be really serious about this thing but I can't figure it out. Let's just see what happens at the club. Can't too much be happening because they can't have a shootout in there." That was easy for her to say.

"Somebody might sneak a gun into the club."

"The owner said that he's checking everybody and is going to have extra security." Sally pushed him.

"All we can do is wait, Sally. The whole city knows about the situation. She's probably going to be with Clarence. Our people say that Danny Boy has Jezebel with him." Bambi accepted that the situation was too complex and things were happening too fast for her to make a prediction.

"I just don't like it. She's about to get away with something right under my nose." She lit up another Black and shook her head as she took a long drag. "Let's just see what happens."

Sally had a lust for catching killers. The feeling it gave her was almost as good as having an orgasm. Preventing a murder was also taken seriously. Usually that was easier than solving a murder but this situation was different. She had no idea of what might happen or who it may involve other than her two prime suspects. There were too many choices for her to be able to make the kind of move she wanted to make, arrest somebody for murder or attempted murder. It wouldn't be happening tonight but she would try her best to keep up with Keisha.

20

◆　◆　◆　◆　◆

When Clarence, Keisha and their entourage arrived at the club, it was one o'clock. Ten of his top people were with them on the inside and five stayed outside in case of an emergency. Clarence was prepared for whatever popped off.

The owner wouldn't let them in until he talked to Clarence. "I got to scan you and all your people for guns and weapons Clarence." Usually he let Clarence bypass the metal detector. "I have to check her also. We also checked Danny Boy and his people."

"We're all clean. It's your house." Clarence expected such. It was nice to know that Danny Boy was already there.

The Platinum was over capacity, and the VIP was overflowing. Instead of there being ten police officers for security, there were twenty. Snoop Dogg's "Drop it Like it's Hot" was moving the crowd.

Two of Clarence's soldiers walked through the door first. They were dressed in green and gold sweat suits. When they bobbed their heads up and down, it meant things were good. Before they gave the signal they scanned the club. They already knew where Danny Boy was sitting. He was sitting by the stage so he could be close to the entrance.

Clarence's appearance put the club on pause. Keisha walking in behind him caused people to start whispering and talking. They were just walking and trying to keep it as normal as possible.

Still drunk, Danny Boy stood up and his people stood up with him. Jezebel wrapped her arms around him to keep him still. He turned a bottle of Moet up to his mouth and started swallowing.

Clarence had it on his mind to just show his face and pass through. He only stopped when he saw Danny Boy standing up. It was the glaring that made him stop.

Along with that, people stopped dancing and the music stopped playing. All eyes were on Clarence and Danny Boy. Clarence and his entourage weren't even twenty yards from the entrance and people cleared the path between them. Security came as close as possible.

"Just be easy, Danny Boy," Jezebel whispered in his ear. He finished off the Moet. "You can get him later."

Danny Boy looked back at her with disgust and pushed her back. "Sit down and shut up, bitch."

She took her seat without saying a word or changing her expression. Being called a bitch wasn't appreciated. Her ex-pimp used to call her a sorry-ass bitch.

Danny Boy also told his boys not to move. His intentions were to take Clarence on, one-on-one, right in front of everybody. Clarence coming to the club was just like disrespecting his turf. Clarence showing up with Keisha was like saying all of last night meant nothing. Danny Boy was not about to let his work be denigrated and disrespected. He couldn't see the situation any other way. Danny Boy planned his course of action before he got to the club.

He walked across the dance floor. There were about forty yards between them. "Meet me in the center, Clarence."

Sally and Bambi were in the VIP, directly above where Clarence was standing. She knew security wasn't going to let them fight.

Clarence let Keisha's hand go and started walking toward the center. Security started walking toward the center, too.

"I feel good off that pussy last night," Danny Boy hollered to disrespect Clarence. He took one last drink from the Moet bottle. Keisha and Kevin stopped LCP from rushing the dance floor. Four security officers kept Danny Boy's crew at bay.

"Well, you won't be eating that anymore or anything else that makes money in this town." Clarence was walking slowly to maintain control. He planned to use Danny Boy's anger against him. "You'll be broke real soon, you clucka."

Danny Boy knew that Clarence had that much power in the district. Though he was walking fast, security was about to stop him. "Fuck you bitch," he hollered as he threw the Moet bottle. He looked like a quarterback throwing a touchdown pass.

The bottle was sailing directly at Clarence's head with a perfect aim and spin, like it was a football. Nobody in the club was blinking. Keisha closed her eyes as many hollered for Clarence to duck. In less than a second, the butt of the bottle would be at Clarence's forehead. With Danny Boy's strength, many already envisioned the bottle knocking Clarence clear the fuck out.

Clarence couldn't just duck. He feared that the bottle would hit Keisha or one of his people. As he dipped, he put his right hand up with his palm open to slow the bottle down. A loud "*thack*" echoed through the club when the bottle hit the palm of his hand. The velocity of the bottle was so strong that Clarence's arm was pushed back far enough for the middle of the bottle to be at his shoulder. Once Clarence absorbed the impact, he pushed himself back up and the bottle came forward. Clarence caught it with his left, and tossed it back into his right, and slammed it into the floor and said, "That's your ass, Danny Boy," while pointing his right index finger at him.

Sally was the first one to start clapping. She was wearing a black, two-piece skirt suit with gray pinstripes. Bambi joined in immediately. She had to admit that she just witnessed one hell of a show. It only took seconds for the rest of the club to start clapping.

Danny Boy was hollering and cursing at Clarence. He was also trying to break free from the security officers.

Clarence was shaking his head with a walk that said he was satisfied. He came just to be seen and ended up making his mark, again, without even trying. He felt totally satisfied with all aspects of the situation. With his ego salvaged, it was time to go.

Danny Boy was still struggling with security when Clarence and his crew were walking out the door. The first thing he noticed when he turned around was that Jezebel was nowhere in sight. He was so angry with the situation that he decided to say fuck her. It was time for him to get some sleep. Security let him leave after Clarence left the premises.

Sally and Bambi made sure they watched Clarence and his crew drive off. "What do you think we should do?" Sally asked Bambi.

"We could pick up Danny Boy and Clarence for their own protection." It was past her bedtime by several hours.

Sally ignored the comment because they didn't operate that way in the district. "Those girls worked the hell out of those boys. They planned the entire thing."

Bambi looked over at her with sleepy eyes. "I disagree.

"What makes you say that?" Sally quizzed.

"I saw Jezebel disappear after Danny Boy started walking toward the dance floor. If she cared about him, she wouldn't have missed the action. She's the one to watch."

"Take me home Sally. We can talk about this tomorrow or Monday at work." Her brain shut down.

Sally stopped talking. She didn't expect to see a murder but was intrigued with what she did witness. Something big was about to go down and first on her agenda was to find everything she could about Jezebel. The fact that she was Keisha's roommate made it a simple matter. She saw the picture in Keisha's room.

Keisha went from being the good little girl to a woman with a vendetta who pitted two cats against each other. The way she did it was the most impressive thing. Nice girls just don't flip the script the way she did. Jezebel had to be the source. Maybe that would reveal the rest of the plan.

Keisha couldn't wait to get Clarence's clothes off. She was caressing his dick as he was unlocking the condo door. "Slow down Keisha, we got time." He wanted her, but security had his mind preoccupied. He was in a serious beef.

"I can't help it Clarence, I've been waiting too long for this. I've been horny since you put this ring on my finger." To her, what Danny Boy had caused was just perfect. They were walking in.

"Hold up." Clarence pulled his nine out and whispered for her to unlock the door. Slowly, he checked every room and closet as she waited in the living room. She knew how to play her position and he was not about to be surprised.

"It's all clear, come on back," he hollered from the bedroom.

It was about time, she thought to herself. She threw her jacket on the couch and proceeded in that direction. "I'm coming Clarence." She was surprised to see him already in the bed. Karyn White's "Superwoman" started playing. Speakers were all over the room.

"I hope you like my bedroom." Candles were all around and a plasma television was on the ceiling, just above the bed. The walls were covered with mirrors, the little square kind and Egyptian musk incense had the atmosphere and tone just right.

"With me, Clarence, there is nothing that you can do wrong." She was taken off her square by the look of the room. What she said was something she practiced for quite some time.

"Can I get my own private dance?" he said sitting up in the bed admiring how she looked. He regretted that he didn't have a pole in the room, but one would be put in soon, he thought.

The request brought her back to reality. "I was thinking the same thing." She was impressed that he paid so much attention to details. Dancing hadn't been on her agenda. She didn't mind, it was just another part of the mission.

To the beat, she started moving her hips and waving her hands in the air. She didn't have much clothing on so it would be a short dance. Clarence was lying on his side and thinking how good she looked. She came close to him and took her top off. There was only enough of it to cover her breasts. She dropped it right in front of him. Her nipples were standing up and Clarence's dick hardened from looking at her perfect breasts.

Keisha placed her hands over her head to give him a better view of her breasts. Through the sheets, she could see that he was aroused. Getting turned on herself, she made a few dips, turned around and started shaking her ass for him. She had her hand on the zipper of her skirt. Once she unzipped it, all that was necessary was a pull. She was standing before him with nothing on. She stood there for a while so he could take in all of her body.

Keith Sweat's "Make It Last Forever" came on. That was her favorite of all time.

She kicked off her shoes and Clarence slid over. The satin sheets felt great to her. She got on her knees and pulled the top sheet back. She couldn't believe how good he looked with his clothes off. "I'm going to make this a night for you to remember Clarence."

She made him lay back by putting her finger on his shoulder. While inching closer, she caressed his chest. Her fingers were enjoying the hardness and firmness of his chest and stomach. She whispered, "I love you," in his ear.

He touched the backside of her arm. Sensations went through her body from his gliding touch. Her pussy moistened. Instinctively, she grabbed his tool and started to massage it. To keep herself from letting out a moan, she started licking the inside of his ear.

"I'm going to make you the happiest woman in the district," he said while caressing her shoulders. His voice was turning her on.

She couldn't believe how good it was feeling to touch him without any limitations. Things that Jezebel told her came to mind and it was hard to focus.

With enthusiasm, she kissed him down to his belly button. She needed him to stop touching her so she could maintain her focus. She was supposed to be seducing him, not being seduced. She stopped kissing him when she got to his pubic hairs. She was still caressing his shaft.

She sat up on her knees and said, "I'm going to show you

how much I love you, Clarence. I'll do anything to make you happy." Her eyes and expression said the rest.

They just looked at each other. The intensity of the moment kept him from saying anything. All he could think to do was thank God. He knew at that very moment, he had truly given his heart to her. He was blown away.

"Umm," came out of his lips as she licked the head of his dick. Her right hand squeezed while she licked and sucked. She was keeping her mouth moist just like Jezebel taught her. "That feels good, Keisha."

She more she sped up the more noise he made. It was feeling like the best blowjob that he ever had. She stopped to take him to the next phase.

"I need to feel you inside of me baby, I need it *now!*" she said, never letting his dick go. It was time to work his mind a little more as she laid on her back.

With him on top of her, she wrapped her legs around his waist, and guided his eight inches into her love nest. "That feels good. Make love to me Clarence."

Clarence pushed into her slowly. He could feel the walls of her pussy and all its moistness. It was tight, wet and warm.

"That's it Clarence, real slow. That feels so good." She was nibbling on his ear. With all her strength, she put as much pressure as she could on his dick, using the pussy exercises she learned. "This pussy belongs to you."

Clarence sped up, he couldn't help it. He didn't think that having sex with her was going to be that good but was definitely surprised. "That feels good, go faster." She kept the pressure up with her pussy and started throwing it back at him to add to his pleasure. "Oh shit, I'm cumming!" She dug her fingernails into his back. "Fuck me harder!"

Clarence exploded inside of her. The strength of his ejaculation caused him to stop stroking. He never experienced a nut like that. She started kissing, "I can't wait to be your wife. I love you."

Thinking about Jezebel helped her to maintain her focus. She wasn't anywhere near an orgasm when she said it. She wanted to make him feel like he never felt before. Without Jezebel, she would have fallen deeper in love with him. Sex with him was far more pleasing than she bargained for. She took it as a plus to go with her mission. She came just after he got his. Later that night, she got a few more, while she tried to fuck and suck him dry.

Clarence didn't know what hit him. It was the best sex that he ever experienced. It was also with a woman he loved, admired and respected. It seemed like she knew more about sex than he did. He went to sleep exhausted. When he woke up, she had breakfast already prepared.

"Good morning sleepy head. You look cute when you're sleeping." She placed a breakfast tray over his lap. There were pancakes, apple juice, half a grapefruit and blueberry syrup. "My future husband has to keep his strength up."

He sat up against the pillows. "Girl, you tried to kill me last night. I think you took some Viagra. You acted like you were on a mission." He was thinking that she was trying to keep him from fucking anybody else.

"So am I marrying a man that can't hang?" She laughed with an innocent look on her face. "I told you that I planned to do all things to you and for you."

He touched her chin and kissed her lips. "I'll just take my vitamins." They laughed.

"As your future wife, we have to talk about a few things."

He dipped a few slices of pancake into the syrup. "Wassup baby?"

"We need to talk about the money that you're making and you getting out of the game." She got off the bed and started pacing.

He looked up at her. "I ain't been in the game but a year.

I can't even buy alcohol yet. What's up with that?" Retiring was not in his plans.

"Well, if my father retired and done the right things with his money, my mother would be here today."

"I ain't feeling retirement yet but I do need to do something with my money." How to handle his money had been the big question on his mind for some time now.

"How much money do you think you need Clarence? Cats are going to start trying to rob you soon. If you think you need more, let's make more, then leave the district." Most of what she was saying was a charade.

"When you wanted me to work for your father you didn't say a thing about retiring." He finished half of his breakfast. Retirement was out of the question.

"My Daddy did numbers, you're a drug dealer. He didn't have beefs and have to deal with as many problems."

"I grant you that but I'm not ready to retire. We can talk bout what to do with the money because I consider you a partner." This was his way of avoiding an argument.

She sat on the bed with an attitude. "Well, Daddy put all his assets into a trust and corporation so he could invest like he wanted to. Plus, it all passed to me without the state getting a dime for probate."

Clarence wrapped the sheet around himself and crawled to the end of the bed. "He put his what in what?"

She put her feet against the floor. "Everything he had was in a trust, so the police could never take his shit. Jessica schooled him on it and set it up for him. That's why he sent her to college."

"I don't understand." He sat down beside her. "Tell me what she did for him."

"We used a corporation to protect the money and to invest in things. We own a lot of stores in the district that people don't know we own. Many corporations have privacy attached to them, like in Nevada." She was feeding him slowly. "It's all mine now and it'll be ours when we get married."

"We have to go to see Jessica as soon as possible, like today, so we can get started." He got up and headed toward the shower.

"I need to run to the store. Where are the keys to the truck?" She planned to make him wait to see Jessica. There was plenty of time for that.

"Go ahead." He turned the shower on.

"What do you want for dinner?" She was grabbing his keys off the dresser. He didn't answer so she went into the bathroom. She had to open the shower door to ask him again. "What do you want for dinner?"

"So you gon' spoil me like that?"

"We do all things together, with no secrets. Right?"

"That's right. Whatever you want to eat." Clarence had other things on his mind. She dipped.

Her part of the mission was almost complete. His mind and heart were in the palm of her hand. She didn't have total control of him, but just enough to suit her needs. In a few weeks she'd be able to pull him up by telling him exactly what was on her mind.

Clarence felt ready to take things to a brand new level. Last night made him think Keisha was the best thing that ever happened to him. There would be no more women and one-night stands. Her sex put all the others to shame and knowing what to do with money meant the world to him. There was no telling what they could accomplish together. With him making the money, and her handling it, the sky was the limit.

◆ ◆ ◆ ◆ ◆

21

◆ ◆ ◆ ◆ ◆

"Good morning Mr. Jacobs." Keisha was on her way back to Clarence's condo but she needed to put down some game first.

"Good morning to you Keisha. You sure look sexy in that outfit this Sunday morning." Mr. Jacobs was in his sixties and had been flirting with Keisha since she turned thirteen and started blooming. His respect for her family kept him at bay.

"Thank you, Mr. Jacobs. I just need to buy some Tylenol." Tylenol had nothing to do with her visit.

"Here you go." Mr. Jacobs filled prescriptions for Keisha's family for years. He owned a chain of pharmacies in the district. It was all that he had going for him. He worked seven days a week.

"How much do I owe you?"

"That'll be two ninety-five." He couldn't take his eyes off her outfit.

"Here's a five." She caressed his hand when she took the bottle. He brightened up. "Keep the change."

"Thank you sweetheart. You're such an angel."

She did a sexy finger-fanning wave when she left out of the door, "Bye Mr. Jacobs." She'd be calling him later to get what she really wanted.

When she got back to the condo, Clarence was gone. She planned to spend the entire day at his spot to spoil him. She took a shower and put on the extra clothes she had with her. It was time to make that phone call.

"Jacobs Pharmacy," he answered on the fourth ring.

"Mr. Jacobs, this is Keisha," she purred with a sexy voice.

A big smile came to his face. "Yes baby, what can I do for you?" He was feeling young again.

"I can do something for you if you do something for me. I promise you'll be satisfied."

"Well baby, what are you talking about? You know I ain't got no money. What's on your mind?" A vision of her ass popped in his head. That ass turned him on for the longest.

"I don't want your money. You can get some of this pussy and if you're good, I might even suck your dick."

He started rocking back and forth. "Just tell me what you want baby, and when you want it." He was almost willing to find some money to pay her.

"I'll call you tomorrow. Bye sweetheart." She hung up the phone.

It was four o'clock in the afternoon and Danny Boy woke with a splitting headache and hangover. He couldn't remember how he got home. Shortly after he left the club, he fell asleep in the car and his people carried him into the house.

Clarence and Keisha were the first people that came to his mind. He felt that they set him up. Jezebel had some questions to answer also. He vowed to kill Clarence. What Clarence said meant the same thing to him. It was a must that he make the first move and not get fucked up in the process. Since he was on a mission, he figured he might as well get Keisha and Jezebel too.

It took a few hours for him to find the most unexpected of assailants to do the job.

"Yo, Skull, I've been looking for you all day." Danny Boy had been to every abandoned building in the city, and places where base heads hung out.

Skull opened his eyes. He thought that someone came to put him out of his misery. His two hundred and forty pound frame had shrunken to one hundred and eighty. He couldn't believe who was looking at him.

"What the fuck you want?" Bad memories came back to him. The news about him traveled fast. When he heard the news, he laughed all that he wanted.

"I got some work for you. Here are a few grams on good faith." Danny Boy threw him three grams of crack, already cut into small pieces and ready to be smoked.

Skull stood up and walked over to the window. He saw Danny Boy's Benz and a few boys around it. He didn't recognize the other rides. Looking out the window was his way of avoiding looking at the package but it didn't work for long. His taste buds watered when he looked at the creamy whiteness of the cocaine. Acting weak in front of Danny Boy was out of the question.

"I can't help you, I'm a walking dead man." He already knew what Danny Boy wanted.

"I can change that, kid. It's a brand new day in the district. I'll make sure all your debts are paid."

Skull could hardly think straight with the cocaine in his hands, it was calling his name. He knew that he wouldn't be able to argue with Danny Boy for long. Whatever he was offering, he had to take it. Even if it was an ounce.

"I don't know, Clarence has a lot of soldiers."

"I'll pay you twenty thousand if you can get him before the week is out. That'll be enough to start paying off the people you robbed." Danny Boy was one of the few that were bold enough to find Skull. Most drug dealers wouldn't venture into certain abandoned buildings where hordes of cluckas were. The insides of the buildings were always dark but Danny Boy related to base heads.

"When do I get paid?" He was hoping to get half up front or just a little.

"As soon as you get it done."

"We have one problem." Skull still hadn't looked at him.

"What's that?"

"I don't have a gun."

Danny Boy pulled a package from under his jacket. There were two nines and a case of bullets. "Your problem is solved. If you get the job done, I'll put you back in the crew if you handle it this week. You'll be my head of security." Danny Boy dropped the package on the mattress.

Skull looked at him and they made eye contact and stared at each other. It was like time stopped. Danny Boy knew that the offer of redemption meant a lot.

Skull looked back out the window. "I'll be holding you to your word."

"Word is bond, Skull. Here's a thousand dollars." Danny Boy started walking out.

"D & C needs you."

Skull walked over to the package to see what he had. The nines felt good in his hands. He put the package back down and walked back over to the window. By the time he got there, he had his pipe in his hand and was warming the tip with a lighter. Before Danny Boy and his boys pulled out, Skull was sucking his glass dick.

Danny Boy made up his mind to be a playa. He was regretting that he lost his temper at the club. After thinking about it, he felt that it was himself, not Clarence, that made him look bad. Slowly, he was learning that his position required that he have more control of his actions.

If it weren't for his status, he would have hunted Clarence down himself. That wouldn't be cool. He wasn't a banger anymore. In his position it was all about staying clean while letting others do his dirty work. These are things that Clarence kept reiterating to him. His plan was rather simple, have Skull kill Clarence, kill Skull then take Clarence's slack.

"Drop It Like It's Hot, Drop It Like It's Hot." It was Danny Boy's favorite ring tone. When the caller ID showed who was calling, he thought that it might be a mistake. He was still in his Benz, heading to Virginia with his boys, to chill for a couple of days.

"What?" Danny Boy stated with authority.

"Hey man, we need to meet somewhere so we can talk." Clarence was at his Pennsylvania spot.

"You started a war, and now you want to talk." He turned the music all the way down so his boys could hear the conversation. "What kind of game are you playing, *Clarence?*"

"What good is it going to accomplish if one of us kill the other? Sally will definitely make an arrest. So when do we meet?" Clarence was trying to do the best and right thing for the present. A few certified killers volunteered to knock off Danny Boy and all his people but they were the last alternatives.

"I don't know man. You threatened me at the club, and all of a sudden my supplier has put me on hold until Thursday." Danny Boy felt like playing with him a bit but what he said about his supplier was the truth.

"So what you want, an apology before we meet and call a truce?" Clarence raised his voice. "I'm not your supplier, what I got to do with that?"

Mentioning the part about the comment in the club would be a little childish. "An apology would be nice."

"So you want to be slick. It sounds like you're playing games. If you apologize, I'll apologize." When the music was turned down he figured that others were listening. He was tempted to mention the bottle being thrown.

"I don't think we need a truce, I ain't trying to kill you. You aren't trying to kill me, are you?"

"No. Since you feel that way, let's call a truce. I apologize, if that's what you want."

"Well I'm not, I'll be back on Thursday." *Click.* They all laughed at Clarence.

Clarence felt that he put forth the best shot that he could have. It now became a matter of survival. If he didn't get Danny Boy, Danny Boy was sure to get him. It would be less than forty-eight hours that Danny Boy had to live. Clarence planned to be out of town the entire time. That way he would have an airtight alibi. None of his people would know what was happening. Sally was too slick for that.

Clarence called an emergency meeting. He needed to talk to all of his top people. He told them that he was taking Keisha out of town for a few days and left Kevin in charge. It was ten o'clock when the meeting ended. He called Keisha to tell her that he was coming home.

Skull was across the street in a cab waiting for Clarence to come out. He was watching them for three hours. To keep the cabby happy, he gave him two hundred dollars for his time. Finally, the light upstairs went out which meant the meeting was over. He got out of the cab to make it across the street before they came out to get into their vehicles. With thirty-two shots, he figured he'd be able to easily put two in Clarence.

Before any of them came out of the building, Skull made

it to the other side of the street and was walking up the block. His plan was to walk by and wait a few minutes, a few stores down, if necessary. When he walked by the door he saw a few of them about to come out of the building. He sped up so he could hurry up and turn around.

The bodyguards came out first and Kevin was right behind them.

Skull was three car-lengths away. He took two more steps then turned around. He saw Clarence coming out of the building.

Clarence looked to his left and recognized the figure. "That's Skull," he said in a voice just loud enough to alert Kevin. "It's a hit." The hand movement and stance alerted him.

The bodyguards and Kevin only looked at his back and didn't pay attention to him turning around. Clarence was moving back into the building, pulling his gun out but Skull was already pulling the triggers. *Boom, boom.* A deafening sound was heard repeatedly before anybody knew what happened. A bullet caught Kevin in the arm before he could get back in the store. The two bodyguards got behind cars in the street to shield themselves from being shot, but to zero in on Skull, as well. Skull started running away down the block but the bodyguards couldn't get clear shots because there were too many people on the street running for cover. Skull was moving too fast for them to catch up. Crack heads tend to have that extra speed going for them.

Kevin was taken to the emergency room where the bullet was removed. It would be a matter of time before he healed, but in the meantime, he had to deal with the police and their questions about what happened. Hospitals always alerted the police when they received gunshot victims to see if their injuries were a random act of violence or retaliation from a beef.

It was twelve o'clock when Clarence got back to the condo and Keisha was up waiting on him. She was sitting on the couch with a worried look on her face.

"Are you okay?" she asked as she walked toward him. "I heard about the shootout." She was glad to know that he wasn't the one shot.

"Thanks, boo. I'm okay but we have to talk. We're going to stay in Maryland for a few days. That was Danny Boy's work." Essentially Clarence's plans didn't change. What happened let him know that he made the right decision.

"Okay, we can stay at Jessica's house." Keisha was tired. She was truly worried about Clarence and was relieved when he came home. She cancelled the candlelight dinner she planned. It was cool because her plan was working better than expected.

"I'd rather get a few hotel rooms but we still have to go see Jessica about the business we talked about. I got one and a half million for her to incorporate and invest. In case something happens to me, I want my mother to be taken care of. She'll be going on vacation in the morning."

Clarence wasn't about to lose the war. He came too far to fall now. "Get dressed Keisha, we have to ride."

Keisha did as she was told.

A slip by his people almost cost him his life. If he weren't a detailed person, he and his people would have been full of holes. He knew the police, and Sally, would be looking for him to ask all kinds of questions, so it was a good time to lay low. In less than two weeks, all problems would be solved. His mother was put on the first thing leaving town.

22

◆ ◆ ◆ ◆ ◆

"What happened to you, Mr. Big Dick?" Sally already knew about the shootout but she didn't hear of anyone getting shot. Kevin's arm was in a sling.

Kevin walked through the door. "You got to do something, Sally. Skull tried to kill Clarence tonight." He took a seat on her couch.

"Who the hell is Skull?" She loved to act ignorant to get more information.

"He used to be Danny Boy's right-hand man. He's been in hiding because he robbed a few cats for their drugs." He didn't realize that he was ratting.

"Are you sure that it was Skull?"

"Clarence noticed him first by the way he was walking. I could tell after he told me. Clarence kept us all alive."

"So what do you want me to do? I can't just arrest Skull because ya'll want me to. I need something … I need a reliable witness." This is what she really wanted. Arresting Danny Boy could help her get his lips loose.

"So, what are you saying?"

"I'm saying you have to be a confidential informant if you want to save Clarence's life." Whether or not he turned into a rat, he had good value. He helped her keep up with a lot of Clarence's moves.

"You know I can't do that. You'll be pimpin' me for life. Just save a brotha's life for the hell of it."

"So you came over trying to pimp me?" She laughed as she started rubbing his leg.

His mind became confused as he gained an erection. "So you want me to testify that Skull tried to kill us. I'll get murdered." Her hand was now on his dick.

She could tell by the expression on his face that she was getting to him. "Nah, just tell me what Clarence has planned for Danny Boy." Lightly, she started kissing his neck.

He jumped up. "I don't know. What are you going to do? Clarence just told me to collect all the money while he's out of town. I'm not a rat, Sally."

Sally started thinking what Clarence would be doing out of town. She blocked Kevin out.

"What are you going to do Sally? Talk to me."

She looked up at him. "I'll let you know, I'll call you tomorrow. Get out." She started pushing him toward the door. She needed to think. When he said Clarence hadn't told him anything, she knew there was no more juice in the grapefruit.

Sally knew that something else was about to go down. It was a must that she be up to speed. So far Danny Boy attempted a murder. That was enough to pick him up for questioning. Skull would be the first person she planned to arrest and question. That was happening first thing in the morning. With enough pressure, he'd spill his guts. To make the case stick she would record Kevin talking to her about it. She also planned to use the tape to make him her next confidential informant.

There was still much work to be done. She still wasn't satisfied with Keisha. She could have easily paid one of her father's people to murder Clarence and Danny Boy. A few hundred would do it in the district. There had to be much more to it and she had to find out.

It was about eleven thirty when Keisha returned to her room after taking an English exam. She was relaxing until Jezebel returned after finishing her biology exam. She heard keys in the door and jumped up when she saw the person coming through the door.

"I miss you," she whispered in her ear.

"I missed you too Keisha. Girl, I'm so tired." Jezebel was been busy the entire weekend. She didn't expect Keisha to be that excited to see her. It hadn't even been three days.

"I have so much to tell you. Our plan was almost spoiled. Danny Boy put a hit out on Clarence but he saw it coming." She just left Clarence at a classy hotel. She convinced him to drive her Escalade while she pushed his Suburban. They figured the killer wouldn't be looking for them in Maryland. Skull wasn't that smart.

"So where is Clarence?" She sat on her bed.

"He's at a hotel not far from here."

"Where is Danny Boy?"

"Clarence says he's out of town. Clarence tried to call a truce but Danny Boy told him to wait until he got back in town to discuss it." Keisha couldn't make her next move until she got with Jezebel. If Clarence were murdered, all the planning would be for nothing.

"I'm exhausted. Cleopatra had me up all day Sunday, then I had to drive back and get ready for my exam. I'm ready to finish those niggas and move on." She was ready to take a nap.

Keisha wanted to ask her what Cleopatra had her doing. Maybe later. "Well, did you get it?"

"Yes, I got it. It's brand new."

"Where is it?"

"It's under my bed." She reached under her bed and pulled out a wooden case and opened it. "It's a big motherfucker."

"It's pretty." She closed it by placing her hand on top of Jezebel's.

"So what's up with the pharmacist? I know he was easy."

"I got him waiting, let me call him right now." She reached on the table to get her cell phone. There was a pick-up on the third ring. "…. This is Keisha Mr. Jacobs." She was using her sexy voice. "You got what I need? …. Be at the hotel at five o'clock. I'll call your cell …. Be sweet, big daddy." Mr. Jacobs was in the bag.

"I'm going to need your help Jezebel. He makes me want to puke." She had been trying to psych herself up since Sunday morning.

"If he's that old, I can feel you. I felt like that the first time I did a prune. But they cum in less than a minute."

"I think I'm going to need a few drinks. He's old and ugly." They both laughed.

"I have to get a nap first. I'll be your designated driver, now what else do we need to do?"

"We need Danny Boy to get back in town. How do we do that? Sally might arrest him too." The pivotal part of the plan was still him. He had one more part to play.

Jezebel sucked her teeth. "That's going to be easy." She dialed his cell number. "This is Jezebel, Danny Boy."

"Where the fuck did you go? You just disappeared." Danny was pissed because he felt that she played him also.

"I had to go. I can't be getting caught. I told you I have open warrants in Jersey." She wasn't about to let him get close to her.

"So what's up? You tricked me. You just leave after cats buy you shit. I've been sending people by your spot." Danny Boy was just playing it cool, testing the water.

"If I tricked you, why would I be calling? I'm trying to get some of that tongue and dick." She cut her eyes at Keisha.

"I don't believe that's why you called." He didn't want to just act like he wanted the pussy as bad as he did.

"What you did to Keisha made me jealous. You passed all my tests."

"Where you at right now?" He was planning when and how to bang her, and then dump the body.

"I'm in Maryland, at a hotel. I'll be back in the district before the week is out." She needed to get the damn thing set up so she could get some sleep. The weekend was catching up with her.

"How about I shoot over there so we can get busy."

"I'm a little stressed at the moment. How about Wednesday or Thursday evening at your spot. Just you and I."

"Oh, yeah, why we got to meet at my spot? I like that condo you invited me to." Danny Boy was trying to see if she was trying to do a hit on him.

"How about we meet at a hotel. A spot that's on the outskirts of town where there are fewer police." As long as they met in the district it was all good.

"Wednesday night, I'll call you." Killing her at a hotel like that would be perfect. He didn't peep the test.

"I'll get the room, then I'll call you. I'll make sure it'll be worth your while." It was perfect, she had a trick for him.

"So where's Keisha? That bitch really put one over on

me." This was a test. She had to be nearby he thought.

"She called me from New York. She and Clarence are on their honeymoon. Clarence wanted to split." She was almost caught off guard.

"So when are they coming back?" He didn't think to ask how they met.

"She said in about two weeks. Clarence is really trying to lay low. I think he's scared."

"He better be scared," he said in a loud voice.

She put a smirk on her face. "I heard a cat tried to air him out. Heard they missed him by an inch."

"I heard that too but anyway, I'll be waiting for you on Wednesday. Don't disappoint me." *Click.*

Danny Boy was planning to send his boys to rape and kill her. With Clarence out of town, he figured it was safe for him to hit the streets. Word had it that all of Clarence's spots were closed. He figured that by Wednesday he would have laid low long enough. One by one he planned to kill them, even if he had to handle it himself.

"Keisha, I need to get some sleep. I got a trick for him. I'm not going to no hotel." She laid back on the bed. "That nigga is probably trying to kill all of us." Jezebel closed her eyes.

There was one last piece of business that Keisha needed to tell Jezebel. She opened the box and put the key to Clarence's condo inside.

At that moment, Keisha realized that she was a totally different woman. She was jealous over another woman. She never saw Jezebel so exhausted. She was never this tired after studying. It had to be what Cleopatra had done with her. All the things that Jezebel said about Cleopatra came flooding to her conscious mind. She just sat there and stared at Jezebel.

She wanted to make Clarence pay that much more. It

was his fault that she became a freak. Nothing could make her have negative feelings toward Jezebel. She knew for sure that she had to accept Jezebel's offer to join *The Clit*.

◆ ◆ ◆ ◆ ◆

Sally and Bambi were been riding around the district trying to put the puzzle together.

"We've got to go to Maryland." Sally and Bambi were standing in front of Danny Boy's crib. Sally ran out of places to get information.

"The only thing in Maryland is Keisha. She spinned you the last time ya'll talked." Bambi was tired of working on this case. They asked any and everybody that kept up with the streets what they knew. All they got was the same information. Nobody saw Clarence or Danny Boy.

"Jezebel is also in Maryland. I'm sure they're both at school taking exams. I did a little research on Jezebel."

"Okay, spit."

"She's from Queens, New York, with a record for prostitution. The cops I talked to said she joined a group called *The Clit*."

Bambi looked at her with her eyes squinted. "So you think she's the mastermind and what's driving Keisha."

"Bambi, something is about to happen. This isn't just about Clarence and Danny Boy beefing with each other." Sally couldn't help but to spend all the time she could on the case.

"Did you just say she belongs to a group called *The Clit*?"

"Yes, that's what I said. Don't ask me what it means. I can say this much though; she and Sally are about to meet."

Bambi started laughing. "That's funny."

"What's funny?" Sally wanted to smoke a Black. They had already smoked a box and a half.

"The Pinstriped Bitch vs. *The Clit*. That sounds like a wrestling match." She was still laughing like it was a joke.

Sally laughed. "For now, it's the Pinstriped Bitch vs. Jezebel and Keisha. You ain't worth shit today." Bambi had been telling her to sit back and wait but Sally disagreed.

"I can't help it. It's funny that none of the suspects are in the district, but we're trying to run them down before they get back in. This isn't by the book." Bambi felt that Sally had started to take a big personal interest in the case. It wasn't their fault that they met a lot of dead ends.

"We have to keep scratchin' for clues. There's no telling what we might find. I know that it's simple. Just arresting Danny Boy for attempted murder isn't going to do it." They had also looked for Skull. He wasn't to be found.

"Listen. She wanted revenge. She puts them in a battle. One dies. The other goes to jail. She goes on to live her life. So what she did a striptease and let a guy eat her thing." Bambi was happy with that theory, especially being that she figured it out.

"Maybe it's a Black woman thing. Keisha was betrayed. If she would have been happy about them just battlin' she didn't need to be with Clarence. She has more than that in store for him." There was nothing that could change her mind. They just pulled up in front of Keisha's dorm.

"I guess a white girl would be happy with Clarence's death. We do know that one of them is bound to get killed. It's hard to catch a killer at times."

"Let me go see if they're inside."

It was five o'clock. Sally knew they had to show up before the night was over because they both had two exams to take on Tuesday. If necessary, she would wait all night to see them. When she walked back out of the building, they were arriving. She saw them get out of what looked like Clarence's Suburban.

"Damn, if it ain't Sally." Keisha took another drink of Alizé. Sally was the last person she wanted to see. With the package from Mr. Jacobs, she was ready to execute the rest of their plan. The rest was simple.

"I've been expecting her. Anything else wouldn't be like a bitch." Jezebel had driven so that Keisha could get her nerves right. They were at the hotel for less than ten minutes. "Let's go deal with her. Jessica is going to pick you up in two hours."

Jezebel opened the door as Sally walked toward them. Jezebel put a smile on her face, it was game time. By the time Sally got to them, Keisha was walking around the front of the truck and leaned on the hood. It would take a while for her buzz to wear off.

"Hello ladies, I've been looking for ya'll." Sally was acting a tad aggressive.

Jezebel put out her hand. "My name is Jezebel. I don't think we've met." This was meant to throw Sally off.

"I'm Sally. I'm a homicide detective," she said as she shook hands with her.

With a slight giggle, Keisha commented, "You came to harass me about Clarence and Danny Boy again?"

Sally noticed she was slightly intoxicated. "There are a lot of new things that have happened, and I need ya'll to tell me what you're up to."

Keisha and Jezebel looked at each other. It was as if they had practiced.

"Did I say something wrong?" Sally folded her arms. It looked like she was holding them hostage.

Keisha stepped closer to Sally. "We are trying to get some rest and prepare to take our exams tomorrow. Is that alright?" Jezebel looked from Keisha to Sally. She hoped that Keisha didn't get too mouthy.

"What ya'll all did at the club was real slick. The owner

told me that ya'll paid him so you could do that lil dance. What was the purpose?" It was one of those questions that were meant to make a suspect say the wrong thing.

Jezebel held up her bracelet. "This is the profit from that night. I plan to get more this week." She was pretty quick on her feet most of the time.

"So what, are you a prostitute or something?" Jezebel was turning out to be the adversary that she expected.

Jezebel turned to Keisha. "Should I tell her?"

Keisha shrugged her shoulders like it didn't matter. "Might as well, she asked."

"As a member of *The Clit*, if a man don't lick, he don't stick, and if he ain't rich, then he don't get shit. Some call me a high-priced prostitute. I call it being an empowered woman." She had a smile on her face like she was doing an interview for a magazine.

Sally hadn't taken the time to craft questions that would get specific responses. There was no time to wade in now, the mood was been set.

Bambi had just walked up as Sally continued her questions. "So why did Danny Boy eat only Keisha? You have a pussy also."

"She's teaching me the game. Can't you see we're driving Clarence's truck? And look at this ring." Keisha held up her hand.

"Okay ladies." Sally let out a breath. "I know that ya'll are trying to get revenge on them. I can't figure out exactly what ya'll are trying to do, but I will tell you this much, I'll be on the trail for a long time. Don't do anything ya'll will regret." She turned around and Bambi followed suit. They jumped into the BMW and headed out. Sally was so mad that she didn't say a thing all the way back to the district.

When the BMW was out of range, they high-fived each other and said, "Fuck that bitch."

The I's had been dotted, and the T's had been crossed. So far all parts of the plan had been executed perfectly. It seemed that luck was on their side. Things actually went better than they planned. They were grateful for Clarence not getting shot and murdered. Revenge was just a matter of a few more moves. If it took all summer, that would be okay.

● ◆ ◆ ◆ ◆

Clarence had a suite at the Hilton. He was laying low until he heard about Danny Boy getting hit. All of his calls were made on his cell and the room was in the name of an alias.

"I thought that ya'll forgot about me." It was nine o'clock, and he had expected Jessica and Keisha by five. They kept telling him that they were on the way. "I hope ya'll didn't forget the food."

Jessica walked through the door first. She couldn't manage a smile. Asking him why he did it was on the top of her head.

Keisha gave him a hello kiss. "I got you some orange juice and a pizza with extra cheese. There's a whole case of orange juice in the car." She walked past him and placed all the food on the living room table. Jessica had already taken a seat.

Clarence popped a can of orange juice and started guzzling. "Ya'll have some. I might eat and drink all of this." He put down the orange juice and grabbed a slice of pizza.

"We ate some Kentucky Fried Chicken on the way over here," Keisha added.

"Oh yeah, we don't have enough time to eat and talk. We have to discuss –" Jessica said like they were ignoring her.

"I'm sorry Jessica, Keisha, tell her what we are trying to do," Clarence stated.

"We want to start a trust and a corporation in one of those places that have privacy, like Daddy did with all his stuff. It's going to be all of my money and his money. We'll be equal partners. Right Clarence?" This conversation was done to appease Clarence but Jessica already knew how she was going to structure the corporation and trust.

"That's right. We're equal partners." Clarence had absolute faith in Keisha. He felt that he had no reason to feel otherwise.

"Okay. Let me write a few things down." She opened her briefcase. With pad in hand, she was ready to go. "What is the name of the corporation going to be?"

Clarence stated, "LCP for the corporation, and C&K for the trust." Clarence had already eaten another slice of pizza. "This pizza is good. I can eat this every day. I might as well, since I'm going to be here for a few days."

"Listen Clarence, let me tell you how this works," Jessica continued. "All of these companies are going to be based in Nevada. That's what I did for Sherlock. I'll have an attorney make out a million shares, half for you, and half for Keisha. What are your positions going to be?"

Keisha proudly said, "He'll be the CEO and Chairman of the Board. I'll be the President. We'll make you our Treasurer and Secretary."

"Sounds good to me," Jessica stated.

"That's perfect," Clarence added. He was on his third slice of pizza and a third can of orange juice. "Where do we sign?"

Jessica finished writing in the information. She passed the form to Clarence and he signed. Then he passed it to Keisha and she signed.

Jessica needed to explain a few details. "You know I get five percent of all money I launder." Clarence shook his head like that wasn't a problem. "It only takes a few hours to set this up because they have dummy corporations and trusts. So where is the money?"

"I'll be right back." He went into one of the rooms.

They started whispering about how many tainted meals and juices they needed to feed him. He couldn't taste it or smell it. They could have eaten a little with him without having any problems. Keisha was bringing him all his meals. Once the money was deposited, she would be in the fourth quarter. Jessica willingly participated in the plan. Keisha wasn't going to tell on her for laundering the money. She felt safe.

Clarence walked back in with a leather travel bag. "All of one point five mil is in here. I have another two hundred thousand out in the streets. I'll be getting it when I get back to the district."

Jessica stood up to leave. "I'll be taking care of all of this in the morning." Keisha planned to take a cab back to school in the morning. She had to be there to feed him his breakfast. She was too tipsy earlier to drive the Suburban.

Clarence walked with her to the door. "I really appreciate this Jessica. I can't wait to start buying houses and buildings." Because he was new to the game, he had a lot to learn about handling money and investing. He felt better knowing his money would be safe in a bank. He also liked the idea of putting all of his assets into a trust.

"This is what I do for a select few. See you later." He closed the door behind her.

Keisha started taking her clothes off. By the time he turned around, she had her blouse off. Quickly she let her skirt drop to the floor. Making love to him would cause him to eat more. She had already been started earlier with Mr. Jacobs.

In the morning, she made his breakfast and fed him by spoon. She told him that she had eaten before he got up. She had an antidote for the poison that she was feeding him. She got it just in case she had to eat some of the food. Before she left she took his lunch and dinner requests.

Clarence wasn't worried about Danny Boy or anybody else finding him at the hotel. Danny Boy didn't know that Keisha and Jezebel were college students in Maryland. Still, he took it as a blessing and stayed in his suite to study real estate investing. On the Internet he had found some good properties to purchase in the district.

Danny Boy and his boys couldn't take it anymore. They came back on Tuesday. They ran out of weed to smoke. Before his workers started getting rowdy, he figured one more day wouldn't change things. He was also ready to start looking for Clarence and his people. They had a war and he intended to win. Skull may have missed but Danny Boy planned not to.

It was twelve o'clock at night when he drove his Benz up in his driveway. He had to ride around town for a few hours to let people know that he was back.

Jezebel played him just right. She hit on the second night that she waited on him. She knew he couldn't stay in Virginia but for so long. She called him every day to make him think that she was really interested in fucking him. The rental car was well worth the money. She called Keisha.

It took her less than five minutes to get to his back door. She dialed his number on her cell.

"Hey Danny Boy, I just had to hear your voice. Where are you?" She needed to know his location in the house. She was on his back porch.

"What you mean where I'm at. I'm in the district. I thought we were getting together tomorrow. Where are ... Hold on, I hear knocks on my back door."

She knocked a little harder. "So can a girl see you tonight? We can get a quickie." She knocked a few more times.

"I don't know. Let me find out who is at my back door knocking like they crazy." He had his .45 out.

"I can be at your house in less than five minutes. I'll meet you there."

"Do that." He walked into the kitchen and laid his cell on the table.

Knock, knock, knock. She was standing in the door so he could see her face. When they made eye contact and he smiled, she knew she had him. He started laughing. Might as well fuck her, and then have his boys come over. He put his gun in his pants.

As he opened the door, he said, "Isn't this nice. We –"

Fire came out of the end of the ten. That was all he saw before he felt his legs collapsing. The third shot caught him in the stomach, along with the fourth in his heart, as he fell to the floor. Target practice makes the difference. For good measure, she shot him in the forehead from two feet away. Death was instantaneous.

"Where you at Keisha?" Jezebel called her as soon as her feet hit the block.

"Just another block and I'll be at his house." Keisha was driving Clarence's Suburban. She planned to circle the block three times.

Jezebel was two blocks away and just getting back in the rental car. "I'm on my way to do the other thing."

"Later sister."

"Later sister." *Click.*

Ten minutes later, Jezebel was in Clarence's condo. The Glock in the new case was placed inside of Clarence's closet. She left as quickly as she arrived, heading back to Maryland. When she got to the DC/Maryland line, she called the police about a disturbance.

On Keisha's third drive around Danny Boy's crib, she saw the police coming.

Jezebel and Keisha celebrated with a bottle of Moet when they got back to their room. All night they licked and sucked on each other. It didn't matter that they each had to take an exam the next day, they were excited. They had done more than just pull off a murder. They rested at two o'clock as exhaustion set in.

It was a quarter after two when Sally got to the murder scene. She refused to answer the phone until she and Kevin finished fucking. When she finally took the call, she rushed to get dressed. She made Kevin freak a Black for her.

Bambi had filled her in, per procedure, while she rode over.

Sally walked all around the bottom floor before she went to the kitchen. Once she walked into the kitchen, the other officers walked to the front of the house.

"What's up Bambi?" She passed her the Black. She looked down at Danny Boy. "He got hit four times from the back door."

"Not exactly. He got hit five times." Bambi was ready to break the whole thing to her. It was an easy scenario.

Sally picked up one of the bullet casings. "This is a 10-millimeter casing."

"Yes, it is. I wonder if he was shooting hollow points." Bambi had already made arrangements for an immediate autopsy.

"Clarence is our prime suspect. We aren't going to put this on the news. He hasn't been seen lately. In the morning we're searching his and his mother's condos, and all of his spots. If we find a ten, that's his ass." Instincts were telling her that it wasn't that simple. It was too simple. Clarence had to be slicker than this. Still, a lead is a lead.

"I already have warrants prepared." She had filled in the blanks on the computer. "After you sign them, we'll just have to go see the magistrate." Bambi was way ahead of Sally.

"That means it's time to ride. I'll just have this crew go with me to the condo. We'll go to his spots after that." They were out.

24

◆ ◆ ◆ ◆ ◆

Clarence was packing his bags when Keisha arrived. "Where are you going Clarence? I have your breakfast right here." It was eight o'clock.

"It's time to get back to the district. Danny Boy got nailed last night." The first thing on Clarence's agenda was to find Skull and air him out.

"It's early in the morning. We can relax until about ten o'clock. Math is always easy." She needed him to eat his breakfast. She put his breakfast on the table.

"I do have some time. Hey, is the money in the accounts yet?"

"Jessica said it'll be there when you check at nine thirty. So you need to hang out." She needed to dose him up a few more times. "Why do you look so tired?"

"I've been feeling a little sluggish lately. Look at my hand, I got the shakes or something. I'm just stressin' I guess." His face was looking a little raggedy, like he was drained, and had aged a few years.

She smiled at her work. "It's all this good pussy that I've been putting on you." She grabbed his hand and led him to the table. "You just need something to eat."

He had become spoiled by all of her attention and sexin'. "I'm sorry that the wedding got spoiled. We can get married in Cancun if you like." He sat and started drinking his orange juice.

"It's okay. It's like we are already married and this is our honeymoon. I'm just glad that you are alive." She sat in his lap. She caressed his neck and the back of his head.

"As soon as I get the operations back up and running, I'm going to treat you real special. You've been taking real good care of me and it doesn't go unnoticed." He took a bite of his cheese omelet.

"Can I count on that?" Eat boy, eat. Just a few more doses.

"When the time is right, I have to tell you something." He kissed her on the lips before he took another bite. Guilt was eating at him. He needed her forgiveness.

She kept kissing him on his face. When her lips reached his ears, she whispered, "I also have something to tell you when the time is right." It wouldn't be that long.

"Oh yeah?" He started smiling. "You can tell me now." He took in the last bite.

"Patience, patience," she teased. "I need some sex before you head out." She moved closer to him and rubbed his crotch. "Afterwards, we can check on our money." Leading her to the bedroom, he swallowed his last bite, and agreed.

At that same moment, Sally was filing charges against Clarence for the murders of Karyn Langston and Danny Boy Perry. She almost couldn't believe that he had a 10-millimeter in his condo. Seeing that the bullets left in Danny Boy weren't hollow points really excited her. People in the neighborhood said they saw a black Suburban in the area at the time the murders would have went down. She figured she had a perfect case against him, she was just waiting to get a ballistics test.

They took everything out of his and his mother's condo. This included one hundred fifty thousand in cash.

Clarence checked his cash at nine forty –five and it was all there. To him, all things seemed to be perfect. It was all just a matter of dealing with a few ends. Then he'd be back to making money, and he could start buying properties. With Keisha as his wife, life couldn't be better, so he felt.

As she hopped in her Escalade, she took off for school to take her exam. Just a few more steps, she thought to herself.

Sally was alerted the minute Clarence's Suburban was spotted. She had it followed to make sure he was driving. The moment that it was established that it was him, an arrest team was activated. He was at his Pennsylvania spot.

"So why did you do it?" Sally just walked in his office and started talking.

"Why didn't you knock?" His breathing became shallow as he banged on his chest to cough.

She sat her purse on his desk and took a seat. "Why did you kill Danny Boy?" She was hoping he'd give her some extra evidence.

"I didn't kill Danny Boy. I just got back in town."

"Stop playing, Clarence. This is all off the record. What made you kill him? Was it about Keisha? Was it about money?" Sally noticed that he looked older and pale. The sparkle he normally had in his eyes was non-existent.

"I've been in a hotel for the past few days." He felt too

weak to stand and already made plans to see a doctor in a few minutes.

"Can you prove that?"

"You damn right I can, I have witnesses. Good witnesses." He was growling as hard as he could.

"I got hard evidence on you Clarence." She was dangling her left leg over her right. Her purple and gold pinstriped two-piece pants suit was brand new – just for the occasion.

"I don't want to play, Sally."

"Clarence, the 10-millimeter that was found in your condo was the weapon that killed Danny Boy. Tell me about that."

Looking at her in disbelief while struggling to get air in his lungs he said, "We can play games tomorrow? Can't you see that I'm sick?"

The look on his face took her breath away. Intuition told her that he was being sincere. She could see also that something was really wrong with him. She stood.

"I'm sorry Clarence. You are under arrest for the murders of Danny Boy Perry and Karyn Langston." On those words, four uniformed officers walked in with their guns drawn.

It took several hours to process and book Clarence. As usual, the police made a big deal of making an arrest, especially one for murder so quickly. The body wasn't even that cold yet.

Clarence used his first phone call to call Keisha. She didn't answer. His mother was still on the cruise, so he called his lawyer. He informed him not to talk to the police, and that he probably wouldn't get bail for a few days. The magistrate denied him bail an hour later.

Clarence was blessed when they placed him with the other prisoners. They congratulated him on killing Danny Boy. He didn't tell them any differently. Being that he was a major playa, they put him down with how to get contraband and food in. They knew he could make things happen. In a day or two he promised to get them some dro.

He knew most of the cats in there. They told him that Skull was in the protective custody wing. He had been involved in a robbery. Clarence planned to catch up with Skull when the opportunity presented itself. He wanted to talk to him first. Depending on what he said, Clarence planned to pay someone to shank him. He also had to pay a guard to arrange it. One way or the other, Skull would be shanked to death if Clarence had his way.

Keisha smiled when the recording said she was getting a phone call from a jail. "Hello, who is this?" she asked acting clueless. She got Jezebel to sit beside her on the bed. They already saw the news and were waiting to get the call.

"It's Clarence. I'm in the county jail."

"What? What for? You got a speeding ticket or something?" She cut her eyes at Jezebel, and she smiled.

"Nah, they charged me with Danny Boy's murder." He planned to tell her later about the other charge.

"Why the fuck they do that? You were with me in a hotel in Maryland. We just got back in town this morning." Over the phone, she sounded like she was really upset. Jezebel held her thumb up for the great acting skills.

"I don't know. They didn't give me a bail." She already knew this. "My lawyer said that he'd be able to get me a hearing by Friday." He sounded hopeful but he knew he may as well get comfortable. The publicity for the case was too big and he already made his initial appearance.

She started thinking that she needed to give him just a little more thallium sulfate to kill him or permanently disable him. "Clarence, I'm scared. We found our way back together and now this happens."

"It'll be okay. Just knowing you have my back is all I need right now."

"Have you eaten yet? I know the food in there isn't that good."

"Damn girl, you must be reading my mind. I ain't eat this shit they tried to give me. You spoiled me," he mused. The more she did for him, the more he wanted to purge his heart to her. "A cat is going to call you, just hit him off."

"Okay, I'll take care of you. I'll send you some music and put some money on your books."

"I had ten grand on me, just send the food and the music."

"I'm going to miss you, boo. When are visiting hours?"

He hollered at another convict. "Saturday, Sunday and Wednesday. By the time you get here, visiting hours will be up. I'll be out by Saturday, but I still need to eat."

"Okay, I'll get you a few pizzas and some orange juice. I know how you like to ball." The orange juice would contain just enough thallium sulfate to give him permanent nerve damage for life.

"I know I got this case beat. I melted down my gun. If there was anything in my condo, it was planted there." He could barely stay awake. He had fought it all that he could.

"So that's why they arrested you. Just as soon as you beat the case things will be back to normal. You don't sound too good. Are you okay?"

"I'm tired as a motherfucker. I just need something to eat. I'm out." *Click.* Clarence laid on his bare bunk. Sheets weren't even on the mattress.

He didn't want to tell the police that he was sick. They were treating him like he was a terrorist. Naturally, he felt that they weren't going to do much for him. It was a time for him to be strong. It was his first challenge with the system. The police had to be behind Danny Boy's murder. He knew for sure that he had a solid defense. The system was now his number one enemy and turning to the enemy for health care wasn't a choice for him.

He laid on his bunk and waited for his packages to arrive.

Sally waited all day for Kevin to meet her. What she needed to talk about couldn't be done over the phone. She didn't want to chance that a tap was in effect.

"What took you so long to get here? I've been waiting for an hour." He wasn't in the car good before she started with the interrogation.

"I had to do some things for Clarence. That's my dawg till the end. What's up?"

"Look, it's like this, and tell me the truth. I know that you ain't gonna be a rat and I respect that about you, but I don't think that Clarence killed Danny Boy." Being outside of her usual character was rather different.

His expression said "what the fuck?" "So why in the hell did you arrest him?"

"I had to because of the evidence. The murder weapon was in his condo. I do have a job." The ghetto in her came out.

"I don't believe that he did it. Too many people have volunteered to do it for free. I know when Clarence is lying. Plus, he ain't stupid."

"That's the same thing that I was thinking. He knew I'd be all over him, so why take the chance of taking the murder weapon to your own house." She had her head on the steering wheel.

"So, are you going to let him go?" This was the kind of

conversation that only happens in books and movies.

"I can't. I think that he killed Keisha's mother. I believe this is all a part of a revenge plot."

He laughed. "I don't want any of that dro you smokin. They love each other and Clarence loved Keisha's mother." He started to get out of the car. His man's welfare was on his mind.

She grabbed his jacket. He glared at her and she let go. "I'm dead serious. I can't prove it all yet, but I know it's true."

"I know Keisha changed a lot in the last year but she ain't diabolical. Clarence is too smart to do a hit like that and slip. I've seen his work." He moved too fast for her to stop him.

It was going down right in front of her face. She knew who and she knew why. What she didn't know was how to prove it. She had been looking the entire time, looking for the one clue to help crack the case. What was missed? There had to be something, something that would make others see what she was seeing. Bambi had gotten to the point that she didn't want to hear any more about the case. There was only one more chance for her to find something, anything. She had to try.

25

◆ ◆ ◆ ◆ ◆

Clarence picked some cats to get Skull and he planned to bond all of them out. In the meantime, he would feed them whatever they and the rest of the tier wanted to eat. He didn't let any of them drink his orange juice. He needed to get out to make it to a doctor. He was feeling worse by the day. He only got out of bed to eat, use the bathroom and the phone. All day he felt drained.

Friday morning finally arrived. Just as his lawyer assured him, the judge set a bond. He didn't care that it was a one million-dollar bond because he only had to pay ten percent.

"Keisha, you got to hurry up and come get me. The bondsman is waiting for you." He forgot about saying "hello." It was a state of emergency.

"I got you, baby." She was packing her things. Her first semester of college was over.

"You need to call the bondsman and wire him the money."

"Alright. I haven't let you down yet, have I?"

"I'm sorry, no you haven't. I love you Keisha."

"I love you too. I got you." *I got you* is what she meant.

"I need to see a doctor."

"Why? Did something happen in there?"

"Nah, I'm short of breath and just really weak. I'm tired all the time too."

"Okay, I'll be there as soon as I can." *Click*.

She was glad. He was almost dead. She had taken him to the edge and left him there. He was dead broke too. The condo, the cars, his jewelry and clothes had been sold or destroyed. The only thing that he owned was the money in his jail account. She only had one more thing to do.

"Clarence, you have a visitor," the guard yelled. Clarence thought that he was hearing things. He opened his eyes to see what was happening. "Get up, you have a visitor."

"Alright man. Give me a minute." It was seven o'clock at night and no bond was made yet. He called Keisha repeatedly, but she didn't answer her phone.

The green with yellow pinstripes suit caught his eye before the face confirmed who his visitor was. It was Sally. He noticed that she didn't have the usual expression on her face.

She motioned to him to pick up the phone. "I need your help Clarence."

There wasn't much fight in him. "You just arrested me as an innocent man."

"I have doubts about you killing Danny Boy. I know what's happening, but I need you to help prove it." She had seen the county jail make people age but his situation was an exaggeration. He looked five years older.

"So who killed Danny Boy?"

"Keisha and Jezebel. It was a setup. You need to get medical attention Clarence, she may have poisoned you. You look terrible."

"Nah, I can't believe that. She'll be here in a minute to

get me out. Keisha ain't a murderer, I know her." He felt like he had an unquenchable thirst and his leg wouldn't stop shaking.

"Listen Clarence, all of your stuff has been sold. Real cheap. I need your help to get them." If he got off with Karyn's murder, so be it. More than likely, one case would prove the other. It was the motive.

"I don't believe that Sally, lay off." He hung up the phone and walked away.

She did all that she could do.

When Jezebel and Keisha pulled up to the jail on Saturday, late in the afternoon when visiting hours were almost over. Sally had been expecting Keisha to visit and she was waiting for the call. It was made when Keisha asked to see Clarence. She was a few blocks away.

Clarence's walk was stiff and slow. He was moving just fast enough to keep the guards from thinking that he was sick. Keisha was satisfied with her work.

"So why ain't I out on bond?" he asked in a low growl. This was all the anger that he could muster. He kept from shaking by pressing his feet to the floor as hard as possible.

She just looked at him. Death was in his eyes, no shine, no glitter. He had aged tremendously and his bottom lip was quivering. He barely looked like Clarence. His skin looked pale. A bum from the street is what she was reminded of. She loved all of it. Perfect. She didn't say a thing for minutes.

He ranted, cursed and banged on the table and window. The more he yelled, the lower his head got to the table and the plastic glass. He could barely hold the phone up to his ear. "Talk to me Keisha."

"I know that you killed my mother. I always knew, she told me." He raised his head up a little. "Clarence, you betrayed all of us. How could you do that? Do you realize how much pain you've caused me?"

"I'm sorry," he whimpered in a low tone. "I love you Keisha. I didn't mean to hurt you. Let me explain. I'll make it up to you. Just get me out of here."

"I love you too Clarence." He brightened up. "That's the reason I didn't kill you. I couldn't. I tried to kill you that day in my Escalade." His eyes opened wide and his head lowered a bit. Drool started coming out of his mouth. "The ultimate payback is slow and painful. I'll let you figure it out." His mind went back to Sally's visit and all that she revealed to him. His chin hit the table and he was out for the count. With closed his eyes as thick slobber began dripping from the corner of his mouth, Keisha knew she got the ultimate revenge.

"I know you can still hear me Clarence. The subconscious mind works like that.

"You were the perfect man, I mean perfect. I put up with so much but I was blinded by my love for you. The line was crossed when you pulled the trigger and killed my mother. Funny as it may seem, I still had love for you. I still do. I must admit it took me a minute to get myself together because I was on the verge of a breakdown. I still have you in my system, but if it weren't for Jezebel and her tongue, your dick almost made me want to forgive you."

His eyes opened when she stopped talking. He was wishing that she had killed him. Guilt was setting in.

"I can't forgive a Judas. I did what I had to do. I got all your money and all of your shit has been sold. Make it how you live. Payback is a bitch, then you die!!!" He drifted into an unconscious state.

Keisha felt like a new woman. It was time for her to start her new life with *The Clit*. She was satisfied with her revenge.

◆ ◆ ◆ ◆ ◆

Sally caught Keisha just before she got to Jezebel's Jaguar. "I got to hand it to you, you got them."

Keisha was too happy to get the smile off her face. "What are you talking about?"

"I'm talking about what you did to Clarence and Danny Boy. How long does Clarence have to live? You can tell me."

Keisha put her hand in front of her face. To keep from laughing, she twisted her body. She felt like she had almost been caught. That made getting her revenge that much sweeter.

"So you think it's funny that you just committed two capital crimes. I'll be searching for evidence to get you." It became personal.

"I respect your gangsta, but Sally, I have things to do. Are you finished?"

Sally stepped to the side and proceeded. "There is no statute of limitations on murder."

Keisha stopped and turned around. "I know that. I didn't murder Clarence." Before she got in the car she waved at Sally.

"She's still using that weak press game?" Jezebel asked.

"You know it. Play our song."

R. Kelly's "When a Woman's Fed Up" started playing. They sang along while they waved to Sally.

Sally was smoking. "La di da di da, la, la la la, oh oh oh oh oh..." was all she heard. Sally couldn't help but to hum with it. "When a woman's fed up, there ain't nothing you can do about it." Sally watched, shook her head and sang the song. Mad as hell, she still respected their gangsta.

See you in the next one. ......